GUZZI DUET, BOOK TWO

EnTANGLED

BETHANY-KRIS

Dedication

For my newest son, Devon.

Contents

Chapter 1

It was possible to be entirely alone in a room full of people.

Gian Guzzi had never had that experience before, but now it was all too common. He had wrongly assumed that taking the highest seat in his Cosa Nostra family would leave him with very little time to consider or wallow about his personal problems, but that couldn't be further from the truth.

Already, it was August. A hot, humid summer month that Gian had planned to spend with someone else, ignoring the heat as best he could. Three months had passed since his last encounter with Cara Rossi, but not a single fucking day went by where he wasn't reminded of her in some way.

Part of that was by his own hand, of course.

Being a boss, on the other hand, forced Gian to keep his personal issues quiet. He certainly couldn't afford to let the men around him think that he was distracted by his emotions, never mind a woman that he could no longer have. He needed for them to think that at all times, he was on his very best game, no matter what.

Duty first.

Legacy second.

And only then, love.

Gian finally understood what his grandfather, Corrado, had been trying to tell him for years. He had assumed that it was a sacrifice all made men needed to make for the sake of *la famiglia*, but he was wrong.

Only the boss made that sacrifice.

Cosa Nostra had to be his one constant. He had to breathe the business. He had to bleed the life. He was the one who was expected to repeat the rules and enforce them. He was the only one who was looked to when something needed to be heard. His voice spoke for everyone.

That was what a *good* boss did. Then, if he did his job well, the boss's men would never know that he was just like them, affected and ruined by silly things like love and a woman.

Duty. Legacy. Love.

Always in that order.

Always.

Oh, yes.

Gian understood those words perfectly well now.

It was better to listen to the people around him, let them talk, and then form his own opinions and give orders from what he learned. He learned that quickly enough as a boss. It also left him with too much time, when he was alone with his thoughts.

All he ever did was think.

"Happy birthday, boss!"

Gian tried to smile as a hand clapped his back with enough force to shake him from his inner hell. It brought his attention forefront to the VIP section of the club and the men, again. Men celebrating *his* thirtieth birthday.

He should be celebrating, too.

"Here, another drink," Stephan said.

A whiskey was shoved into Gian's hand.

He sipped at the strong liquor, as it gave him something to do. *"Merci."*

Stephan said something else but Gian wasn't listening. He was not a big partier to begin with. He had only agreed to this night with his men because they had asked for it. Given how quickly tensions could flare in the family, peace-keeping was a constant part of the business. Especially for Gian.

Earlier in the day, he had spent too many hours sitting around a dinner table with the older generation of Capos in the family and their important people. They, too, had wanted to celebrate their boss's birthday in some way, but not like the younger men did. Which was understandable.

While the divide between the generational lines had closed enough for Gian to consider it comfortable, he still preferred to keep the two groups separate. He allowed everyone their voice, and their chance to express it. As much as was acceptable, anyway.

"Happy birthday to you! Happy …"

Gian was urged forward in the group of men as a server strolled forward with a cake in her hands. It was a two-tier cake, gold in color, with black trim. The Guzzi family colors. His name and the proper birthday greeting had been scrawled across the side. It certainly looked good, but even his appetite was seriously lacking lately.

Happy birthday, boss.

Dirty thirty, Gian.

The platitudes kept coming from everyone. Gian smiled and nodded, laughing when he needed to. He wasn't shocked anymore that no one seemed to notice his cheer and good-nature was nothing more than a carefully-crafted lie.

He had perfected this shit in no time at all.

"Set it down," someone told the server with the cake.

A table was pulled over, and the cake was set down. Another man passed Gian a knife, while paper plates, napkins, and plastic forks were set out on the table by another one of the girls who worked in Gian's club.

"This one is all you," Domenic said, nodding at Gian, and then to the cake. "Go for it. Might as well add some diabetes to the alcoholism these fools already have."

Gian smacked his brother in the back of the head for that one. "You're one to talk. How many nights a week are you in a club drinking, never mind at home alone?"

Dom shrugged. "It's how I meet people."

"Right. Good excuse."

"Just cut your fucking cake, Gian."

"You know I didn't ask for a cake," Gian said to his brother, lowering his tone so only Dom would hear. "I only agreed to a few drinks."

Dom nodded. "They want to celebrate you, man. Let them."

Gian sighed.

Right.

Celebrate.

It was only *him* that wasn't feeling the party.

"Just cut the cake," Dom said. "After that, they won't even notice when you go. They'll be too drunk and working on a sugar-high."

"You get to be the lucky—or unlucky—fuck that stays behind to make sure they don't tear my club apart," Gian warned.

"I can do that."

Fine.

As long as Dom knew …

Truthfully, Gian was grateful for his brother. Dom had been one of the very few constants at Gian's side since he'd taken over the family. He had made his brother, as he promised to do, and given Dom his proper *in* to the family business. Besides, it was a hell of a lot easier to make Dom his consigliere when he was already a made man.

Dom became Gian's right-hand man practically overnight. But that was how it needed to be, and Gian didn't give fucking anyone the chance to argue or question it. Dom was better suited for the consigliere position rather than a Capo or underboss, simply because the men knew him, Gian trusted him, and he was not in the family for everyone else, only his brother.

As he had always been.

His underboss, on the other hand, had been something he allowed the men of the family to pick. It was unusual, and certainly not the norm, but they had their voice and vote in *someone*.

Stephan was who they chose.

Somedays, Gian wanted to kill the bastard.

Other days, he was worth his weight in arrogant, ignorant gold.

"Hurry up!" someone shouted from behind Gian.

Dom chuckled. "Let them eat cake, Gian."

"Didn't saying that get someone killed once?"

"She didn't give them the cake, though."

Gian didn't think that was the point.

Still, he went ahead and sliced into the cake. While the outside had been a gold and black-trimmed masterpiece, the inside was a vibrant crimson color. Red velvet, it seemed.

Like blood.

It was oddly appropriate, considering how much blood he had already spilled.

"All right, move over, let me handle this," Dom said.

Gian willingly gave the knife to his brother, and let Dom get to work. If there were two things Dom liked, they were food and good conversation. Gian was able to step aside, and barely anyone noticed as they were too busy drinking their liquor and shoving their faces full of cake.

Gian knew, in that moment, he should take the time to appreciate what he was seeing. Calm and peace. Content men. Vanishing violence. A family ready to *work*.

He should have been happy.

He should have been ... a lot of things.

Being a boss was not as easy as he had thought it would be. He had only been given a glimpse of what the position was like when his grandfather filled the spot. Now, sitting in the seat himself, Gian had his eyes wide open.

It was fucking lonely at the top.

Gian was constantly surrounded by people.

He had too much work to do.

He never stopped moving.

His time was thin.

His patience was thinner.

And yet, more than he cared to admit, he found himself entirely alone. No amount of work, Cosa Nostra, or distractions would help with his problem.

Only one person could—Cara.

She was out of his reach, now, to an extent. Physically, she wasn't his to have, no matter how badly he wanted her. Emotionally, she had every fucking one of her claws buried into his heart, and she didn't even know it.

His soul was entangled with a woman who no longer wanted him, even if he would still die for her.

Gian had no one to blame for that but himself.

Gian buttoned up his suit jacket as he stepped out of the back of the black town car. Chris held the door open until Gian stepped away from the vehicle, and then promptly closed it shut once he could. Standing in the middle of the large, circular driveway, Gian stared down the mansion that had become a private hell of sorts for him.

He did not want to enter that house.

He couldn't even call it a home, now.

Once upon a time, it had been exactly that. A *home*. His grandfather and grandmother's home, filled with memories of years long past and happier times. Now, whenever he entered the mansion, invisible weights fell on his shoulders, while a pressure built in his head, ready to burst at any moment.

That could happen to a man when he was expected to share a space with his wife, especially when said wife was Elena Guzzi. Gian was expected—in his current position—to behave a certain way regarding his wife and marriage. It looked better on his image, and his family, when he treated his wife *as* his wife. Regardless of how he felt about it, he needed to be seen with his wife. Out and about, at the mansion, and more.

Elena was no happier about Gian's presence in her life than he was, frankly.

And that only made it that much more difficult.

Gian could have moved Elena into his penthouse, and sold his grandfather's mansion for a few million, but he had chosen a different route. For one, because neither he, nor his wife, wanted to be together in a smaller space than they had to be. And for two, because the penthouse was his, much like her previous penthouse had belonged solely to her. They were not accustomed to living together, and Gian had built his life around the fact that his wife was not going to be involved.

He was not going to change his lifestyle entirely, simply to suit the desires of a few people who watched him like a hawk.

Thankfully, Elena didn't put up much of an argument when Gian suggested the mansion as a sort of middle ground. He spent a couple of days and nights there, though usually in an entirely different wing from his wife, and a few nights at his penthouse in the city where he was easily assessable to his men and business.

That certainly didn't mean either of them liked the arrangement, which only made nights like these that much fucking harder to get through.

"You good, boss?" Chris asked.

Gian kept his features schooled as he replied, "Why wouldn't I be?"

"You just seem … quiet."

"When have you ever known me to be loud?"

The enforcer chuckled. "Point taken."

"Are you in the mood for dinner?" Gian asked. "You're more than welcome to join us. Elena does seem fond of you."

Or at least, the woman was slightly more pleasant when someone else was nearby.

"I could eat."

That was that.

Elena barely blinked a lash at one of Gian's men entering the mansion behind him. Wearing one of her usual dresses, with her blonde hair perfectly done and her makeup flawless, she greeted Chris first, and only turned to Gian once the enforcer headed toward the dining area of the right wing.

"I didn't know you were coming tonight," Elena said.

No greeting.

No hello.

Nothing.

"It's Saturday, Elena. I always come here on Saturday nights."

"Not usually this late."

"Do you want a daily update for when I plan to come and go from different places, and when I might show up here?" Gian asked.

Because if that would keep her from meeting him at the door, he would happily try to provide her with those details.

"You're being a smartass," Elena said, "and I could do without the attitude."

"It's been a long day."

"Well, you certainly had a long night, didn't you?"

Gian resisted the urge to roll his eyes. "If you're talking about the dinner, and then the birthday party at the club last night, yes, it made for a long evening."

Elena crossed her arms, her jaw stiff as she stared at him hard. He always thought blue eyes would have fit his wife far better than her brown eyes did—the iciness in her gaze couldn't quite be matched by any other woman he had come in contact with. Sometimes, her brown gaze gave off a sense of warmth simply because of their color, but it was a lie.

She was colder than ice.

"And why wasn't I invited?" Elena asked. "I am your wife, Gian."

"Because it wasn't a family thing," Gian replied dryly.

"Still—"

"I wasn't asked or invited to bring you, so I didn't. Don't act like that bothers you because we both know it doesn't. The only thing that might bother you is not being able to buy something pretty to wear out for an evening. If that's what you want, decide where you want to go *next* weekend, and I will take you. Not for my birthday, though."

"Fine."

Gian sighed internally, taking that as a battle won.

"Also, my birthday is coming up," Elena added quickly.

"And what would you like for it?"

She smiled sweetly, as though she was pleased with his question. Another false invitation into her web.

It never failed to surprise Gian how easily men could be caught up and then subsequently killed in the maze of Elena's games and manipulations. He had been one of those men, once. Years ago, it had been him who saw her distant eyes and perfectly-styled appearance and thought, *something is wrong with her, she never smiles.*

She seemed sad, alone, and too quiet. She had been young at just twenty-three, with no siblings and only her father raising her. Her mother had died long ago.

Her beauty, sweet nature, and soft voice had drawn him in easily enough. Her world had been a malevolent place, and certainly not meant for her.

He had been stupid.

A foolish man caught up in a hero complex.

It was a mistake Gian would never make again.

Not with Elena.

Gian wrongly perceived what he thought to be Elena's innocence and naivety as a direct result of her upbringing, under the hands of her violent, awful father. He had never once considered that every single thing that Elena offered to a man, whether it be emotionally, verbally, or physically, was a game. Her words were meant to placate and soften. Her touch was meant to disarm and trap.

For her, men were a means to an end.

She had simply found the *right* man in Gian to use.

It was a particular sport that she had been taught all too well, and had yet to lose.

Gian hadn't realized he had been playing Elena's game until it was too late. He had fallen for all of her lies, they were only a few weeks short of being married, he was stuck in the agreement made, and his life *shattered.* Just like that, she ruined what should have been his free choice and will.

And she had done it for no other reason than to be free.

She trapped him so that she could fly.

"Well?" Gian asked. "What do you want for *your* birthday?"

Elena shrugged. "Nothing spectacular."

"But something amazing."

"That is what your wife deserves, isn't it, Gian?"

"She certainly deserves *something*," he said as he moved past her.

Elena reached out to pat his cheek. It took every ounce of willpower he had not to flinch away. He did not share a life with this woman beyond the one they were forced into, and they certainly didn't share affection. He didn't want her touching him, and he had no interest or desire to touch her.

Once, before they'd married, all he had wanted to do was touch her, and to save her. And then he'd figured out her games, but it was already too late.

"Don't," Gian murmured, stepping out of Elena's reach.

"So touchy, Gian."

"I wonder why, Elena."

"You're no fun tonight."

With her, he was never fun.

"If you want something, then ask for it. Don't, however, try to manipulate me into giving you something by pretending to be nice or that you give a shit. You don't. I don't. It's that simple."

Elena shot him a look. "Fine, whatever. Shiny and pretty things, people to sing me happy birthday, the usual."

Gian nodded. "It'll be done."

"*Out* somewhere, too. Not here."

"Pick a place."

Elena was the one to walk past him that time. Her smile was serene and her sarcasm oozed as she spoke over her dainty shoulder. "You're too good to me, Gian."

As he should be.

As he *had* to be.

Because she was his wife.

Little else had to matter, apparently. Certainly not his *feelings*. Those disgusting fucking things were meant for weaker men, and Gian had no time for weakness. The only time he did indulge his feelings were when it came to a certain woman that was out of his reach.

"Well, are you coming to eat supper, or are you going to stand there in the entryway all night?" Elena asked.

"Did you cook it?"

"God, no."

"Then yes, I'll eat," Gian said.

He didn't even trust his wife not to try and kill him with food, honestly.

This was how their life was lived, now that they had to be together in some shape or form. Carefully, circling around each other with the occasional sharp word quick to show itself and cut the other person standing too close. Maybe it was easier for them both this way.

If they stuck to what *was*, they would not dig too deep into what had *been*.

Neither of them wanted that mess brought up.

Not again, anyhow.

The priest waved his hands upward in a sweeping motion to the parishioners, and everyone stood at the same time to be blessed a final time. Gian was grateful—it was almost over.

And by *it*, he meant his time with his wife for a couple of days.

Church was meant to be one of his peaceful times, but even that was becoming tainted by the fact that he now sat in a pew with his wife, instead of with his family like he once had. Appearances were everything, after all.

Some needed to be kept happier than others, in that regard.

"Finally," Elena grumbled under her breath as the priest dismissed the congregation. She stood, brushing down the skirt of her cream-colored, knee-length dress that matched her shoes and hat. "Mass never ends. I hate it."

And yet, she was one of the best dressed in the entire congregation.

"Church is good for the soul," Gian replied tiredly.

"People like us have no souls, Gian. This is nothing more than a farce, and if there is a heaven, we will only be allowed entrance because we paid our way in."

Touché.

"Chris can drive you home," Gian told his wife as he picked up his aviator sunglasses from the pew. "I have things to do today."

Elena pursed her lips. "I'm sure."

She didn't push him or argue his demands, though. Chris would be waiting outside to return Elena to the mansion, and she had another driver on speed dial to take her wherever in the hell she wanted during the week. She had a license and could drive perfectly well, but she preferred to be chauffeured about like a queen.

Gian didn't give a shit, as long as it wasn't him doing the driving.

It wasn't long after Elena was gone down the aisle that Dom slid in beside his brother in the pew. Gian allowed a few more people to head down the aisle, opting to stay behind with Dom to get his weekly update.

It always fucking hurt.

15

It sucked like nothing else.

Gian did it to punish himself, surely.

It still helped him to *breathe*.

"Well?" Gian asked.

Dom sipped from a to-go cup of coffee like he had all the time in the world. "Nothing new, really. Cara's been pretty quiet the last week. She's still working at that women's shelter over on the Fifth."

"Carolina's House," Gian said, naming the shelter.

He knew it, because he'd donated to it often over the years, given his family's history with the place.

Cara didn't know that, though.

She didn't know Gian watched her at all.

Dom nodded. "Still there. She'll be back in school next month, probably. I'm not sure about the shelter after that."

Knowing Cara, and what she wanted to do with her life, if the shelter allowed her a position while she remained in university, she would take it in a heartbeat. Gian hoped they gave her the chance. Dreams were worth following, after all.

"That's about all I have to tell on that side of things," Dom noted.

"*Nothing* else?" Gian asked.

Dom gave his brother a side-long look. "She's not been out with anybody, you know. And you could just outright ask that, instead of posing it like it's something else. I don't think she's even got time for a man, Gian."

He doubted that. Cara had time, if she wanted to make it. For whatever reason, she just hadn't made the time.

Yet.

Jealousy burned hot and heavy in his gut at the thought. Gian ignored the reckless, violent emotion, because what in the hell else could he do?

He couldn't force his wants upon Cara.

Hadn't he already hurt her enough?

"You could go see her," Dom suggested.

Gian scoffed. "Our last encounter did not end well. I doubt me showing up would go over spectacularly, either."

"Then why not leave her alone, man?" Dom nodded down the aisle where Elena had disappeared to. Most of the people had also cleared out of the church. "You do have a wife, Gian. Focus there, maybe."

"Right, my wife."

Fuck that.

Gian decided their conversation was going nowhere, and turned around to leave, only to come face to face with his father and mother. Frederic and Celeste made no attempt to hide the fact they had been standing there eavesdropping on the brothers' conversation.

"Do you have something you would like to add?" Gian asked his scowling father.

Frederic had no qualms about sharing his opinions with Gian, especially regarding his unconventional marriage, and the affair his son had had with Cara for months.

"Your brother has a point," Frederic said. "Don't go getting yourself caught up into another mess with the Rossi girl. Not now, Gian. You have better things to focus your time and energy on, and Elena is just one of those things."

"Or you could mind your fucking business."

"Gian!" his mother said, horrified and glancing toward the pulpit.

Gian wasn't in the mood to tone down his attitude for the sake of sensibilities. "I said what I said, Ma. I meant it."

"You married your wife," his father said, paying no attention to his wife or what his son had told him. "You chose to marry that girl, and now you have to live with it."

"I never got a choice, actually. I was given the illusion of a choice, which you're aware." Gian slid on his aviator sunglasses, and pushed past his father to head down the aisle. "It still makes no difference to what I told you. Mind your fucking business."

Chapter 2

There was something about the city of Toronto in the summer that Cara Rossi loved. People seemed happier in the summer.

It was definitely *not* Chicago.

Speaking of Chicago …

"Seems my sister is so busy, she can't even be bothered to phone me on a regular basis," Tommas said the moment Cara picked up her brother's call.

"I don't even get a hello, huh?"

"Do you think you deserve one?"

"I think I'm your only living sister, so a hello would be *nice*."

"Hello, Cara. Call me more often, please. I like to know you're still alive and kicking. Without having to call to ask if you *are*. Okay?"

Cara rolled her eyes upward. "I'm sorry I haven't called in a while; I *have* been busy, regardless of what you think."

"Do tell."

"I beg your pardon?"

"What has you so busy that you can't afford a five-minute phone call?" her brother asked.

"You're such a nosy little shit. I think you get that from your wife."

Tommas snorted. "Believe me, out of the two of us, it is me who is the nosiest. Abriella gets all the dirty details from me."

"I bet."

"I worry about you, Cara. That's all."

She slowed a bit in her walk to allow an older couple to go ahead of her. "You don't need to be worried about me at all. How was the wedding?"

"That was a month ago."

"I did call to congratulate you. You were gone. I left a message on the house phone."

"I have a cell phone, too."

"Which you turned off for days," Cara argued.

Tommas grunted under his breath. "Fine, my bad. I'm shit at keeping in touch, too. I get it."

"So, the wedding?"

"It was wonderful," Tommas said. "I waited a long time for that day."

Cara smiled. "Good, Tommy."

"We headed to New York after the wedding, and then took a trip to Italy for a bit. It took us a good two weeks after we got home to settle back into a routine. That, and Abriella had to find a new doctor that she liked and we had appointments for that to catch up on."

"A doctor, for what?"

Tommas cleared his throat. "So, we might have found out some good news the morning we got married."

"Like?"

"Like Abriella is pregnant," Tommas said quietly.

Cara came to a full stop on the city sidewalk, and people blew on past her like nothing was amiss. "*What?*"

"We haven't told a lot of people, but it won't be long before the news starts to travel. I wanted to be the one to tell you."

"Congratulations, Tommas. You're going to be a great dad." Then, Cara thought to add, "I don't talk to anyone from Chicago who would tell me, so no worries there."

"Word still has a way of getting around," Tommas said. "Which happens to be part of the reason I am calling you."

"I don't understand."

"I should have called the week after the wedding, when something got brought up in New York, but with Abriella and the honeymoon—"

"I don't need details on that," Cara jumped in fast.

Tommas laughed. "Relax, that's not what I'm talking about. I just meant to say my mind was elsewhere for a bit but now that I'm back home and shit is settled, I figured it was time to call."

"Again, not understanding, Tommy."

"Is something happening up there in Ontario that I might need to be aware of?" Tommas asked.

"Not that I know of."

"You visit Aunt Daniele and Uncle Claud."

"Yes."

"And nothing seems off in the family business?"

Cara sighed. "Tommas, you know I don't stick my nose in the mafia side of the family business. I stay far the hell away from it, and for good reason."

For one, because her twin sister had been killed by the mob. For two, because the last person she did get involved with, who happened to be mixed up with that, tore her fucking heart out and might as well have laughed about it.

She was *not* making that mistake again.

"Yes, but—"

"Tommas, you're seriously asking the wrong person. I don't have any idea what's happening in the Guzzi family. I haven't ever known, even when I was with Gian. Which by the way, haven't seen him in three months, and it'll be a few more before I do, if I can help it."

"Three months?"

Cara hummed out her confirmation. "I'm not any man's *goomah*. I don't give a fuck who he thinks he is."

Tommas coughed. "I'm not sure Gian ever thought that's what you were, either."

"You don't know that and besides, he didn't have to see me as his anything. What he did made everyone else see me in that way. That is bad enough."

"Point taken," her brother agreed quickly.

Cara was never going to allow another man to make her blind and stupid to his real life. She didn't give a shit how good-looking and charming he was on the outside. Gian Guzzi had seriously damaged Cara emotionally and publicly. She loved him—still did, really—but that meant nothing when his lies came into play.

She hoped he was happy with his wife.

Tommas' voice brought Cara from her thoughts. "But it was strange not to see someone from that family at the New York meeting. Do you remember what I told you three months ago?"

Cara didn't even have to think about it. "You said if I ever found myself in over my head with anything, all I needed to do was tell you and you would fix it."

"Good. Nothing's changed with that, Cara."

"I got it, Tommy."

"And call me more, for fuck's sake."

The first thing Cara had learned about Carolina's House was that it had been named after its unintentional founder. Carolina Demaske had taken in over a hundred women during the span of her ninety-four years of life. Women who were old and young, sick and helpless. She had nursed their bruised faces, cleaned their sick bodies, and helped raise their young children without ever asking for a single thing in return.

After Carolina had passed away, *her* daughters began the foundation that would eventually lead to the women's shelter Cara stood in front of.

Carolina's House was quiet when she strolled through the front doors. It wasn't unusual for a mid-week day. The women's shelter took in victims of domestic abuse, along with older teenage girls, and young mothers who needed help in various areas of their lives. Some needed the ability to safely get away from their abusive partners. Others needed a place to sleep, and the chance to get on their feet.

Cara had been incredibly lucky to be offered a spot at the shelter as a counselor of sorts. She worked alongside a registered therapist and counselor to help the women get their lives, business, and futures sorted out. Whatever they needed regarding legal things or even just *surviving*, Cara helped.

Or, she tried.

Cara wanted to be one of those people who *helped*.

She stopped at the drop-off room—a daycare-like space in the center where two volunteers watched over younger children while the mothers did whatever they needed to do for the day. She dropped off a bag of snacks she knew the kiddos loved. One of her favorite children noticed her presence instantly.

"Cara!"

"Hey, Mikey," she said, letting the three-year-old boy hug her around the legs. "What are you building today?"

"A train station."

"A train station, huh? Can I help?"

Mikey nodded enthusiastically. "Momma said she would help when she was done with Miss Jenny, but you can help, too."

Cara didn't hesitate to get down on the floor and help Mikey begin the building of what looked to be a huge train station. It was only once the kiddos noticed the treats that she was able to sneak out.

Carolina's House survived because of volunteers. Amazing men and women who came in with no expectations, only the desire to make life a bit better for someone struggling. People brought food. Some brought items for the babies and kids, or things the women needed. Every little bit helped.

Cara had learned something incredibly important since beginning her co-op program with the shelter. Money could only go so far, and while it could buy a hell of a lot for those in need, sometimes care, love and support helped even more.

"I hear someone wanted to see me today," Cara said, leaning in the doorway of her boss's office.

Jenny smiled from behind her desk. On the other side, Tiffany flipped through documents in a folder.

"You weren't busy, were you?" Jenny asked. "I know it's your off day."

"Nope. Never too busy for this." Cara slipped into the office, closed the door behind her, and took a seat beside the seventeen-year-old Tiffany. "Mikey is working hard on his train station, by the way."

At the mention of her son, Tiffany beamed. "I'm trying to save up enough to get him the big Lego set he wants for his birthday. It's a whole train. He saw it at the store. Killed me to tell him no."

Cara held back her frown. She had so much, when others had very little.

"When is his birthday?" Cara asked.

"Two months."

"You'll get it."

Cara would make sure of it.

The teenaged mother hadn't been given an easy life, and Mikey had been one of the final things to send her running from her abusive father. She had hopped from couch to couch with her son, never staying in school, and barely being able to hold down a job. Child Services had eventually caught up to the teen, and sent her home to live with her father.

Tiffany ran away with her son *again*. The second time, she came to Carolina's House. So far, Tiffany had gotten a job, and her GED testing was a month away, which Cara had no doubt the girl would ace. Tiffany's court appearance to be legally emancipated from her father and keep him from trying to take her son away, was in just two weeks.

"So, what's happening?" Cara asked Jenny.

Jenny nodded to Tiffany. "She had something she wanted to ask, and while I could have done it over the phone, I felt it better she ask directly."

Cara turned to the teen. "You have my cell number. You know you can call me anytime, right?"

Tiffany nodded. "Yeah, of course."

"What do you need?"

"I know the House set up a volunteer to take me to and from court, but I was hoping ... well, that *you* might do it, Cara. I know you're busy, and you start back at university next week, too. But—"

"Absolutely," Cara interjected quickly.

She was honored that Tiffany felt better having Cara there than anyone else.

"You won't have to miss anything?" Tiffany asked.

"It doesn't matter if I do," Cara replied. "Lots of stuff can be worked around. This, for you, is one thing that can't be. No problem at all."

Tiffany's hesitance left her eyes. "Thank you, Cara."

"Don't worry about it."

They fully suspected that Tiffany's father likely wouldn't even show up to court, but either way, *they* still had to go.

"I'm going to go find Mikey," Tiffany said.

Cara said goodbye, and once the girl was gone, turned to Jenny. "That's all? Did you want me to stick around and help with dinner or anything?"

"Extra hands for dinner would be great, but there is one more thing."

"Oh?"

Jenny shrugged. "Tiffany did mention something important. Your classes are starting up next week."

"So?"

"Your co-op term actually ended last week, Cara. You've already gotten your grade for this, sweetheart."

Cara just stared at the woman. "I'm here because I want to be, because this place is amazing and so are the women and the people who run it, not because of a grade."

Jenny nodded. "I know."

"Why mention it?"

"I wanted to ask if you would like to stay on, even after your classes start. We can work out days or evenings, weekends. It doesn't have to be a five-day-a-week thing, or whatever. The women love you, and the staff—"

"Yes." Cara didn't need to think it over. "You don't even have to ask."

The first day back to class was always a shit show for Cara. It meant rushing between halls and buildings to be early for professors that were almost always late, but had zero issue with calling out a student for coming in *after* they finally showed up. It also meant orientation for smaller classes, plus going over what could be expected for the coming semester.

Cara had another year left, and she was done. Not only did she already have her Masters of Social Work, but once the year was up, she would also add her master's degrees of science and in public health. *If* she decided to take her education further, she could choose a residency program for psychiatry and continue on that path. But for now, her three master's would allow her the ability to work in several fields, including with children and mental health.

It was every goal she had wanted to achieve, and it was almost a reality.

She wasn't used to the early morning routine after the summer, though. Cara had even managed to forget to feed herself, which sent her running to the café she liked just a couple of blocks away from the university, when she had thirty minutes to spare.

Cara groaned at the sight of a long line when she stepped into the café. Unfortunately, another swarm of people came in right behind her. She quickly filed into line in order to not wait any longer.

By the time she did get to the front of the line to place her order, Cara was damn near terrified to check her watch and see how late she already was for her second to last class. She quickly asked for a coffee, bagel, and cookie to-go. Though she was hungry for more, her stomach would have to wait until she got home.

"Your order will come up down there," the barista said, pointing at the end of the counter.

"Great, thanks."

Cara fiddled with her bag as she waited for her order. She kept glancing down at her watch to check the time, but her solitude didn't last long.

"Are you waiting for someone?"

Looking over her shoulder, a pair of striking blue eyes met her gaze. The man was handsome enough, with a disarming smile and a sports coat slung over his arm. He leaned against the counter right behind Cara.

"Are you talking to me?" Cara asked.

The man nodded. "Sure am. It's a friendly thing to do, when the only other option is standing around waiting and talking to yourself."

Cara managed a laugh. "That's true. And no, I'm not waiting for someone."

"You kept looking at your watch. I just assumed."

"I'm late," Cara explained, "and getting later by the second."

"I'm Nathan," the guy said.

Cara spun around to take the hand he offered, noting his short-trimmed nails and smooth skin. He looked to be in his early thirties, if that. "Cara."

"Well, Cara, I'm glad you're not waiting for someone. At least no one is standing up a beautiful woman."

She arched a brow. "Are you working toward something?"

Nathan shrugged. "Would it get me anywhere if I was?"

"I'm not on the market for dating, sorry."

He glanced down at her hand, still firmly held in his. "No ring."

"None on yours, either."

"To be fair, a lot of surgeons take their rings off when they're on a shift. I just got off mine, though. But no, there isn't a ring."

Cara smiled. "A doctor."

"You don't sound surprised."

"Your hands give it away."

Nathan chuckled. "I'm going to take that as a compliment."

"Miss, your order is ready."

Cara dropped Nathan's hand with a shrug and turned to grab her waiting goods. "Thank you for the conversation, but I really am late."

"No problem." He flashed her a smile. "Have a good day, Cara."

"You, too."

Cara had only taken a couple of steps toward the door, when a familiar figure passed by the café's windows outside the business. She recognized the man for two reasons—one, he shared similar features to his brother, and for two, she had seen his face on the news over and over again several months earlier.

Domenic Guzzi.

Gian's younger brother.

For a second, Cara simply stood there, watching Domenic pass by the café without as much as a look inside. She didn't even know if the guy would recognize her, but it didn't much matter. He didn't matter, really. It was just the fact that Cara almost expected to see Gian, too.

How long could they be in the same city without running into one another? And she *really* hated how a part of her wanted that run in, too.

Move on, she told herself.

Before she could think better of it, Cara turned on her heel to approach Nathan again. It didn't have to mean anything, but a date was a date, and it meant she wasn't wallowing on a man who had severely fucked her over in the emotions department.

"Did you forget something?" Nathan asked when Cara approached him. He already had his order in hand, and looked like he was ready to head out, as well.

She held out her phone, the screen unlocked and ready to input a new contact. "Plug your number in—no guarantees, though."

He glanced down at her phone before taking it from her. "No promises here, either."

Cara could work with that.

Chapter 3

There was nothing more irritating to Gian than seeing a pair of Royal Canadian Mounted Police detectives waiting for him at the front desk of his building. At least, the managers and ladies working the front desk knew better than to allow the RCMP detectives straight up to Gian's penthouse.

Ever since Corrado died, the police attention on the Guzzi family was … rough. Damn near constant. It didn't help that following Corrado's murder, several more deaths followed in the organization, and most done in a public way.

For the most part, the Canadian crime family managed to keep their heads down and their noses clean where police were concerned. They lived under the rule that less attention was better. This, unfortunately, was blowing that all to hell.

"Gian," the taller of the two detectives—Seeley, Gian thought his surname was—greeted.

The shorter of the two, the one with wide-framed glasses and a suit that always needed pressed, hung back from his partner. He was usually that way whenever the detectives showed up for another round of *make-Gian-talk-and-get-shot-down*.

"Detective Seeley," Gian replied dryly. Then, he nodded to the quiet detective. "Shaw."

Seeley glanced upward at the tall ceilings of the building, and then quickly back to Gian. "*Je voudrais*—"

"English only, please," Gian interrupted.

Seeley's jaw clenched.

Gian made pissing these men off into a game.

"You speak French," the man said firmly.

"Today I want to speak English," Gian replied. "Serve me in my language of choice, as you're *supposed* to do. I know how the police works in this country. We're all on a nod and greet basis out there on the streets, aren't we? Use English."

"Fine, English it is."

Gian stuffed his hands in his pockets, and rocked on his heels, pleased as fuck to have once again, annoyed the cops. Maybe if he did it enough, they would leave him the hell alone for a week. He doubted it, but he figured the risk was worth it.

All Royal Canadian Mounted Police were required to speak both official languages of the country. English and French. Gian found the detectives assigned to irritating him preferred French, and because *he* spoke French fluently, they expected him to converse in that language.

Gian was just as unpleasant in French when it came to cops as he was in his other languages. Cops all held the same distinct stench. Their job was to *seem* nice to him, to placate his distrust with them, and bring him in closer to their schemes. They put men like him away all the damn time, and Gian refused to be their next foolish sheep.

"I want to discuss some things that came up in your grandfather's case, and see if you could confirm anything for me," Seeley said.

Gian passed the man a look. "Corrado has been dead for months; you should leave him that way and let his soul rest in peace."

"Don't you want justice for your grandfather?"

How little they knew …

Justice had already been served.

"What information do you have?" Gian asked, determined to get these idiots out of his building so he could get back up to his penthouse. "And what do you want from me?"

Seeley took a folder from Shaw and opened it up. The very top item happened to be a photograph of a man with half of his face blown off, but the other side was perfectly recognizable. Gian focused on the recognizable part instead of the grisly bits with brain matter and fluids soaking into the green grass under the body.

"Nik Tradek," the detective said. "Hired gun. We did a bit of digging and found some interesting emails and numbers between him and another dead man of the Guzzi Cosa Nostra—Constantino Rossi."

"And?"

"It wasn't exactly made quiet *why* Constantino was killed, I mean, not when it came to rumors on the streets."

There was a reason for that; Gian wanted it made clear that anyone who came up against him or his family would meet the same fate. Their closeness to him mattered for *nothing*.

"Rumors are not admissible in court," Gian reminded the detective.

"Be that as it may, word only travels when there's a ring of truth."

"Again," Gian drawled, "*and?*"

"Nik showed up dead last month. As you can see, his face was blown off, or most of it."

Yes, because it'd taken two months to find the bastard. He lived his life underground and off the grid.

Gian wanted him dead.

He got his wish.

Gian made a dismissive noise. "Well, I guess that's one less killer in Canada, then, isn't it?"

Seeley sighed, closing the folder and passing it back to his partner. "Gian, I know you're not a stupid man."

"You're right, I'm not."

"Then let's talk."

"I'd rather not, I'm not stupid, after all. You said it first."

"Then let *me* talk," the detective said.

"You did waste your time coming all the way here, so be my guest, Detective Seeley."

The man gestured at the file his partner held. "You should be aware—if you aren't already—that this really is no longer about Corrado's murder, or the many deaths that followed after his. This is about the Guzzi organization as a whole, and putting an end to the reign your family has had in this city—"

"Country," Gian corrected smoothly. "We're the largest organization in this country, at the moment, and for the unforeseeable future, too. We have always been the reigning organization, and that isn't going to change. Even when the cops couldn't handle something like the biker gang wars, *we* did. And for the most part, the Guzzi organization keeps a tight leash on gangs and other violent entities that cause us issues, which in return, cause the people and *you* issues."

Seeley tipped his chin up, defiant.

Gian smirked in response.

"I mean, you could be grateful," Gian added.

"Right, that's the word police are known to use for *criminals*."

Gian waved that off. "Those are semantics. If you're here to tell me that the focus of the police has changed from putting away murderers, to bringing my family down, then you're too little too late. You see, I took care of the issues that needed taken care of, and *you* can take that however you want to. What it means, however, is that you're left with the rest of us on your side of things, including me. So, here I am. I've even made it easy on you."

"I beg your pardon?"

Gian held out his wrists, offering them to the detective. "You didn't even have to ride an elevator to arrest me. Here you go, do your job."

"I—"

"Can't," Gian interjected. "Yeah, I know. But hey, I'm really starting to look forward to these weekly meets and the games we play, so maybe in a few more, we'll actually get to the point where we can sit down and have coffee. Or maybe not."

"And how are those growing pains coming along in the organization?" the detective asked, moving an inch closer. "How difficult it must be for a boss of your age—even with your last name—to gain any traction with some of those men?"

Gian let his cool, calm expression take over as he answered, "So you're watching, then? Good, see if you can keep up. *Je suis désolé, mais je dois y aller,* Detective. Have a good day."

"We're not done talking, Gian."

Gian had already turned back and was heading for the elevator. His response was a flick of his hand over his shoulder, even when the detective called out for him again.

Oh, they were done.

Entirely so.

"Explain to me, boss, how a man who gets driven around ninety percent of his time, has managed to get two parking tickets and one for speeding, in three months?"

Gian glared at the back of Christopher Basso's head from his spot in the rear seat. "You know they only pulled me over on the speeding ticket just to get a look inside my car."

"Says you."

"I wasn't speeding," Gian muttered.

"You are aware I know that you drive like a bat out of hell, right?"

"Shut up, Chris."

"What about the two parking tickets?" the enforcer asked.

Gian scowled. "I couldn't find a spot. I used a fire lane a couple of times—whatever."

"You'll be lucky if they don't demote enough points from your license to take it from you today."

"They're not going to take my license, for fuck's sake."

"Well, if they do, I'll still be here to drive your ass around."

"You sound like you're enjoying this," Gian accused.

In the rearview mirror, Chris flashed a grin. "I *enjoy* keeping you on your toes, sure. You're the only made man I know who doesn't spend all his time in court for offences related to the organization, but instead, his shitty driving habits. I'm serious, they're going to take your license one of these days."

"You know what, fuck—"

"Here we are," Chris said, pulling the car over to the side of the road. "You've got a half an hour to get through security and see the judge. Tamper down the attitude, and pay your fines again."

Gian flipped the enforcer off as he pushed out of the car. Leaning back in, he pointed at Chris and said, "This isn't over."

"Maybe they'll send you for Driver's Ed, boss!"

Gian slammed the car door closed as hard as he fucking could in response to that nonsense. Chris wasted no time pulling back onto the road, likely knowing he had pushed his luck with his boss enough for the day. Turning, Gian faced the courthouse and the busy steps filled with people coming and going. This wasn't his first rodeo at the place, and likely wouldn't be his last.

It took Gian twenty-five minutes, just to get through security because of the long line of waiting people. He slipped into the courtroom designated for traffic offenses and had just enough time to sit his ass down before his name was called. Like a robot, he went through the motions of the court as he had done many times before.

The only ticket Gian chose to dispute was the speeding ticket, because fuck, he had *not* been speeding that day. Since the officer in question didn't show up, the judge tossed it out. Gian was still left with two demerits off his license, and a nearly thousand-dollar fine.

"Pay within thirty days, or on floor four," the judge ordered, his gravel hitting down with a loud enough bang to make Gian's headache pound.

Great.

Chris was going to have a field day with this nonsense.

Gian wanted to get the whole day over with, and while he could pay at home on the government website, he headed through the maze of people for the bank of elevators. One elevator opened, and a flood of people came out. Gian bolted for that one, not wanting to wait for the next. A few climbed in behind him, and the doors closed. From ground floor, the elevator went up one, stopped, and dropped half of the people off. Only one other person climbed in.

At the third floor, one used mainly in the courthouse for private consultations before appearances, the only other person got off the elevator. In their haste, they bumped into the one person coming on.

Cara Rossi.

She didn't see him right away, as she was too busy glaring at the asshole over her shoulder who hadn't even bothered to apologize for running into her. But when she did see him, the door was starting to close, she was already on the elevator, and Gian was frozen in place.

Cara seemed to be in the same state.

"Gian," she said.

That was it.

That was all she said.

Just his *name*.

And good God, how he missed that sound coming out of her mouth.

The elevator moved up, closer to his floor.

Gian didn't know *why*, as he knew better than to corner Cara, but the part of him that hadn't seen her in three months, the piece of him that had been lost and torn and so fucking useless, made him move. He pulled the emergency switch, and the elevator jerked to a halt. A red light came on, illuminating the space. A bell-like sound dinged through the speakers.

He was well aware of the camera just above his head, but since he didn't plan on doing anything that would get them in shit, he ignored it for the moment.

Cara shifted in her heels, the black dress she wore showed off all kinds of leg and skin, but was still long enough to be appropriate. "This is a courthouse, Gian, not your personal place of business or something. You can't just shut off an elevator."

"I just did," he said quietly.

"And someone will start it back up if you don't push the switch again."

"So be it, but it gives me a minute."

"To do what?" she asked.

Gian wasn't sure how to answer that, so he went with the blunt truth that had been stabbing at him for months. "To just look at you, say hello, anything, Cara."

"And if I'm not interested in any of that?"

"Then say so."

Cara only stared at him, pain reflecting in her blue eyes. It killed him that he had been the one to do that to her—that his lies did this to *them*. He no longer wanted to excuse his actions, and he knew they couldn't be explained away, but he still wanted *her*.

He loved her.

So badly.

"I did tell you," Cara whispered, "three months ago when I left your penthouse. I told you then, Gian."

"And I've left you alone, haven't I?"

"Yes, but—"

"You should know that I think about you all the fucking time, Cara, even when I know it's the last thing I should be doing. I miss you, constantly. I'm alone all the time, too, even when I'm not, and it's not even your fault. I know I did this. I fucked up, I know. I'm sorry, *mon ange*. I would do it a thousand ways differently, if I could, now."

"Except you can't," Cara said, a fire returning to her eyes and a heat in her tone. "You lied and lied and lied *more*, Gian."

"I didn't tell you the whole story, but I didn't purposely keep it from you."

"It, you say. *It*. Come on, say what *it* is. Your *wife*."

Gian drew in a slow breath, murmuring, "Yeah, my wife. Estranged, spoiled, difficult, hateful, bitter, but yes, *my* wife, Cara."

"And how is she? Your wife, I mean."

"Pleased in her place," he replied frankly.

He had nothing else to offer in that regard.

Elena wasn't worth it to him, not after everything.

"I hate you," Cara said so softly he strained to hear the words. "I hate that I want to say things right now to hurt you, *only* to hurt you, Gian. I hate that I want you to know what it felt like to trust you, and then watch you fucking ruin it like you did. I hate you for doing that to me."

He could work with hate, maybe.

Hate was passionate, too.

Like love.

"You broke my heart, Gian."

"Well, I hope my heart has been a suitable replacement, Cara. Because you still have mine, and you didn't bother to give it back. It's like waking up with a giant hole in my chest every single day. I can't *not* know it's gone. I always know. And maybe I don't have any right to say that at all, but there it is."

Cara glanced away, but he saw the wetness in her eyes all the same.

"I'm sorry," Gian said again as the first tear slipped from the corner of Cara's eye. "I hate me, too."

Tears meant something—she wasn't numb and she wasn't cold. Not to him or what had happened, anyway. It meant there was a part of her that wasn't done or hadn't entirely moved on from everything. She hadn't moved on from them.

"Are you done now?" Cara asked. "Have you gotten what you wanted? Can I go?"

He wanted to say no. He had her barricaded in an elevator, and God only knew how long he would be able to keep her there. He could finally force her to listen to the shit he had to say, if he wanted to.

Gian had a feeling that would not help him with Cara, only hurt him. He couldn't force her back to his side, he couldn't demand her there, and he wouldn't ever lie to her again to have her with him, either.

If she wanted him, wanted to be *with* him, he needed her to do that on her own. She would then understand it was because she wanted that, too, and had done so, knowing exactly what it meant for both of them.

He couldn't give her what she deserved. He couldn't be her husband, or live with her in a public fashion. She would never be looked at with the same respect his wife would, and in fact, would face a barrage of shit *just* because she wasn't his wife.

And the titles she would wear because of his selfishness?

Homewrecker. Whore. Mistress. Slut. *Goomah.*

Gian could keep going, too. He'd heard them all be slung at the woman his grandfather had loved for decades, a woman Corrado barely spoke about to anyone. How could those same people justify shaming someone, when they didn't even know her or why she made her choices?

Why would Gian knowingly do that to Cara?

He loved her, so why hurt her more?

Gian stepped closer to Cara, and she didn't move away. Instead, she watched him carefully, with a stone-still body, painted red lips, and eyes that cut him to the core. He reached up, the side of his hand brushing along her cheek to push back the stray curl, before his thumb swept under her eye to wipe away the tear stain.

She was still so beautiful.

Like fucking life in his hands.

"I didn't mean to do this," he told her.

Cara nodded. "Yeah, I know, but you still did, Gian."

"And what I said, before you walked out on me that day, remains the same."

"You tried to say a lot."

"I have only ever loved you," Gian murmured as he leaned forward and pressed a soft kiss to Cara's forehead. His thumb stroked her cheek, and she didn't move away, but he felt the wetness of her tears slip down to his skin away. "And I'm sorry that it hurts you, Cara. I'm sorry that I hurt you. I'm sorry that I love you."

"Me, too."

Gian reached behind Cara and pushed the emergency switch on the elevator. It took a couple of seconds for the machine to respond, for the red light to go off, and for the elevator to move again. Cara turned away from him, then, pressing the second-floor button.

At his floor, Gian expected the people and security waiting there as the door opened to let him out. He shrugged off their questions, giving no answer as to what happened to stop the elevator.

Behind him, he heard Cara whisper as he walked out, "I miss you, too."

For them, he had been sure it was far too late. He had done that, not her.

But was it?

"Drive," Gian demanded the second he shut the car door.

Chris glanced at his boss through the rearview mirror. "Shit, that bad?"

"*Drive.*"

Quickly, the car pulled off onto the road, but the enforcer was still keeping one eye on Gian. It made him feel like a bug under a microscope. He couldn't hide the fact he was emotionally unsettled—sad, haunted, and angry all at once.

He couldn't hide shit when it came to Cara.

"You know I was just joking about the whole losing your license thing, right?"

"I didn't lose my license. I paid the fucking fines. Take me home."

"Boss—"

"Shut up and drive," Gian snapped.

"You got it, boss."

Chris didn't ask or say another thing. The man made no jokes as he navigated city traffic, and headed in the direction of Gian's penthouse. Gian, on the other hand, stewed in his fucking mess of emotions the entire way, alternating between glaring out the window, and hiding his clenched hands in his pockets.

He had paid his fines, and then gotten the hell out of the courthouse as fast as he possibly could. He feared that if he ran into Cara again, he wouldn't have as much control the second time around. He thought it was very possible that he might just grab her, make her listen, and have her talk to him more than what she already had.

Gian was an *idiot.*

It was only the ringing of his phone that brought him out of his frustrated daze. He didn't even bother to check the caller ID as he swiped the screen and then put it to his ear. The usual, causal Italian and French greeting he answered with was gone because of his current mood, leaving a rude bark in its place.

"What?" he snarled into the phone.

"Well, hello to you too, asshole."

Gian's anger kicked up a notch or two at his wife's voice. "What do you want, Elena?"

"Rough day?"

"Do you care?"

"Not really," she answered sweetly.

"Why are you calling me on a Tuesday?"

He wasn't due back at the mansion until tomorrow evening, at the latest. He didn't spend every day and evening there, if he could help it. Usually, he found excuses. As long as it *appeared* that he was in a relationship with his wife, then no one would bother to look too deeply into what was actually going on.

That was good enough for Gian.

As it was, this façade took enough work.

"Dinner, with my father. It's coming up. He called, and wanted me to remind you."

Fuck.

Gian's irritation managed not to spill over into the phone when he said, "Great, anything else?"

"Nope."

Wonderful.

He hung up without a goodbye, and didn't feel guilty for it. After all, Elena would do the same for him.

Chapter 4

"Quaint little place, isn't it?"

Cara's head popped up, and her nerves instantly bloomed at the sight of Frankie Ricci. He seemed relaxed, with his hands shoved in his pockets and a small smile on his face.

The coffee shop buzzed with noise around them.

"Frankie, hey," Cara greeted.

"Studying?"

She closed her spread-open books. "Trying. Sit."

He did, taking the only other chair at the table. She couldn't help but wonder, when he looked at her, was he seeing Lea and not *her*?

"You all right?" Frankie asked.

Cara shrugged. "So, so."

"I didn't expect to get a call from you, and especially not one to meet up."

"I, uh ... was in a shitty place for a bit."

Cara packed her books away. It had taken her months just to gain up the courage to contact Frankie, never mind considering what they would actually talk about. She had *lots* to ask and say. Whether he would answer ... that was the question.

"Thanks for agreeing to meet me," Cara said.

Frankie leaned back in the chair, his posture softening. "No problem. I noticed you've been quiet lately."

"Quiet?"

"Not so ... out and about." Frankie smiled, adding, "With the boss."

"Gian."

He lifted a hand as if to say, *who else.*

Cara cleared her throat. "I haven't been out with Gian in three months."

"Ah."

"You don't sound surprised."

"Because I'm not," he replied. "I'm even less surprised because I know his wife has taken a more active role in his business side of life. More than she ever did when they first got married. Kind of forces you into the back seat, doesn't it?"

Cara bristled. "I'm not *with* him at all."

"I didn't assume that, either."

Cara checked her impulsive defensiveness. "I'm sorry, don't mind me. It's a knee-jerk reaction. I feel like everyone I met knew what was happening, everybody except for me. No one thought to tell me that he was married, or that I was an affair."

Frankie's expression didn't change. "Define 'affair' for me, Cara."

"Why?"

"Because your definition of it won't fit with a lot of people's opinions of the word."

"Really?"

Frankie nodded once. "That's what I said."

"He's married."

"Yes."

"He was involved with me in a relationship."

"Again, yes," Frankie said.

"Then that is an affair," Cara pointed out.

Frankie still didn't look entirely bothered by Cara's reasoning. "I mean, technically, sure. But only because men who join our … thing, aren't allowed to be divorced, for the most part. Some do, sure, but they know they're never going fucking anywhere. Gian, being an underboss at the time, couldn't afford something like a divorce, given the circumstances of his marriage."

"Circumstances like?" Cara pressed.

"That's something he'd have to answer. I just know arrangements aren't usually made to be broken."

"He was still having an affair with me. He made me his mistress and he didn't even have the decency to tell me."

"Because he didn't have paper stamped from a proper divorce," Frankie replied softly. "After how many years of being separated from his wife, is he allowed to have a relationship with someone else? Even though they were clearly separated, why do words like affair have to be tossed into it? Why does the fact he's married—but again, separated—have to be the first thing to be brought up in conversation? Seems unfair to him."

"That's easy for you to say, to defend his actions, sure. But people still consider her to be his wife. They are still married." Cara glanced away. "Does it seem unfair because you, too, were miserable in your relationship with your wife, and occasionally found a happy pause with my sister?"

Frankie blew out a slow breath. "A happy *pause?*"

"You're still with your wife, aren't you?"

"Yes. We have one child, a girl. Our first boy is on the way, due in a month. We're very much together. Happily, I might add."

"Happily. Even after what you did?"

"My wife and I were a lot like Lea and I were, before the pregnancy thing got in the way. Casual, no strings, and we didn't get too deep with one another on an emotional level. And then the pregnancy came, so our family forced us to do the *right* thing." Frankie's tone twisted bitterly, and his lips curved into a sneer. "We didn't want to be married. She didn't want me around, and I didn't want to be there, either. You think she *didn't* know? She knew, but she didn't care. She didn't consider us together, even if everybody else did because we weren't divorced."

"Oh," Cara murmured.

"Our unhappiness meant nothing to everyone else, as long as we continued doing the right thing for who we are," Frankie continued with a heavy sigh.

"And so, Lea ..."

"Was there," he said, "and it was stupid and easy, but it hurt us both a lot, too."

"And what about your wife?"

"Our daughter was born, and I was over there a lot more. I stayed with her, to help with the baby and whatever else. You could say the baby brought us closer, as silly as that might sound. It'd been a while since I had seen Lea at all when she died," Frankie admitted, frowning. "There was no proper breakup or goodbye, whatever. It was hard, and it set me back for a while with my wife because I felt like I couldn't explain what was happening inside my head. Circumstances being what they were, and all."

"But did you?"

"Eventually." Frankie chuckled. "She's pretty amazing, my wife."

"Did you love my sister?" Cara dared to ask.

"Not in the right way," Frankie said without even thinking about it. "Not in a way she should have been, not like I do with my wife now. It took a while to figure that out, too."

"In an unhealthy way?"

"Exactly."

Cara tapped her fingernails to the table, settled in her heart, yet restless in her soul. "Thanks for meeting up with me to talk about this. I know it's private, and you really didn't need to tell me anything, if you didn't want to."

"I don't think this was only for you to talk and learn about Lea."

"Well—"

"I mean, you can say that, but I don't think it is. I think that you've gotten yourself tangled up in your own situation with a man, and like your sister, you keep running—"

"I haven't gone back once, actually."

"But you consider it. You *want* to."

Cara wouldn't look Frankie in the eye. "I'm not like Lea, and I'm not like your wife, Frankie. I have a line that I don't want to cross, and I didn't appreciate being forced over it without even knowing what was happening."

"Fair enough. Question for you, then."

"Sure."

"Had Gian said upfront that he had a wife—estranged for years, basically separated from, whatever—would you have continued seeing him?"

"I don't know," Cara answered.

But her voice wavered.

She had taken a second to answer.

Frankie continued staring at her, and in that moment, she didn't think he looked at her and saw Lea at all. He just saw a confused, sad woman.

"I think you do know, Cara. Again, circumstances, and all. They make all the difference."

Cara made a dismissive sound. "Well, it certainly does now, anyway. Like you said, his wife is present, apparently."

"Public opinion counts for too much in this life, unfortunately, and we made men are entirely to blame for that, too."

She didn't reply to that.

She didn't know how to.

Cara fidgeted in an attempt to soothe her nerves as the maître D' of the posh restaurant scrolled through reservations on a tablet. It didn't help, and considering it had been months since she had dressed up and gone out on a formal date, she felt all kinds of awkward.

"Name?" the man asked.

"Rossi. Cara."

"Ah, here we are. Follow me."

Cara managed to get distracted by the high-vaulted ceilings of the restaurant, and the crystal chandeliers hanging over every single table. She was led closer to the open concept kitchen of the restaurant, and further away from the bar.

"Miss," the maître D' said, bringing Cara from her daze. "Your table."

Cara thanked the man, and sat down at the empty table. Checking her phone, she noted she wasn't early, but she wasn't late, either.

Nathan—the doctor she met at the café—arrived less than five minutes after she had sat down, wearing a proper suit and a smile. "Cara."

He took her hand, bent down, and kissed two of her knuckles, allowing her to stay seated. Then, he too took the only other chair available at the table.

"Why do you seem surprised to see that I showed up?" Cara asked.

Nathan laughed, taking the menus from the server before shooing the man away. "No promises, remember? That's what you told me when we met. I get a random text, just as I'm coming out of a routine surgery, that asks about dinner, and nothing else. That doesn't seem a little on-the-fence to you?"

Cara had to give him that. "All right, fair enough."

"You look beautiful."

"Thank you. And this place is …" Cara waved a hand high. "Amazing."

"It helps to know people sometimes," Nathan joked. "The owner is a friend from way back. I always get reservations last minute, when others can't.

"Nice to know."

"Drinks before food?"

"No on the drinks. I think I'll let you order the food for both of us. Surprise me."

Nathan flashed her with a smile. There was nothing necessarily wrong with the man. He was charming, good-looking, and decent, by all standards. He looked fit, well-dressed, and had a good path in his life. He was everything that she should want in a man, because he was safe and nice and appropriate.

Cara felt nothing looking at him.

Nathan did nothing for her.

Sad, really.

She just wanted to feel normal again.

It didn't help that it felt like someone was watching her. Cara tried to brush the odd sensation off and ignore it. Despite regretting her spur of the moment decision to text Nathan for a date, Cara decided to stick it out.

It was only after the food had arrived, and Cara picked at the dish set in front of her, that Nathan cleared his throat loudly.

Cara glanced up at him. "Yes?"

"You didn't hear a word I just said, did you?"

Had he been talking?

Ouch.

"Sorry," Cara said. "I'm not very good company, am I?"

Nathan smiled, but she could see the truth in his stare. "Let's be honest here, Cara. We're not going to repeat this, are we?"

"Probably not. It's not you … it's me, really. I've got no business going on dates at the moment, I think. I thought trying might help. It didn't."

"Yet, you asked me out tonight."

"A shitty attempt at something different," Cara said in explanation.

Nathan didn't look like he understood, but who could?

Cara was a mess.

And not in a good way.

Nathan took her rejection in style, thankfully. Although, he was quieter through the rest of the meal. He offered to walk Cara out of the restaurant once they were done, but she only agreed to let him walk her to the bar. She didn't want a drink, just a second to sit alone and think.

At the bar, Nathan leaned in, his hand resting on her lower back, and kissed her on the cheek. "Thank you for coming out with me tonight."

Cara laughed lightly. "You've got to be one of the strangest men I have ever met. Rejection doesn't bother you a bit, does it?"

"We win some, we lose some."

"Thanks for … not being an asshole."

Nathan's grin widened, and Cara let him kiss her cheek once more. "Enjoy the rest of your evening, Cara. You *do* have my number, in case you ever want to use it."

But she wouldn't use it.

Cara watched Nathan stroll out of the restaurant with his hands in his pockets, and no worse for wear than he had been when he first arrived. The bartender took her order for ice water in a glass, and Cara surveyed the rest of the restaurant while she waited.

It was only when her gaze landed on a familiar pair of dark eyes that she finally understood why it felt like someone had been watching her.

Gian.

He sat at a corner table, tucked away in a quieter part of the restaurant with dim lighting, and what looked to be a glass of whiskey in front of him. Across from him sat an older gentleman, dressed just as well as he was, although the man was several pounds heavier around his middle. His guest seemed entirely oblivious to the fact that Gian was no longer engaged in their conversation, but rather, focused on Cara at the bar like she was the only person in the room.

His stare did not feel like it usually did.

It was hard.

So cold.

Angry, even.

Those dark eyes of his pinned her in place, lips smoothed into a thin, grim line, and his sharp jaw tensed as he looked her over. She didn't miss the slide of his gaze darting to the left, in the direction Nathan had gone. His hand clenched around his glass tight enough for Cara to see his knuckles go white.

Great.

Cara would recognize that look anywhere, even if Gian had no business sporting it. He was fucking jealous.

All over, unnecessarily, completely *jealous*. And fuck, it looked good on him. Like every other goddamn expression he wore, from his indifference to his rage, to his sweetness in the mornings, and the way he looked when he fucked her. It all looked damn good.

She had just spent a little more than an hour with a man who was everything that Gian was not, in certain ways. She hadn't managed to feel anything for him, not even an ounce of the confusing mess she felt with just a *glance* at Gian Guzzi.

How was that fair?

She should be over this ridiculous mess by now.

Even *Gian* had told her that she would be fine—that she was the kind of woman who could fall again and again, yet manage to brush herself off and move on with her life. Yet, there she was, *not moving the fuck on.*

Frustrated, Cara turned away from Gian, refusing to meet his stare again or acknowledge his presence. She had gone months without running into him in the city, and now, in a matter of just a couple of weeks, she had run into him twice.

Someone from up above was laughing at her. Clearly, she had no guardian angels looking out for her.

She snatched up the glass of ice water when the bartender finally brought her the drink, and took a sip. Maybe, if she just pretended like she hadn't noticed Gian twenty feet away, he would opt to go the same route she did.

Cara hoped for too much.

Just as she finished her water and slid the glass back across the bar, she felt his presence slip in behind her. It was fucking crazy and stupid and intense how that worked. The very fact that he didn't even need to speak, or make a noise, and she just *knew*.

Knew that he was there.

Knew that he was looking at her.

Knew him.

"Are you going to corner me somewhere and make me talk again?" Cara asked without turning around.

"No," Gian said, his voice a rough murmur.

"Good, because I'm about to leave."

"Is your date waiting outside?"

"That's none of your business," Cara replied.

"Maybe not, but I asked, Cara."

She turned slowly to face Gian, taking note that he still seemed a hell of lot more tense than he normally did. Even with his hands shoved in his pockets, she could still see his unease in his narrowed gaze and tight jaw.

"You have no business asking anything," Cara reminded him.

Gian's jaw ticked. "So you don't want to answer, then?"

"There's nothing to tell, and you *don't get to ask.*"

"I—"

"Don't you have a guest at your table?" she interrupted, her annoyance rising fast.

"It was over ten minutes ago, but it took him this long to realize I wasn't interested in the conversation he was offering. Enough about me, let's get back to you."

Cara bristled. "Excuse me?"

"Who was that man?"

"None of your bus—"

"Cara." The quiet way he said her name, so heavy and thick, made her back straighten as a shiver crawled up her spine. *Damn him.* Gian took one step closer to Cara, ensuring she couldn't move, as she was backed into the goddamn bar. "At least tell me who he is, that's all."

"A date, someone I met. Happy?"

Gian's eyes flashed with his jealousy, and she hated him for that, too.

"No, I'm not *happy.*"

"Well, don't ask if you don't really want to know."

"How long?" he asked.

"I'm not answering that one."

"I've seen him here before, with the owner. I could always … ask around."

Cara stiffened a bit. "You have no right to do that, Gian. Whether or not I see someone, or go out with someone, or *fuck* someone, isn't for you to know or have an opinion on. I'm not yours, now. You don't get a say in anything I do. Learn that, and fast."

By the time she had finished her tirade, her voice had turned into a harsh whisper.

Gian barely blinked a lash at her rage.

"It fucked me up," he said, shrugging one shoulder, "seeing you out with somebody else. Smiling like you do, and it just … fucked me up, Cara. I thought, who the fuck is he, and what in the hell is she doing, and *why?* And it's fucking disgusting how fast I thought about finding out who he was just to kill him. And you—Jesus, Cara—you don't even realize how pissed off it makes me that you *smiled* for him, *mon ange.*"

Cara sucked in a low breath, willing it to give her some sense of calm. It didn't help.

Screw him for the fact he made her hot and bothered, and all he had to do was *threaten* a man he didn't even know. God, she hated this and the confusing way it left her feeling.

"You don't get to say those kinds of things to me. We're not together. I can date whoever I want. I already told you that. And stop calling me your pretty French pet names, Gian."

"Why? It still fits. My angel."

"I'm not *yours*," Cara snapped. "Not anymore."

Gian smirked, his arrogance becoming all the more apparent. "Oh, Cara, you're always going to be mine. *Sempre, amore.*"

"I beg to differ."

"Do you want to play this game?"

"Gian—"

"You *are* mine, Cara, even if you're not with me. And do you want to know how I know that, sweet girl?"

Cara refused to look him in the eye. He stepped close enough that his body pressed against hers, but she couldn't move away. She kept her head turned to the side, even when his hand slid up to cup her cheek and his fingers threaded into her hair.

"I know you're still mine, because there's no way on earth you could tell me that man, or any other man, knows anything about you worth knowing."

"Stop, Gian."

Why was her voice so goddamn weak?

And why did she want to turn into his palm, not away like she was? *This isn't fair.*

"Has he, or anyone else, even touched you since me? Can you even *stand* to let someone have you the way you let me have you?"

Cara's gaze cut to his fast. "*Gian.*"

"Tell me."

"No."

"No, you won't tell or no, no one has touched you?"

Both of them.

Cara refused to say that out loud. Gian only smiled like he already knew the fucking truth, like he could see it written all over her face.

"Right. I would be willing to bet he knows *fuck all* when it comes to you," Gian said with a dark, husky laugh. "Like the way you won't get your ass out of bed in the morning, or all the little secrets you like to hold onto because you're locked up way too tight in your heart, and it takes a fucking sledge hammer to get through."

Gian inched closer, his unique scent soaking into Cara's lungs like a familiar drug. Liquor and leather and *man*. "Let's be honest, Cara, he doesn't know the shit that matters, really. He probably doesn't know what you like, either. I bet he doesn't know how you liked to be choked when you come, or the way you beg like a good little slut to have your ass filled when your—"

Cara's hand came up swift and *hard*. She didn't even think about it. Her palm cracked against Gian's cheek with enough force to silence the nearby tables of people.

"Excuse me, miss, do you need anything?"

The sound of the bartender's voice had Gian's burning gaze flying over Cara's shoulder, probably burrowing a fucking hole into the poor man who dared to intrude.

"It's fine," Cara said. "We're perfectly fine."

"If you're sure …?"

"She's sure," Gian uttered through clenched teeth.

Emotions warred within Cara, heating her cheeks and making her body vibrate. Her palm stung, but she didn't care. She glared at Gian, daring him to say another word, even when her hand dropped back down to her side. He didn't look away, but rather, his smirk grew sinful, like he had gotten exactly the reaction he wanted.

"I can say more, if you want," he said.

"Shut your mouth. How dare you, Gian?"

"Tell me I'm wrong. Tell me any man, except *me*, knows those things, and owns those things where you're concerned. *Tell me.*"

She couldn't.

"You can't say it, can you?" he asked.

"Fuck you."

"Tell me to get the hell away from you, then."

Cara didn't.

She hated herself for that, too.

What she despised even more, was when he kissed her—hard, demanding, and rough, just the way she liked the most—she didn't push him away. No, she fisted his jacket and bought him closer, she sighed at the familiarity of his hand curving around her throat and his tongue dancing with hers. She soaked in his scent, reveled in his taste, and hated herself for every second of it.

She wanted more, so she just pulled him closer.

Every bit of anger and disgust came out in Cara's kiss, and even more bled away the longer she didn't force Gian to stop. Not when his thumb pressed into her racing pulse, or his teeth bit into her lower lip.

She couldn't breathe, but fucking hell, she was awake and alive again for the first time in months.

Why did it have to be like this?

Why him and her?

Why?

He provoked her, she knew. His words had been *meant* to provoke her into this. She was weak enough to let him.

Cara's lips tingled from the brutality of Gian's kiss long after he had pulled away. *God*, she loved it.

Gian watched her like a predator, refusing to move his gaze even an inch, and not letting her drop her stare. She saw his jealousy still lit up like fireworks in his eyes, but she found so much more staring back at her, too.

A man she had missed for months. A man she still loved, though she knew it was bad. A man she wasn't even sure she knew.

So, why was he so familiar?

"You did that on purpose," Cara said, her accusation coming out quieter than she meant for it to. "You provoked me on purpose, Gian."

"I did nothing that you didn't want me to, *mon ange*."

She hated that pet name, too, because she didn't hate it at all when he said it.

Cara had damn near forgotten they were still in the restaurant, standing at the bar. It became impossible to ignore when the sound of clattering utensils from a nearby table broke her from her daze, and she realized how very public of a scene they had just made.

She finally dropped Gian's stare.

"Come with me," Gian murmured.

Cara shook her head. "No, and you know why."

"Don't do that, Cara. Don't refuse me when you know damn well that it's the very last thing you want to do. Come with me, be with me for a night, and fuck the rest. What's the issue?"

"You know exactly—"

Gian stepped away from her, cocking an eyebrow high as he did so. "We both could be doing far better things than standing here, arguing about nonsense and details that will never matter to me when it comes to us. And before you even spit it out of your pretty mouth, I don't think they matter all that much to you right now, either. I am leaving, my car will be waiting at the curb. I'll give you ten minutes, and then I'm gone. Come with me or don't, but I won't stand here and argue with you for another second."

Cara thought he was joking, or bluffing.

She should have known better.

Gian didn't joke or bluff.

He gave her a soft kiss on her cheek, and then he turned on his heel and headed for the front of the restaurant. There was so much she had wanted to shout at his back in that moment. Fuck him for the *details*, as he called them. Fuck him for making her choose like this. Fuck him for making her love him, breaking her heart, and then doing this to her too.

Why wasn't she stronger?

Why wasn't she a better woman?

When it came to Gian, apparently Cara was nothing more than a stupid, foolish girl who had no control over herself, nor did she want to have limits where he was concerned.

She watched the clock behind the bar.

At eight minutes, her heart won out.

Gian said nothing when Cara slid into his car.

Chapter 5

"I thought you didn't do angry sex," Cara said from her perch on the edge of Gian's bed. "Wasn't it you who said that was unhealthy?"

"I'm not angry."

She might be.

He sure as hell wasn't.

How could Gian be angry when, at the moment, he had Cara stripped down to nothing but her skin, in his penthouse, on his bed? How could he possibly be *angry*?

"You're not even a little bit mad?"

"About what?" he asked, shedding the final bits of his clothing.

"I did hit you."

He shrugged. "I *did* provoke you."

"I knew you did that on purpose."

"And look where you are now, my sweet girl."

Cara's eyes flashed with her desire and irritation. "Yes, how stupid of me, I fell right back in your bed."

"Where you belong, Cara."

Her red lips curved at the edges in a half-hearted smile. "You're impossible."

"So you've said a few times before."

Gian shoved his boxer-briefs down, not missing Cara's gaze dropping to his prominent erection. He'd been as hard as fucking steel from the moment he'd touched her at the restaurant.

It was a serious problem. He intended to rectify it as soon as possible.

Gian crossed the small bit of space between him and where Cara sat on his bed. She stared up at him, still and waiting. He wanted nothing more than to feed into the dark, debasing shit running through his mind. All the urges he couldn't fulfill elsewhere, and the needs that weren't helped with his memories of Cara.

He held back.

Barely.

"Could you snap your fingers for me?" she asked sweetly.

Too sweetly.

"Why?"

"At least then I can say I came running for something when you called."

Fuck.

Gian let out a hard breath. "Cara, stay or go."

She didn't move, neither did her blue gaze—the window into the most beautiful soul he had ever had the pleasure of knowing.

"But don't sit here and make it seem like I'm not giving you a choice," he continued when she stayed silent. "I want you here. I have wanted you here since the day I let you walk out, but don't make this into some hate-fuck session. It's never going to be that and if you need that to justify how you're going to feel tomorrow, then leave. Right now."

Her stare slid away from his. "You can't let me have anything, can you?"

"Not when I can see right through your shit, *bella*."

"You're making this hard on me."

"From where I'm standing, it seems pretty fucking easy."

"Of course it would, to *you*."

Gian opened his mouth to respond, but his air caught in his throat when Cara's hands reached for him, her fingers circled tight around his cock. She slid her palm under his sac to cradle his balls. Firm, long strokes of her hand—tight as fuck at the base, and a little looser at the tip—had his head falling back, and a thick groan escaping his chest. His cock jerked in her hand, when her thumb rolled one of his balls between her soft palm and her fingers. Gently, and not too rough, but shit if that didn't make him flex his hips forward into her strokes for more.

He didn't give a shit if it was her hands, her mouth, or her cunt. As long as his dick was on it, in it, or soaked by it. As long as she was touching, fucking, or doing *something* to him, all was well in his world.

Whatever it was, she was his heaven.

It was his *drug*.

How long had it been since she touched him?

Too damn long.

"You were right," Cara said, "at the restaurant, I mean."

"Do tell."

"There's been no one since you. There *can't* be. They're not you, Gian."

"I'm not sorry for that," he murmured.

"I didn't think you would be."

He was *far* too pleased about it, actually.

"Don't be *nice*," Cara said softly, making him look down at her. "Don't be soft, and sweet, and *good*. Don't do that tonight because you want to fuck with my head after everything that happened. *We* don't do that, Gian."

"Cara—"

"*Don't.*"

"Cara," Gian murmured in a half-groan, his fingers weaving into her hair and tugging firmly enough to make her stop. He found a familiar lust and love swirling in the blues of her eyes, but he saw a wariness there, too. It cut him deep. "When have I ever done that to you?"

She didn't hesitate. "Never."

"And I won't."

A single nod answered him back.

"Now … *Jésus Christ*, get that mouth of yours on my fucking cock. I better see those goddamn lipstick stains of yours where I like, Cara. Be a good girl, like I know you can be, and suck my fucking dick."

She did what he demanded, and it was glorious. A warm, wet familiar bliss that cleared his mind and made him silent in one single second. All she had to do was wrap her pretty red lips around his cock, suck him hard and deep enough into her throat that her muscles contracted along his length, and he was done for.

God, did she know how to suck cock.

It made Gian *crazy.*

Her tongue flicked against the throbbing vein on the underside of his dick, while her sharp teeth scraped along his length on the withdrawal. Gian didn't need to urge or help Cara on when it came to sucking him off. She knew exactly what to do. That didn't stop him from tugging harder on her hair to feel her happy little moans vibrate his shaft. It didn't stop him from flexing his hips forward when she took him deeper, just to see her sly grin form around his dick as her eyes watered.

"You're so good with that mouth, *mon ange. Succhiami il cazzo.*"

Suck my cock.

Suck my cock.

He said it three times—once for each language he spoke.

It was only when his spine started to stiffen and his balls got too fucking tight that he finally pulled Cara away. As much as he wanted to watch her suck him dry, he *needed* to be buried as deep as he possibly could be into her cunt when he finally came.

Too damn long, he reminded himself.

Cara was already reaching for him before he could push her back to the bed, her thighs opening for his body to fit against hers as his mouth slammed down on her parted, wet lips. She sighed when he pulled her hair, making her head tilt back so he could kiss her throat, and bite her shoulder hard enough to leave a mark. He could feel her heart race like thunder when she slipped a hand between their bodies and fitted his cock to her cunt. The wetness of her arousal soaked the head of his dick, and he thrust in.

Home, and *heaven*, and *bliss*.

Those were the things he found when he finally buried his cock balls-deep inside Cara Rossi for the first time in months.

Love, and *selfish*, and *more* were the words that slipped through his mind when she shuddered under him, and her nails raked stinging lines along his back.

"Fucking take me," he ground out against the hollow of her throat. "Take all of me, Cara, and show me how much you want it. Show me how good you are for it, sweet girl."

Cara only mumbled a broken cry of his name. Her back arched hard from the bed while her legs opened even wider. She pushed her head back farther into the sheets, and her teeth clenched around another whine as he fucked her harder.

He couldn't get deep enough.

He couldn't fuck hard enough.

Not enough to feel like he was ever going to satisfy how much he needed, loved, and wanted this fucking woman.

"I want … *I want* …" Cara's words melted together in a gasping breath that he couldn't understand. But with every thrust of his body against hers, with every slide of his cock inside the wet clenching heat of her cunt, he knew what it was. She wanted to come, and he needed that too. More than his own pleasure, he needed *hers*. "*Please*."

He knew what she wanted for that, too.

Not nice, not easy, and not soft or slow.

She wanted his hand on her throat, taking away her air, and a brutal fucking that would ache when she was finally done coming. He gave her exactly that, reveling in the way her cunt clamped down on his cock when his fingers curved tightly to her throat and how the blues of her eyes sparkled with bliss when his rhythm turned harsher.

Shit, her orgasm came on fast.

Even with his hand on her throat, her scream was *beautiful*.

Gian thought he might be able to hold off his own need to come long enough to fuck her through it, and then get her on her knees to finish him off.

He was *wrong*.

He came hard, emptying every bit of cum into her cunt as the last shudder racked its way through Cara's body. His fingers loosened their hold on her throat—he'd never trusted his control to choke her while he came and he wasn't about to start testing the waters right then.

"Fuck, fuck, *fuck*," Gian mumbled.

He was too fucking sensitive and too damn weak all of the sudden. Pulling out of her warm pussy was the hardest thing he ever had to do, but he needed to so he could breathe.

Cara's light, breathless laughter echoed into the room. His cock—covered in their fluids—rested semi-hard against her thigh. He felt her fingertips slide along his length, and looked down to find her using their mingled cum to lubricate her clit as her fingers started stroking fast circles.

"Shit," Gian breathed. "That's fucking hot, Cara."

Her smile was sinful. "Watch me come again."

Jesus Christ.

His cock was already perking up.

"Watch me, Gian," Cara whispered.

All. Fucking. Night. Long.

"*Tabernac.*" Gian's curse came out as a low rumble, his irritation rising as he was forced to roll away from soft, naked skin in his bed. He couldn't let go of Cara completely, so he picked up the ringing cell phone on the nightstand and stroked a hand up her spine with his other. All of his frustration leaked into his tired voice when he answered the call with, "Do you know what goddamn time it is, and what in the *fuck* do you want?"

"Yeah, it's after nine and *Sunday*, Gian. Since when do you sleep in and where in the hell are *you*?"

Dom's voice made Gian sit up in the bed, but he still didn't stop touching Cara as he moved. She grounded him—her presence calmed him. He had been a mess for months and for a moment, he was okay.

"It's Sunday, Gian," Dom repeated. "Mass started already. Elena put out a call to a couple of people when you didn't show up this morning at the mansion, though you were supposed to be there last night. What the fuck?"

Saturday at the mansion.

Sunday at church with his wife.

Merda.

Gian had entirely skipped those plans after seeing Cara the night before. He hadn't intentionally done so, but something better came along, and those plans no longer mattered. He was surprised that Elena cared enough to call anyone and ask around about him, but that was probably because she was hoping his body showed up somewhere.

"Weren't you having dinner with her father last night?" Dom asked.

"Yeah, I had dinner with Gabriel."

"*And?*"

"And nothing. I forgot, I guess."

"You for—"

"Gian, is everything all right?"

Cara's question came out too loud in the quiet bedroom to be hidden. He shot her a reassuring smile, and stroked her back again, saying nothing. She tucked back into the blankets, happy as could be, but Gian knew his brother had heard her.

"Oh, well, shit," Dom said quickly.

"So, something came up," Gian muttered.

"Some*one*, you mean."

"Semantics."

"If you say so. Cara Rossi?" Dom asked.

Gian sighed, scrubbing a hand down his face. "I'm not in the mood, nor do I have the patience, to listen to anyone's bitching this morning, man."

"Yeah, sure. When did that happen again? How long?"

"*Or* your questions," Gian added. "I answer to God, my priest, and the Pope, but certainly not to you. Don't expect me to."

And Cara …

Gian answered to her, too.

"What do I tell Ma and Dad … or your wife, for that matter?"

"Apologize, say I wasn't feeling well. I'll be at the mansion before noon to deal with the other bit, since I need to grab some stuff anyway."

"Sure, sure," his brother said, sounding anything *but* sure.

"*Au revoir*, Dom."

Gian didn't bother to give his brother the chance to say goodbye back, before he hung up the phone. Setting it back to the nightstand, he immediately went back to Cara, his arms ensnaring her warm body and bringing her closer to him under the white sheets.

He didn't want to talk or think.

He just wanted to *be* for a while.

Cara's rhythmic breathing was too light, telling Gian that she hadn't fallen back asleep. He waited out her inevitable questions, but what she eventually said was not what he expected.

"I don't want to be that woman, Gian."

"Cara—"

"I don't want to be the other woman."

He swept her wild curls off her shoulder, giving him soft skin to kiss. He felt Cara's shiver work its way through her body, and so he kissed her again, just to feel it once more.

"I know," he murmured, his lips still pressed to her body.

"But here I am."

"Those are details, and I know they're the kind of details that matter to some, but they are *only* details, *bella mia.* You're not the other woman for me. You've always just been mine. There is no *other* here. There's one man and one woman. One man who loves *one* woman—I love you, Cara. That's it."

"One man with a wife," Cara said softly.

"She's certainly not mine, not in that sense," Gian said dryly. "On paper, maybe, but the rest … no."

"I'm not sure if that makes it better, but I want it to. I wish it did, and I'm pretty sure that makes me a horrible person."

He pulled her closer still, letting her legs tuck in around his under the sheets, while his arm tightened around her midsection to keep her in place.

"Do you want to know anything about her or the—"

"No," Cara interjected swiftly, shutting him down.

Gian kissed her shoulder again. "All right."

"Do you have to go?"

"In a while, yes. I have to go to the mansion and grab some things for the week. I missed church, too, so my mother needs a visit now, to be sure I'm not dead."

"So, the mansion. Is that where … Elena, right?"

"Mmm."

"Is that where she lives?"

Gian let out a slow breath. "Yeah."

At his quiet confirmation of her suspicions, Cara stiffened in his arms.

"Would you stay, though?" Gian asked.

"For what?"

"I'll be back later today or tonight sometime. I'd like to come back to see you. We should talk, or something. Just talk, Cara. Without yelling or slapping, or fighting and fucking. Just *talk.*"

"I don't want to be that woman, Gian," she repeated.

She hadn't refused his request, though.

Gian took that as a win. "But?"

"But I love you, too. I love you, and I want to hate you."

Yeah, that was the hard part.

It was every single reason why she was in his bed, instead of in her own. Because had he loved her even a little bit less, or perhaps in a better way, he would have left her alone to her business and life the night before.

Except he couldn't.

Because *love.*

Or, that's what he was going to keep telling himself. Otherwise, he would be forced to admit how selfish of a fucker he truly was.

"Stay," he said, kissing along the curve of Cara's shoulder. "Stay for me."

"Maybe."

It wasn't a no.

Gian grabbed one of the five new garment bags hanging in the walk-in closet. He used the second largest bedroom in the mansion, while his wife used the master bedroom, just across from his. He only kept clothes when it came to personal effects at the mansion, so that he could come and go as he liked, and it actually appeared as though he lived there.

Occasionally, he did business at the mansion, too. He had dinners for the men, and other nonsense that invited people into his "personal" space, though it was complete bullshit. Home was his penthouse, not this mansion.

He stripped down from the jeans and leather jacket he had tossed on before leaving the penthouse. He'd called his mother and promised dinner to make up for missing Mass, but she wouldn't appreciate him showing up in jeans.

A suit it was.

He had just pulled the shirt up over his head, when a clearing throat froze him in his tracks. Turning slightly to face the opened doorway of the walk-in closet, he found Elena standing there, staring at him.

"Do you need something?" he asked.

"It's good to see you're still alive."

"Is it?"

She just shrugged.

"Where were you when I came in?"

Elena flicked a loose, blonde curl over her shoulder. "Changing out of church clothes. I saw your car, so I came looking for you. Also, I could ask the same, Gian. Where were you last night and this morning?"

"Busy. Something came up."

Gian turned back to the suit he had set out, picking up the pants as he said, "Ma is expecting us for dinner. You don't have to go, but I would appreciate if you did."

"Whatever. How did dinner go with my father last night?"

"Same as it always does. Gabriel is ... Gabriel."

Elena made an agreeable sound under her breath. "Did he want anything specific?"

"You have more contact with him lately than I do, so you tell me."

"He asked *you* to dinner, not me."

Gian rolled his eyes. "Like I said, it's the same shit it always is. Business, family, and you. Nothing new, nothing to worry about. He isn't about to climb through a window and steal you back in the night."

Elena didn't respond immediately and Gian shot a look over his shoulder to find she was staring at the floor, silent. She was as cold as ice, but there were buttons that a man could push, and she reverted into a shell of herself.

Gian had pushed that button.

"I could have phrased that better," he said.

Elena shrugged one shoulder. "I choose not to underestimate my father. He used me from the time I was fifteen to do his bidding and play his games, right up until the day I met you. It's only because he believes I'm no longer useful to him that he keeps a distance now, you know."

Gian grunted, displeased. "Yes, and then you used me. So how different are you two, really?"

"I used you to get away."

"It doesn't justify the mode, Elena."

She only smiled. "It got me what I wanted. I never needed to fuck another man to benefit my father, I only needed to fuck you. And after that, I didn't even need to do that, Gian. So yes, I got what I wanted."

"Yes, stuck in a marriage with me. Where we despise one another, where you lied to me about everything and tricked me with a fake pregnancy, and then losing—"

"I apologized for all of that!"

Gian spun fast on his heel, not hiding his anger. "That's the problem. You think because you spit out a few sad words, that it fixes what you did. It doesn't fix it, Elena. You've trapped me into this fucking hell with you. I'm so goddamn happy that you don't mind because of all the wonderful things you have, because fuck me, right? Fuck me and everything I might have wanted from life, Elena."

"I was taught that feelings didn't matter in this life, Gian. Only the end goal. Perhaps you should learn the same. My bad, that I happened to meet my goals before you did."

Feelings only mattered when they were hers.

That was what she meant to say.

Gian was not stupid.

"Get the fuck out, Elena."

"In a minute."

Gian snarled a warning at his wife over his shoulder, done with her nonsense and games for the day. Elena barely reacted. In fact, she continued standing in the doorway with her arms crossed and her eyes nailed to his back.

"What do you want that you haven't already bothered me with?" he asked, reaching his limit of patience.

"Who were you really with last night?"

Gian's shoulders stiffened. "I beg your pardon?"

"Who were you fucking?" Elena carefully enunciated each word. "That's why you didn't come here last night or to church this morning, right? You've got scratches all down your back. Jesus, she must have liked whatever it was you were doing to her. Doesn't that hurt? That's one thing you're quite good at—making a woman come again and again, I remember that well. Did she scream your name like a good little whore? Was it loud enough to drown out me and everyone else filling your thoughts?"

Gian reacted only to the fact Elena used the word whore. He spun fast on his heel. Elena took a giant step back, far enough out of the doorway that Gian was able to grab the door and slam it closed without hitting her.

Her voice stopped him before he closed it completely.

"Oh, someone's touchy. Is it her again, Gian, the one from before?"

Gian let the door slam in her face, determined not to give Elena a thing unless she pried it out of his dead hands. When a man gave her an inch, she took a mile and ran with it until he was a bleeding, useless, broken mess trailing behind her. It was just what she did, it was what she had been taught and Gian refused to *ever* play those games with his wife again.

The last time he had, he'd lost. Lost his freedom. Lost his rights. Lost what he thought was his child. He just fucking lost.

So no, fuck her, and her games.

"Cara, right?" Elena asked from behind the wood. "That's her name, isn't it? Are you screwing that whore again?"

"Go to hell, Elena, before I fucking send you there."

She laughed at him.

He wasn't surprised.

Story of their life …

"Elena didn't want to come?" Celeste asked as Gian kissed his mother's cheek.

He readied to speak the lie he had prepared, but whether or not his mother would fall for it was another story.

"She's not feeling well," he said.

Celeste frowned. "She was fine at church this morning. Wasn't she,

Frederic?"

Gian's father nodded. "Seemed so, *Tesoro*."

"Well?" Celeste looked to Gian. "See, even he—"

"She's not feeling well," Gian repeated, "and I can't make her come to dinner when she isn't up for it, Ma."

"Fine."

His mother didn't sound particularly happy about it, though. He wasn't about to complain that Elena stayed home.

"What's for dinner?" Gian asked.

Celeste waved a hand, beckoning her son and husband to follow. Gian walked alongside his father, a few paces behind his mother, as Celeste described the meal that was waiting for him. As good as it sounded and for as hungry as he was, he only wanted to eat, spend a few minutes talking, and then get the hell out of there.

Cara would be waiting at his place for him.

Maybe …

He'd sent her a text earlier and gotten a reply. She had been at the penthouse then, but whether or not she still would be was another story.

Cara had a bad habit of overthinking.

Not that Gian blamed her.

"Sounds delicious, Ma," Gian said.

Celeste preened over her shoulder. "Of course it does."

The family had just sat down for their meal when the phone call came in. His parents' maid handed the phone over to Gian with wide eyes before she bolted out of the room. Celeste and Frederic watched him like two hawks as he put the phone to his ear.

Gian tried to hear what Elena was saying through her panic, but he could only make out a few words.

They were enough.

They were too much.

Cops.

Warrants.

The mansion.

Get here, now.

Gian only made it outside of his parents' place. The cops were already waiting for him there, too.

Apparently, the mansion was one of many places served with warrants, and he was just one of many men to find themselves in hot water with police. His father-in-law's house that was just an hour outside of Ottawa was another. Gian found himself in the back of a police cruiser and his hands cuffed, before he could even tell his father what to do.

"The charges?" Gian demanded from the officer.

The man shrugged, but before he shut the door, he said, "Ask Seeley when you get to the station. He said you two had missed your meeting this week."

Gian realized then that he was fucked.

He just didn't know *why*.

Chapter 6

Cara had forgotten how comforting and familiar Gian's penthouse was for her. All the tall ceilings, the warm whiteness of the rooms, and the wide windows that could make someone feel like royalty looking down on the city—it was beautiful.

The walls of the penthouse had heard her secrets and given her a safe space, all those months ago. They had shut out the world and let her learn who Gian Guzzi was underneath his charming, mysterious mask. Or rather, who she had thought he was.

He's still the same man, her mind whispered, *but with added baggage.*

Yes, if only it was that fucking simple.

Cara learned, as she snooped through Gian's office and wandered into his walk-in closet, that the penthouse still held pieces of her time from before. One of her chokers hung from a small brass hook in the jewelry case, resting alongside a half of a dozen Rolex watches. Bangles she had slipped off her wrist still sat in a glass bowl. A jacket she remembered tossing over the bedpost one night in her haste to get in the bed with that sinful man had been hung up in the closet alongside Gian's things.

Gian had no reason to keep her things; to leave the items where she had placed them, or to move them to safe spots where she could find them again.

And yet he had.

Gian kept the tiny pieces of her with him. Cara didn't know if that was because, one day, he planned to return them. Maybe he wasn't willing to scrub her from his penthouse or his life.

There was something else that became *painfully* obvious as she snooped. His wife held no place in his personal spaces. The woman was nowhere. No clothes, makeup, pictures, or mementos. It was as though— only here—she did not exist.

Or perhaps he didn't want her to.

Cara also didn't want to think on it for too long. Thinking for her almost always led to overthinking, and that was a problem. She already knew Gian loved her, and she didn't think for a second that he would say something he didn't mean, but it was all the rest of the details that came along with it where she hesitated.

Cara didn't *want* to hesitate.

Not for Gian …

She decided, when it was just after dinnertime and she was *still* at Gian's place, that it was the only reason why she was there. Comfort and familiarity. Nothing more, nothing less.

Cara was also pretty damn good at lying to herself.

And overthinking.

She should have been gone hours ago. Instead, she stayed, putting the shower in the master bath to use, and then ordering in food for lunch *and* supper. She had answered the one text from Gian earlier in the day, but he had yet to send another.

Cara didn't know if that was a purposeful move on Gian's part, or not. It would certainly be smart of him, to let her have the few hours that kept them apart without his voice in her head so she could work through her shit. She was always working through something.

It was only after supper time had long passed, that Cara began to think something might be wrong. She shot Gian another text and got nothing in response.

Cara was just slipping on her shoes to leave the penthouse, after sending *another* text to Gian that explained he could call her when he had time, when the elevator into the penthouse opened. Chris—Gian's man that had kept an eye on Cara months ago—rushed into the place with a black messenger bag clenched in his hand.

He only hesitated when he saw Cara coming down the hall.

"Sorry, I thought you might be Gian," Cara said.

Chris cleared his throat and glanced back at the elevator. "Boss brought you over?"

"Last night."

The man didn't even look surprised. "All right. You should head out."

The lilt in Chris's tone made Cara stay right where she was. "What's wrong?"

"Nothing that you need to worry about, miss."

"It's Cara."

"I still know your name and I still prefer what I use."

Cara frowned. "Because I'm not his wife, or—"

"Because respect matters," Chris interrupted as he slid past Cara in the hallway. "Now, I'm serious. Get out of this building, preferably within the next ten minutes or so."

"Why?"

"You didn't leave anything behind, did you?"

"Why aren't you answering my questions?" Cara demanded.

Chris pulled open a drawer in the decorative hallway table, and yanked out a gun, dropping it into the bag. Cara gaped like an idiot, wondering how she had never noticed that weapon there before and how many others might be hidden in the penthouse.

Then, she had an even more pressing thought.

Why was Chris here?

He *never* used to come inside Gian's penthouse without permission. No one had ever done that, from what Cara remembered. If he was doing this now, was it because of the weapons? Did he know where they were, or most of them, and did he need to get rid of them for some reason?

"Chris—"

"Okay," Chris said, turning to face Cara with a blank expression. "*Cara*, you need to go unless you feel like getting dragged down to a police station to explain why you are in the boss's place, and what you were doing here with him, amongst many other things they'll ask. If you left something that will say *you*, specifically, were here, then get it and go. I don't have the time to baby you out of this place, I have shit to do."

Cara still didn't move. "Where is Gian?"

"Right now, he's either in lock up or being questioned. Based on whatever they picked up at the mansion, their warrant for this place was on the way. Do you want to be standing there when they get here or what?"

Shit.

"I should go," Cara said.

Chris nodded. "Yeah, do that, and fast."

Cara had just walked out of the front doors of the building when the first cruiser and unmarked car pulled up on the side of the road. The officers and one plain-clothed detective with his badge hanging around his neck, walked past her as though they had no interest in the redhead leaving the building.

She hailed a cab, and didn't take a real breath again until she was back at her place, and hidden in her bed.

What just happened?

The question kept banging around in her head. Cara didn't even know how to answer.

"I'm starting to think that you don't know how to return a phone call."

Cara almost fell off the stepladder she was using to put away groceries in the pantry at Carolina's House. "Jesus, *Zia*, make some noise."

Her aunt, Daniele, only cocked an eyebrow in response.

Carefully, Cara climbed back down the ladder, ignoring the way the floor swayed a bit under her feet when she wasn't so high up anymore. Her new issue with heights and vertigo was becoming annoying, but she ignored it.

Ignoring it was easier than dealing with what it meant.

"I've called you three times this week," her aunt said.

Cara shrugged. "I've been busy."

And avoiding.

She had been avoiding everyone and anything related to the Guzzi family, the police, and the current investigation into their business for three entire weeks. That also meant ignoring her own family, mostly her aunt and uncle, who had been just one of many to be dragged into the city for questioning by police.

Cara knew better than to get involved.

Gian wouldn't want her to, she was sure of that.

Of course, Cara *had* been keeping up with what she could. It seemed Gian had found himself in jail under a half of a dozen weapons charges, and according to the news, the weapons had been found at the Guzzi mansion. The weapons didn't entirely relate to the investigation's main objective—whatever that was, as the info hadn't been offered—but the unregistered, illegal weapons were still grounds for charges.

Canada did not like guns on the streets, especially not illegal guns.

Given Gian's name and affiliations, a previous arrest for assault with a weapon, and his ability to up and leave the country, simply because of the amount of zeros in his bank account, he was remanded to the jail until his trial. A trial which was likely going to be sped up when Gian accepted a shorter sentencing term for a deal that was offered regarding the charges.

Or so Cara heard ...

She was trying not to get involved. She was trying to keep her head low and stay the hell out of it all, so then she didn't get dragged into a mess, too. That was the message passed along to her during a late-night visit from Chris. The man had shown up at her door with those instructions from Gian, and very little else.

Cara didn't have much of a choice but to agree.

As it was, her life was already a fucking mess for more reasons than just Gian's arrest. She didn't plan to add to it with stupidity.

"Did you need something specific?" Cara asked her aunt. "Because I really need to get done here, so I can go home and work on my essay due next week."

"No, I just worried about you, Cara. You haven't called, or been around. I wanted to check up on you. I know you're here a lot throughout the week when you're not at school, so I thought I would drop by today since I was in the neighborhood."

Her aunt seemed sincere enough.

Cara decided to placate the woman.

"I am fine, *Zia*. But I am busy, really. I promise, I will make it up to you, and come over for dinner this weekend. I have nothing else better to do, okay?"

Daniele pursed her lips, but eventually smiled and nodded. "Fine, that sounds good. And you are *well*, aren't you?"

"Yes, why?"

"You're looking a little green today, that's all."

Cara swallowed the nauseous feeling building in her stomach and crawling up the back of her throat. It was not the easiest thing to hide— especially when the random vomiting spells hit at the most awkward of times—but she managed.

"I'm fine," Cara assured. "I'll even call you when I get home tonight after work, all right?"

"If you're sure ..."

"Perfectly sure, *Zia*."

Cara's lies and false smiles seemed to do the trick. Her aunt left with a demand that she had better call that night, *and* show up for dinner on the weekend. She barely heard her aunt's footsteps fade away before she made it to the garbage can in the corner to throw up.

Her hands shook as she tried to steady herself for the second wave of sickness that almost always followed the first round.

The biggest question of her life had been answered that morning when she pissed on a plastic stick, and a small window blinked with a single word over and over again. At seven days late, and a multitude of other symptoms, Cara knew the answer. She still took the test, half praying it would come out one way, and yet feeling a mess of relief, joy, and absolute chilling fear when she finally knew for sure.

Pregnant.

The pregnancy test was still in her purse. It was probably still blinking that goddamn word. Cara was too scared to check. She wasn't ready for it to be real.

Not yet.

"Miss Rossi."

Cara stiffened at the sound of Chris's greeting behind her. She turned the lock in her apartment door to close it up, and turned to face the man. He smiled at her. "You could have knocked on the door."

"I just arrived."

"Mmm."

Chris nodded at her messenger bag. "Going somewhere?"

"School, actually. I already missed one class this morning, I'm trying not to miss a second."

"Would it be so bad if you did miss another?"

Cara's hand tightened on her bag. "Well, kind of."

"You look tired," he noted.

"Do I?"

"A bit."

Cara hinted at nothing being wrong. Eight weeks after Gian's arrest, and five weeks after finding out she was pregnant, Cara still hadn't told *anyone*. Not a single soul knew her secret, and for now, she wanted to keep it that way.

She had been going through a rough patch with her early pregnancy. Exhaustion and morning sickness were taking its toll. She slept a hell of a lot more than she normally did, which said something, considering she wasn't a morning person at all, and she still couldn't smell meat cooking without throwing up.

It was not particularly fun.

At only eight weeks pregnant, Cara was wondering how she was supposed to make it another thirty-two weeks. The doctor had assured her that the tiredness would wane in the second trimester, as would the sickness, but she wasn't sure that she believed the woman.

"Care to go on a drive today?" Chris asked. "There's someone who would like to see you."

"Isn't today Gian's sentencing?"

"It is."

"Is it him who wants to see me?"

"He does."

Cara frowned. "How, exactly? He's always transferred directly from the jail to the courthouse, in cuffs and a cruiser with a guard."

Chris shrugged. "Some strings may have been pulled today, that's all I can say."

"He hasn't even called me."

"His calls are monitored and he calls no one. Messages are passed back and forth during visits, and that's how shit gets done."

"Oh."

"Jail isn't a vacation, believe me."

Cara rolled her eyes. "I never said that. A call would be nice, though."

"You probably won't get one. Maybe a visit, once the media fades away a bit, but not a call. He wants nothing on record other than a name and date. So, a drive?"

Cara handed over her bag when Chris offered to take it. "Fine, a drive."

Cara was certain that the midtown alleyway Chris parked in was not anywhere close to the courthouse where Gian would have been sentenced earlier.

"What are we doing?" Cara asked.

Chris slid on a pair of sunglasses, turned the radio on low, and rested his arms behind his head. "Right now, we're waiting."

Given the man's vagueness, Cara had the distinct feeling that she wouldn't get any of her questions answered, so she didn't ask more. She wasn't sure how much time passed—ten minutes or maybe twenty. Then, Chris perked up, his gaze shooting to the rearview mirror. Cara glanced over her shoulder.

A police cruiser parked behind them in the alley.

Chris said nothing, simply exited the car after grabbing a large envelope from the passenger seat. Cara watched from the back window as Chris passed the envelope to the first police officer who left the cruiser. A second officer, younger than the first, headed to the back of the car to unlock and open the door.

Cara's thoughts of the odd scene, and the obvious bribery happening, drifted away when Gian stepped out of the police cruiser. His hands were cuffed in front of him, but the younger officer quickly undid the cuffs when Gian offered his wrists out. The suit Gian wore belied the fact he had already spent eight weeks in a small jail cell, as it looked perfectly pressed and fit him handsomely.

A few words were said, the officers turned to talk between themselves, and Gian headed for Chris's car. Cara didn't realize she had been holding her breath until he slipped into the backseat with her.

At first, he said nothing.

His hands—God, she missed his hands—drifted over her cheeks with the softest touch, and then he was pulling her close. For a moment, a blissful few seconds, all of Cara's stress and fear and worries drifted away. His dark eyes lingered over her features, his thumbs stroked her skin, and Cara remembered how to smile again.

"I missed your face," Gian murmured.

Cara let out a low laugh. "That's all you have to say?"

"No, not all. I'm sorry. I love you. There's a few more, but those stand out the most."

Before she could think better of it, Cara closed the distance between them. The kiss started out innocent and sweet enough, but took no time at all to burn deep with something far more sinful and desperate. She loved the way his fingers tangled into her hair as his tongue warred against hers. She nearly forgot about the people outside of the car, but she still didn't care.

Not when her heart was suddenly thrumming a familiar tune.

Gian, Gian, Gian.

That's what the song sounded like.

That, and *love, love, love.*

Cara knew it was bad and wrong. She had no business being involved with this man after everything, never mind hoping for a future with him that could never *be* anything. Yet she did.

She hoped and wished, and she thought the risk of crashing and burning might be okay, if she could just love him while it happened. Maybe.

"I heard you pulled some strings," Cara said when Gian kissed a soft path over her cheekbone. "Aren't they worried you might run off?"

Gian chuckled, and kissed her mouth again. "Not in the slightest."

"How much did you bribe them?"

"A lot."

Cara let Gian pull her closer, and soaked in the wonderful sensations of his fingers sifting through her curls. It was the intimate, comforting action that he usually only did in private with her, but it was her very favorite thing.

"I don't have too long," Gian said. "A few minutes, that's all."

Cara nodded. "Okay."

"I'll get Chris to bring you in for a visit sometime over the next few months, if possible. I need the news programs and the fucking media to just … lay off for a bit. I don't want you mixed up in any of this nonsense, Cara, not if I can help it."

Cara's heart stopped for a split second.

"A few months?"

Gian let out a hard breath. "Seven months, five with time already served. It'll be done and over with before we know it, no worries."

That was easy for him to say.

That was easy for him to *think.*

"You've gone stiff on me," Gian said. "Why?"

Cara tried to let the words form, she tried to explain her reaction away, but nothing came out. She was still hearing *five months* in the back of her mind.

"Cara," Gian said gently.

She looked up at him, and the words were right there on the tip of her tongue. *Say it*, and *tell him*, she thought. He needed to know about the pregnancy, especially now.

A light knock on the window interrupted her from saying anything at all. Chris stood just outside the door, and then gestured back toward the police cruiser. Gian sighed, but nodded once in response.

"I'm sorry, *mon ange*."

Cara let him disengage from her, though it cut her up. "Wait."

Gian already had the door open, and one foot out of the car. "What, Cara?"

She grabbed her bag, and dug through it, searching for a small paper she had shoved in there. Her doctor had made an appointment for her to have an early ultrasound when she had complained about cramping. As it turned out, nothing was wrong, and it was perfectly normal for her muscles to cramp a bit as her uterus grew a baby. She got a little picture of a peanut-shaped blob to keep.

Cara found the sonogram picture, and shoved it into Gian's hand. The due date of the baby, how far along Cara was, and other information was listed at the top.

Gian's gaze drifted between the grainy, black and white image in his hand, to Cara, and then back to the picture again. "Is this ... uh, what I think it is?"

"Yeah," she whispered, "that's exactly what you think it is."

He didn't question her on a thing, only leaned back into the car, and kissed her hard on the mouth.

"I'm a little scared," Cara told him.

Gian cupped her cheek with a firm hold, but a soft touch. "Yeah, I get that now, *bella*."

"Five months is like almost the whole time."

"But not all, okay? Not all, sweet girl."

"Boss, the cops need to get on the move, so…"

Gian held his hand out, shutting Chris up instantly. Never once did his gaze move from Cara as he did so. "If there's anything you want or need, Chris will get it for you, or Dom. Someone. Do you understand?"

Cara nodded. "I'm sorry, it was busy with school starting and everything. I missed a couple of my pills and—"

He kissed her again, quieting her. The shiver that worked its way through her spine was wonderfully familiar.

"I don't care, Cara."

"Boss—"

"*Fuck off*," Gian barked over his shoulder.

Chris stepped back with hands up. "My apologies."

Gian's gaze was back on Cara in a heartbeat. "Five months is nothing. We already did three months, right?"

"We didn't even fix the problems or talk about all of that, either. We fucked and here we are! Not the same thing, Gian. It's like a big bomb ticking down that's going to blow the hell up one day."

"Close enough, Cara. And who cares if it blows up, as long as it's spectacular? We're pretty fucking spectacular, love. *Je t'aime, ti amo*, I love *you*. Always."

That, she did believe.

He loved her crazy, but she didn't entirely know why.

He loved her stupid, and she liked it too much.

It was all kinds of bad.

They were all kinds of wrong.

Maybe that's just how they were supposed to be.

"You do need to give me a choice in this—in *us*."

Gian laughed in that sexy way of his. "I did give you a choice. You chose to get in my car. You came with me. You're mine, and you know it."

Jesus.

Why was he so damn right?

"Always, Cara," he repeated, kissing her quickly again.

"Always," Cara echoed.

Chapter 7

"This was not what I expected."

Gian waited for Cara to sit at the round table, making sure to keep his hands visible for the watching guards. It was really their only request, besides no overt public displays of affection.

Not that he cared at the moment ...

Gian's attention was snagged by something *far* more beautiful. Cara, that was, and the way her hand curved protectively around the slight swell of her stomach. He wanted nothing more than to stand and greet her the way *he* liked, but the guards wouldn't be pleased.

He enjoyed having visitors. It kept him sane.

Two more months, he told himself.

That was all he had left, and he would be out of this fucking hell.

"And what did you expect, *mia cara bella*?" Gian asked as she sat down.

"A Plexiglas window and phones, maybe," Cara said, taking in the visitor's area.

"It's a jail, not a prison. I'm in on a non-violent offense. The only prison they would be willing to send me to, is halfway across the country, and by the time they got me the spot, I'd only have a month to spend there. It's pointless."

"It's easier here?"

Gian nodded. "Quieter, less issues. Not so many inmate politics. More visitations. The guards aren't ... completely fucking useless."

Cara gave him a look. "It's not supposed to be a vacation, Gian."

He shrugged. "Hey, if they make it easy, then they make it easy."

"I'm also kind of shocked at the attire." She waved at him.

Gian glanced down at the drab, gray uniform he wore on a daily basis. "I miss a good suit, to be honest."

"At least there's no cuffs."

"Not until I'm escorted back to my cell, anyway."

"I wasn't told what to expect here," Cara admitted.

"But you still came."

Her blue eyes flashed to him instantly, a love and wariness reflecting there. "Of course, I came, Gian."

"I'm sorry it took this long for us to have a visit."

"I had a lot going on, anyway."

Gian chuckled. "Or you're making excuses so that I don't feel like shit."

Cara winked. "You'll never know."

Oh, he did.

He loved her for it, too.

"Your brother didn't say much, though," Cara said under her breath, shooting a look over her shoulder. "Not about *anything*, Gian."

Dom stayed just far enough away from the table to allow the two privacy. Gian sent his brother a grateful nod, which was quietly returned. Dom had too many opinions to name where Gian and Cara's odd relationship was concerned.

"Dom is … Dom," Gian said lamely.

"I don't think he likes me very much."

Gian tried to hide his frown. "It's not you personally, Cara."

"What is it?" His gaze dropped down to her rounded stomach, and Cara's hands cupped the swell quickly. "Oh, well then."

"He doesn't know what to think of it all," Gian explained.

Cara nodded once. "So it's more you, that's what you want to say. Not me, *you*."

"In a way, sure. Except he can't say shit to me because I'm the boss, brother or not. He's in a shitty situation where his opinion is not welcome, but he still wants to give it. Not that any of that matters. Enough about this, Cara, tell me about my baby."

The sweetest, prettiest smile bloomed on her features, lighting up her whole face. *That* was one of the things Gian missed seeing the very most. Even worse, he missed being the one to make Cara smile. He felt that he had given her far more reasons to frown.

"Halfway there now," Cara said. "Twenty weeks this week. He's very active, makes for interesting prenatal appointments when he keeps moving away from the wand as they're trying to hear his heartbeat. I would let you feel, but he's quiet right now. For once."

Gian was sure *his* heartbeat had stopped for a split second. "*He?*"

Cara pulled a small roll of sonogram photos from her purse, and slid it across the table to Gian. "A boy. So far, a very healthy, active boy, Gian."

He looked over the sonograms, taking in the shadowy profile of a baby in the middle of the picture. The tiny slope of a nose, and the roundness of his cheeks and lips were the most prominent features. Another photo showcased five small toes of a perfectly formed foot. The final image was a strange mixture of shapes that Gian didn't understand at all.

"What's this?" he asked.

Cara used the tip of her finger to outline the central image. "What do you think?"

His laughter rung out in the quiet visiting area, gaining the attention of several other inmates and their family. "Shit, really?"

"Yep."

"Definitely a boy, then."

"You couldn't miss it if you tried, once it's pointed out," Cara said, shaking her head.

"Thank you for bringing this, Cara."

"I have copies for me, too."

"I know, but—"

"He's your son, Gian, so why wouldn't I bring this to show you? We might have unfinished business, but he's brand new and he has no baggage. You know?"

"Yeah," Gian agreed. "Come here."

He hooked his finger at her, willing to take the scolding or whatever other issue that might pop up for what he was about to do. Cara, always trusting when it came to him, even when she didn't have the first clue of his motives, leaned closer at the table, until he could cup her face and bring her in the rest of the way.

Gian kissed Cara quickly on her painted red lips, feeling her smile grow when he kissed her twice more in quick succession. "God, I love you. You know that, huh?"

Cara nodded. "I know, Gian. I just don't understand why sometimes."

"Because you're *you*, Cara. And you're mine."

He figured that should be simple enough.

It was enough for him.

Having Cara close was not necessarily a good thing for Gian. Now that he had her there, he wanted to drag her into his lap, tangle his fingers into her hair, and hide away from the world that never left him alone. She was his peace, even if she couldn't possibly know it.

Gian settled for resting his palm over the slight, hard swell of her stomach. "Two more months, Cara, and then we'll have all the time in the world to deal with the unfinished business."

"Don't look forward to doing that too much, Gian."

"I love you. The rest doesn't matter."

"It matters," she argued, "to me."

"The details matter to you. The details aren't us in the grand scheme."

"We're part of the details, whether you want to admit it or not."

"Cara—"

"Yeah, I know," she mumbled when he kissed her cheek. "You're impossible."

"I am," he willfully, and happily, admitted. "More so when it comes to you."

That didn't mean that Gian was stupid, of course. He knew there was a lot that had been left unsaid between them. There were details of his life and his marriage that bothered Cara on a moral and ethical level. She didn't want to be the other woman in his life, but his only woman. He knew these were all things that would somehow need to be dealt with, but he believed—stupidly, maybe—that because he loved her, and he knew that she loved him, it would work itself out.

It *had* to.

Gian only noticed the guard approaching when the man was just a few steps away from the table. "My apologies."

The guard gave a short nod. "Hands in view, Guzzi."

Gian put his hands on the table, and moved an inch or two away from Cara. She frowned at the guard, as the man walked back to his previous post.

Before either of them could talk again, Dom had stepped up to the table, and cleared his throat. "We've only got a few more minutes left, Gian."

"Oh," Cara said, looking to Gian. "Well, I'll step out into the waiting area, and let your brother sit and chat for a minute."

"You don't have to do—"

"Sure I do, he's your brother."

Cara gave Gian another quick kiss before she left the table. Dom offered her a strained, awkward smile as she passed him by. Gian waited until Cara was gone completely before he turned his attention on his brother.

"You're here every week," Gian grumbled. "I get ten minutes with her and you interrupt me. *Why?*"

"I always have people with me," Dom said like it was obvious. "*I* never get the chance to chat with you privately. Now seems like a good time."

Gian grinded his teeth, irritated with Dom's justification. "What do you want to chat about?"

"How do you know you can trust her?"

"Who?"

"That woman. Cara."

"Because I just do, Dom. That's how."

"So, she says she's pregnant, that it's your child, and you just believe her, no questions asked?"

"I'm trying really hard right now not to get pissed off at you, but you're making it difficult."

"Why, because I'm asking you hard questions?" Dom asked.

"No, because you question *her*, asshole." Gian looked back in the way Cara had gone, wishing she had stayed right where she was instead. "You question the motives and morals of a woman who you don't know from a hole in the ground. You question her actions and her behavior with me because *of* me, Dom, because of the choices I made. You're so easily willing to think ill of her because I love her, not because she's done anything to deserve it. That's why you're pissing me off. It has fuck all to do with me, and everything to do with her."

"You said yourself that it'd been three months since you two were together. Then what, one night does the trick?"

Gian sighed, and rubbed a hand over his face.

He needed a fucking shave.

"I'm just saying," Dom muttered, "because the last woman who told you she was pregnant with your kid—"

"The last woman was Elena, and Cara Rossi is the furthest thing from her. The two are not comparable. Cara has no motives to lie to me, Dom, not like Elena did."

"One would think you might be a little more careful."

Gian shook his head. "It's my child and she's mine, too. You don't have to like it, you don't have to approve of it, because you don't matter where she and I are concerned. It would be great, if you and a lot of other people learned that fucking lesson, and fast."

"What about everybody else?" his brother asked.

"What about them?"

"Ma and Dad. Your wife. When do they get to learn you've got a child on the way with your mistress?"

Gian bristled at that title being so easily thrown at Cara like she deserved it. Maybe it was then that Gian could truly understand why the details bothered Cara so much. It was never him that would be questioned for their choices or the results of their behavior together, it would always be her that needed to answer for it.

That was unfair.

"All right," Gian said, standing from the table, "I'm done here."

He gestured at one of the guards.

Dom stood, too. "Gian, you owe me—"

"I owe you and everyone else, fucking *nothing*. That's why I'm the goddamn boss, and no one else is. I answer to those I choose to and you are not one of them."

"And your image, your respect, your wife, or our family? What about that? How do you think Ma is going to feel when she finds out you knocked up some woman when she's spent the last couple of months trying to befriend your wife?"

Dom didn't get it.

He wasn't listening like he needed to.

"I gave you the button too soon," he told his brother. "I spent *decades* under Corrado, learning how to be this man who didn't question what he was told to do, or how to do it. I learned how to not speak out of turn, even when it killed me to stay quiet, and who knew his place amongst other made men. *Decades* of my life were spent this way, Dom, from the time I was a child, until he gave me my button, so that I could sit where I am today, and have my given respect. Clearly, you could have benefitted from that same upbringing, but because you didn't, I have to deal with your disrespect and bullshit. I should have listened to my instincts instead of my feelings where you were concerned this past summer. You're not ready for a button—to be a made man—when your disrespect clouds a discussion with your boss."

"You're my brother first."

"Then, when you were unmade and just a man, you were my brother first and could afford to have a damn opinion about my life," Gian snapped back harsh and fast, uncaring of who heard him say the words. "*Then*, I was your brother first, Dom. Now, I am your boss. Learn the fucking difference. Learn it fast, before you force my hand and my gun. If I were any other boss, you would not be alive right now. Do *not* forget that the next time you feel as though your opinion should be shared."

Gian didn't wait to hear Dom's response or for the guard to make his way over. He headed toward the guard, meeting him in the middle with his wrists already out and ready for the cuffs, so he could be transported back to his cell.

He would rather spend the rest of the day in his cell than deal with his ignorant brother.

Another day, he told himself.

There would always be another day.

Gian would have been pleased to say that the remaining two months of his sentence had flown by before he even knew what was happening, but that hadn't been the case. He had never been more aware of how long sixty days could be until that was what his freedom had been reduced to.

It probably didn't help that for the majority of the time he spent in his cell, he was thinking about Cara, and when he would be able to see her next. It gave him something to do, and something to look forward to. Visits had been planned, but shit just didn't pan out properly.

Not even a conversation was had. The silence in his head when he was alone could be deafening.

As he dressed in the three-piece suit that he had handed over to the jail in exchange for their uniform, and fixed the Rolex watch around his wrist, Gian only had one thought in mind.

Cara.

He had come to a few conclusions when he was kept from her—more so than when he had *chosen* to stay away before. She was the blood in his body, the breath in his lungs, and the sun in his life.

She just was.

Everything, for Gian, was Cara Rossi.

Gian had always known those things, of course, but it was a much more intense understanding to come to when a man was alone with nothing but his thoughts and feelings. He had never done particularly well with feelings, after all.

More so, Gian now wanted to make sure Cara understood that she was all of those things to him and more. He wasn't sure if he had properly explained all of that to her, and didn't she deserve to know?

Maybe if she did know, then Cara might finally understand why details never mattered to Gian where they were concerned. The only details that had ever mattered to him were her.

Gian also needed to make sure he kept his ass out of jail, because he had too much time to think, and he didn't want a repeat. He was tired of jail-house nonsense, their fucking schedules, and going to bed when he was told to.

This was fucking ridiculous.

He wanted home, Cara, and a good meal.

It didn't have to be in that order.

So, as he slipped into his clothes, fixed his jewelry to his wrist and slid his rings on his fingers, Gian was more than ready to get his freedom back.

"Sign here," the nasally-voiced woman behind the Plexiglas window said.

Gian scribbled his name across the dotted line.

Just a few steps away now.

Freedom was so close, he could taste it.

Gian collected the folder with his release papers and headed for the doors that separated him from the outside world. It could have been worse, he knew, as those five months could have just as easily been spent in a prison.

It didn't matter.

He was ready to be out.

He wanted his life back.

"You're looking terribly happy about something, boss."

Gian smiled at the voice that greeted him as he walked out of the jail doors. Chris waited there for him, as that was who he had requested pick him up. He didn't want an affair for his release. As it was, his mother wanted a dinner, and he had men to meet and greet after being locked away for five months. Because of those things, he already had to put off seeing Cara for at least a day or two, which was bad enough.

"It's a nice day for the end of April," Gian noted, glancing up at the bright sky. "Tell me you brought the SUV with the sunroof."

"I did," Chris said.

"Good man."

"I also brought your wife."

There went Gian's good mood.

"What?" Gian asked, feeling the beginnings of a migraine. "Why would you do that?"

Chris jerked his thumb over his shoulder at the SUV. The windows were tinted too dark for him to see inside, but he had no doubt that Elena was sitting in the back seat.

"She had to come," Chris said, "and apparently her father knows you're getting out today, and wanted a meeting before you did anything else. According to Elena, he requested *she* be there, too. Sorry, boss."

"I don't answer to Gabriel Canali or his fucking wants, and he knows it."

"Yeah, I know, but you also don't go out of your way to irritate the monster that man happens to be, so I made the middle-ground choice that I figured you would want me to."

Gian scowled. "I'm going to be late for dinner with my mother, now."

Celeste would *not* be pleased about that.

"I already took care of it, boss."

"Oh?"

"She's going to come for breakfast tomorrow, at that restaurant you like downtown. Just you and her, maybe your father, too. Also, I figured if you were in a public place, she would be less likely to make a scene about you getting out of jail or the fact you were *in* jail to begin with."

Gratitude flooded Gian where Chris was concerned. The enforcer was decent. He did his job, even if Gian wasn't always pleased about the way he did it, and he took care of his boss. That was the most important thing.

"All right, then," Gian muttered, shooting a look at the SUV. "A dinner with my father-in-law it is."

And a car ride with his wife.

Fun.

"Here," Gian said, digging his cell phone out of the paper bag. The device was dead, and needed a charge. "You brought something to charge this, right?"

"Sure did."

Chris never failed.

"I should have brought you a new suit to change into," Elena said.

Gian passed her a look, noting the red dress, matching heels, and wide-brimmed sunhat she wore. For the most part, the hat had been a good shield between them, keeping them from needing to look at one another, never mind *talk*.

"Why would you do that?"

"You know how Daddy is," she said quietly.

Gian went back to staring out the window. "He's the one who wanted this dinner, Elena, knowing I was fresh off release. He can deal with a wrinkle in my shirt."

"Still …"

"And you don't need to be bringing me anything," Gian added.

Elena sighed. "Sure."

Gian glanced back at his wife again, taking note of the nervous edge in her posture and her hands fidgeting in her lap. Chris caught his boss's reflection in the rearview, but quickly turned his gaze back on the road.

"You haven't seen Gabriel since I went in, then?" Gian asked.

Elena shrugged. "I didn't have to. He was in for a while, too."

"He was released a month before me."

"I made excuses."

"Two blocks away, boss," Chris said from the driver's seat.

"*Merci,*" Gian replied, though he continued watching Elena. "Smile pretty and nod at whatever he says, because that's what he likes to see from you. Keep your replies quiet and well-mannered, as that forces him to be polite, too. Don't give him shit to pry into, where our lives or this marriage is concerned; neither of us wants or needs that. Thirty minutes, at the most, and I'll excuse you. How's that?"

Elena frowned. "You don't have—"

"What good is your husband, if he doesn't at least look out for you, Elena?"

Her posture softened a bit. "I don't always treat you well, or I haven't, I guess. Don't be surprised when I don't expect the same in response, Gian."

"I have always looked after you where your father was concerned, Elena. Even before I knew that's what you were using me to do for yourself. Let's not pretend like this is anything different. It's the rest—the lies you told, the way you fucked me over, and the shit we don't have together that I can't be bothered with now. I'm not going to work toward any kind of real marriage with you, and you don't want me to, either. I need to stay married to you for appearance, respect, and an oath I took, and you need to stay married to me to keep your father away. Nothing more, nothing less. This, your father, I will always protect you, and you know it. *You* shouldn't expect any different, not when I have never given you a reason to think otherwise."

She didn't reply.

He didn't need her to.

"Well, fuck," Chris grunted as he pulled the SUV over to the side, and killed the engine.

Gian would have asked what the problem was, but he didn't need to. A news van had parked outside the restaurant, with cameras turned in their direction. "Why in the hell are they here?"

"Your guess is as good as mine, boss."

Jesus Christ.

"Your release *was* publicized," Elena pointed out.

"So then a news van shows up at the jail," Gian replied, "not the restaurant where I'm meeting your father."

"Gabriel, then?" Chris asked.

"Why would he do that? He's not in any better of a position than I am at the moment, and could afford to stay out of the fucking spotlight for a bit."

Gian hadn't been the only organized crime boss arrested in those raids. Gabriel's sentence had been lighter by a month, sure, but the man still went in. Besides that, Gian wasn't exactly low profile in the city of Toronto.

Long before his family's name had been synonymous with crime, the Guzzis had become rich by striking gold in one of Canada's only gold mines. They were old money and with that had come a socialite lifestyle that spanned generations, his included. He didn't enjoy that side of life as much as his parents had, or even as much as his sister currently did, but his face was well known, much like his last name.

"Pay them no mind," Chris said, "and I'll scare them off when you're inside, boss."

Gian nodded, thankful. "Great."

Unfortunately, the second Gian stepped out of the car, he could feel the fucking camera burning into him. He was *very* aware that his face would likely be on the news that night, and that didn't exactly make him jump for joy.

The born and bred gentleman he was sent him to Elena's side of the SUV. He opened her door, and offered a hand to help her out. She didn't pass the cameras a single look, but she did lean in and give Gian a quick kiss on his cheek.

Then, just as fast, she murmured in his ear, "For Daddy to see."

For them, it was always a show.

It always had been.

It had to be.

He hadn't expected the kiss, and it took a great effort for him not to pull away from Elena, but he managed.

Elena kept her hand firmly tucked into his elbow as they entered the restaurant. Unsurprisingly, Gian found the place quite empty of patrons, and only a couple of wait staff waiting for them at the front.

"Your father owns this place, doesn't he?" Gian asked.

"Yes."

Wonderful.

"How nice of him to close it down for the day, just for us. That's a great way not to draw any fucking attention."

It was a great way to make a scene, by closing down a busy restaurant for a day, only to have two crime bosses of rival families show up for a sit-down together.

Fuck.

Gian hated Gabriel Canali for many reasons, including the woman hanging on his arm currently. The bastard could not be trusted.

Elena's false smile grew as the woman wearing a standard black dress led them through the restaurant, closer to the front windows. His wife leaned into his side, her hand tightening on his arm with a fierceness that damn near hurt. Yet, her smile never faltered, not even when she first caught sight of her father.

Gabriel was a bull of a man, with his torso as wide as he was tall. Dark-eyed, black-haired, and with a soul as dirty as shit, the man was intimidating at first glance.

A Camorra boss of a clan that liked its violence to the extremes, and its money as dirty as it could get, Gabriel held no loyalties to anyone but himself. He didn't follow the same kinds of rules in life that Gian, or other made men did, as Camorra clans were, simply put, out for the betterment of their own positions.

Gabriel had killed nearly every single one of his rivals off. All except for the Guzzi family.

Gian had too much pride to let a cocksucker like Gabriel force his hand more than he had already done. As it was, he'd married the man's daughter, was stuck with her until the day one of them died, and that was more than enough punishment for Gian, regarding getting mixed up with the Canali Camorra clan.

Far more than enough …

"Gian," Gabriel greeted, pushing his large girth up from the head of a table. "Beautiful day, isn't it?"

Gian nodded, taking the man's hand for a shake. "It is."

Then, Gabriel turned his gaze on his daughter. "Elena, *mia reginella.*"

My little queen.

Gian felt his wife's fingernails dig into his skin through his suit jacket.

"Daddy," Elena greeted politely. "How are you?"

"Well, although not as good as your husband, seeing as how he's free today. You only get one free day to have fun after a sentence, and then it's back to work. I'm happy to see he's spending it with you." Gabriel chuckled darkly. "I can't say I ever did that for my wife when she was alive."

Elena said nothing, but she didn't move from Gian's side, either. She had her sore spots, and her father was one of them. In a way, Gian thought it might do him well if he cared less, that he had a colder heart, so he could send Elena right back to her father's cruel hands to do with as he wished.

Fortunately for Elena, Gian was not that cold, callous, or cruel.

Even if he wished he was.

No woman deserved to be beaten, used as a toy, or traded for the pleasure of men and blackmail like Elena had been for the majority of her life under Gabriel's demands. It wasn't exactly a secret in their family. It was not freely talked about, either.

"Sit, sit," Gabriel demanded, waving at the table. "The food is coming soon."

Near to the second they were all seated at a table, food was brought out from the kitchen by a chef and a waiter, served to each of them. Gian was at least grateful to get a few bites of a decent meal shoved into his face before the Camorra boss began talking again.

"Are you ever going to give that husband of yours a *bambino* or two?" Gabriel asked his daughter. "I might like a grandchild, too, Elena."

Elena kept her head down as she replied, "Someday."

Gian forced the lump of food down his throat. "Not everyone wants children."

"All good Italian men do," Gabriel said. "Although, considering it's been four years since the two of you married, is it more that you don't want any or that you *can't* have any?"

Elena stiffened in her seat.

Gian kept his focus on his father-in-law. "Children are not on the conversation menu tonight."

"Just curious. She did lose your first child, didn't she? Shortly after the wedding. Perhaps those abortions Elena had didn't serve her well, after all. How many was it again, *cara*, five?"

"Daddy, don't start—"

"Elena, are you finished?" Gian asked, interrupting his wife from taking her father's bait. "Eating, I mean."

She nodded. "I am."

"Chris is waiting outside for you."

Elena didn't need to be told again. She got up from the table, said a quick goodbye to her father, rubbed a hand on Gian's shoulder as she passed, and then she was gone.

"I was only asking," Gabriel said with a smirk. "No need to send her out. She can handle her own, Gian, I assure you."

Gian held back from punching the man in the throat. "Yes, and then I'm the one who has to deal with her emotional backlash from *handling* you and your nonsense for the next week. No, thank you, Gabriel. If you're going to throw my wife's abortions in her face, maybe stop to consider who forced her into those, as well. What was she, sixteen the first time? The police chief, wasn't it?"

Gabriel didn't even blink at the accusation. "It kept me from getting tossed behind bars on a five-year sentence."

"Shame. Those five years could have done her a world of good."

"She's not as innocent as you think, Gian. You're under some impression that she didn't understand what she was doing for all those years—she knew. She knew *perfectly* well."

This was an emotional, manipulative game that Gabriel liked to play with his daughter, far too often. He couldn't use her to do his bidding now, so he liked to mess with her in other ways. Sometimes, Gian thought his wife and father deserved one another for their despicable behavior toward each other and other people. Other times, like now, he didn't want to sit back and watch Gabriel hurt Elena simply because he could.

"What did you really want today?" Gian asked. "What did you want by asking me here?"

"To warn you," Gabriel said before he took a hearty sip of whiskey from a glass. "I couldn't do that when you were in jail, and your men are already well versed on staying away from me and mine."

"For good reason. Warn me about what, exactly?"

"I was arrested and put in for four months because of *you*. Or rather, my affiliation to you was enough to have them watching me, and then serving me with warrants that garnered the charges I received. I don't care about the details, Gian, I care about my freedom."

"Don't we all?" Gian asked dryly. "Get to the point, so we can go our separate ways and pretend like this didn't happen until the next time."

"*The point*, you arrogant fuck, is that you've clearly got a rat problem somewhere. Someone, likely one of your fucking men, is feeding information to the police. And that's not surprising, considering all the shit you stirred up after your grandfather was killed. Corrado was a good man, fit for his position. You, on the other hand, are a spoiled, cocky, ignorant—"

"If we're going to trade insults, my demand is that you let me go first," Gian murmured. "It's only fair, considering. Otherwise, I'll take a pound from you for every name you throw at me without it being deserved."

Gabriel ground his teeth loud enough to be disturbing. "You find out which one of your useless cunts are talking to the police, or I will do it for you."

"Who's to say it's not coming from your end?"

"It's *not.*"

"Well—"

"Figure it out," Gabriel interrupted, "or I will tear through your streets and do it myself."

"Are we done?" Gian asked, standing from the table.

"Very much so. Tell my daughter to behave, Gian, though I am sure you're keeping a proper eye on her. Women like Elena need that sort of control. She needs to be on a *very* short leash, because her bite is far worse than her bark, believe me."

Gian didn't bother to respond to that, instead turning on his heel and heading for the front of the restaurant. He was gone from the business, and into the waiting SUV, before the cameras even realized he had stepped back out.

This time, Gian sat in the front seat beside Chris.

Elena sat in the back, glaring out the window.

Chris handed over Gian's charging cell phone, still plugged into the cigarette lighter. "Here, it's been going nuts. Probably trying to catch up with all the shit that it's missed out on these past few months."

"Thanks. Drive."

The enforcer did as he was told.

"What did he say when I was gone?" Elena asked from the back seat.

"Ignore that fucking bastard," Gian replied.

He was more interested in checking his phone. A brand-new message scrolled across the screen, one sent within the last few minutes.

From Cara.

Twenty-eight weeks today, it read. He could see, through looking at her messages for the past several months that she had sent him a text like this for every week that he had been locked up.

Gian smiled.

Elena leaning over his shoulder quickly made his brief happiness dissipate. He turned his phone's screen off, but he wasn't sure if Elena had seen the messages, or not. Of course, if she had, that didn't mean she would understand what they meant.

"I'd like to go to the mansion," his wife said.

"Be my guest. I'm going to the penthouse."

She sat back in the seat, unbothered and cold once more. "Good."

Elena dropped her pretense and her mask, as she had gotten what she wanted where her father was concerned, and didn't think she would have to worry about him again for a while.

Gian expected nothing different.

Chapter 8

"Good God, be careful, Claud!" Daniele leaned over the railing, shaking her head. "You're going to throw out your back again, you stubborn mule."

"I could have gotten the landlord's son to help bring the box up," Cara said, two steps above her aunt.

"Will you *donnas* shut up? Knock it off," Claud barked down below in the stairwell. "It is one goddamn set of stairs and a crib. I can handle this."

Daniele sighed. "I see an emergency room visit in our near future."

"Oh, just go get the apartment door open!"

"Fine, throw your back out! I don't care."

Daniele cared, Cara knew.

Even as her aunt stalked down the hallway, huffing, she still looked back over her shoulder with concern to see if her husband was coming. Cara leaned over the railing to see her uncle scratching at his jaw while he stared at the crib.

"I'll get the landlord's son to come help," she told her uncle.

"*I* had a son to help, but where is he now, Cara?"

She only stared at her uncle, unsure of how to answer that. She had no idea where Constantino was. There had been no funeral, no memorial, or anything to suggest he was dead, yet her uncle spoke like Constantino was buried somewhere, or dead in a ditch.

"So, do you want me to get you help, or not?" she asked.

"Not, girl. *Not.*"

"*Zia* was right, you are a stubborn mule."

"She only uses that word because she's too polite to call me an ass!" Claud shouted as Cara followed the path her aunt had taken.

"I'm not too polite, you fucking ass."

She *was* grateful that her aunt and uncle had been sweet enough to pick out a nursery set for her, as once she was no longer able to hide the fact she was pregnant, they were the first people she had told. She had told her brother second.

A whole lot of questions followed, from both ends. To be fair,

Tommas asked a whole lot less questions than her aunt and uncle. Questions about the father, or the fact she was just a few months off graduating. That led them into the fact the baby would come soon after, or shortly before, graduation. Then, even more questions about the baby's father.

Cara supposed the questions were normal, given her circumstance. She chose not to answer specific ones, while she gave vague answers for others.

She rubbed a hand over her twenty-eight-week pregnancy swell to soothe the jabbing elbows of her unborn son driving into her organs. Inside her apartment, Cara found her aunt moving a few pieces of small furniture out of the hallway to make it easier to get the crib inside what had been Lea's bedroom.

Cara finally got around to cleaning it all out.

She had a reason to now, after all.

"The rest of the nursery set will be delivered," Daniele said, "so at least for the rest of the furniture, you won't need someone to carry it in."

Cara agreed. "Thanks for all of this, *Zia*."

"No need to thank me, Cara. You work hard and I know you'll be a good mother, so you deserve all the help and whatever else you can get, believe me." Daniele went back to her work, randomly asking, "Of course, you could get lots of help by way of the baby's father."

Cara side-eyed her aunt, trying not to be too rude when she replied, "*Zia*, I am sure he will help, but right now, I am handling this on my own. And I am okay with that, as I have told you many times. The father is my business. Please respect that."

"I worry about you, Cara, that's all."

"I'm perfectly fine, *Zia*."

"Yes, yes, I know. You keep saying that." Daniele waved a hand at her. "Go check on your uncle, and make sure he hasn't had a heart attack in the stairwell."

Cara set her purse and phone on the couch, before going to do as her aunt wanted. Just as she reached the end of the hallway, Claud was finally pulling the large crib box through the stairwell door.

"See, I managed just fine on my own," Claud muttered.

"Huffing, puffing, and red-faced the whole way," Cara agreed.

Her uncle shot her a dirty look, but didn't respond.

"I think just setting it in the bedroom will be good enough for today," she added with a smile. "No need to put you through the torture of setting the crib up today, too."

"Who *will* do it for you, Cara?" Claud asked, pulling the box down the hallway toward her apartment. "Gian? His brother, perhaps?"

Cara froze, her back turned to her uncle. "What did you just say?"

"Nothing. I was thinking out loud. It was nothing."

She slowly turned around. "It was not nothing—you specifically said a name, not that I have given you a reason to use that name, so why did you, *Zio?*"

Claud wiped a hand over his face, effectively removing the sweat from his brow at the same time. "Word travels in this business, between us made men, I mean. I happen to know you get occasional visits from the boss's men, and I also know you were seen out and about with him last year before your trip to Chicago."

"*So?*"

"I also know you had a visit with him in the jail a couple of months ago, Cara."

She grinded her teeth in an effort to stay quiet.

It didn't work.

"*Zio*, this is not your business," she said firmly.

"You're right, it isn't. And your brother told me that, too, when I called him to chat about your current predicament."

"You called Tommas?"

"Lower your voice," her uncle snapped.

Cara's back straightened at the sound of a man scolding her.

Fuck. That. Shit.

"I am not in a *predicament*. I am pregnant, and by whom, is my fucking business to handle how I please."

"I know Gian Guzzi is the father, Cara. Or I have a strong enough suspicion to use his name, for good reason. And considering your reaction, I am not wrong. Tell me I am wrong."

"And so what if he is?"

"He's a married man!"

"Do you think I don't know that?" she cried, throwing her hands wide. "I *do* know that, Claud!"

"Have you considered how difficult this road will be for you and the child?" her uncle asked quietly. "To be the mistress of a made man and the bastard boy, born to a *goomah* mother? Have you considered that at all?"

Cara felt the familiar prickling behind her eyes that signaled her tears were trying to fall. She held them back, and settled for hiding the trembling of her hands at her sides.

"I know I made choices that might not be what everyone else would make," Cara replied, level-toned and stone-faced, "and I know this won't be easy, but don't toss those words at me *just* because they're the ones everyone else wants to use. You only see the surface, and how that looks, but you don't care about the rest. You don't care to know the details, about me and him, about us, or *why*. So that also means you don't get to tell me *fuck all*. Not what to do, how to handle this situation, or anything else about me, my baby, his father, or what I should do with my feelings. Take your opinion, and shove it up your—"

"Cara," her aunt called softly from behind her.

She turned to find her aunt standing a few feet down in the hallway. No doubt, Daniele had heard every single word.

Walking past her aunt, Cara said, "Well, there you go. Now you know *who*. Does it make it better, *Zia?*"

Daniele didn't say a thing.

She didn't have to.

Cara knew the answer.

No, it was not better.

Cara dug into a takeout container full of noodles, as the news program on the television repeated the highlights of the day. She checked her phone, seeing a new message from Gian, one in reply to her latest update on the baby's gestation.

I like Marcus for a name, Gian had wrote. *It's my middle name, and my grandfather's father's name. A family name.*

Cara thought to reply, but she decided she would do that after she finished eating. She had just taken a good mouthful of noodles when a shot of Gian came across the screen.

New Guzzi Crime Boss Released, the headline read across the bottom of the screen. That wasn't exactly news to Cara, as she had known Gian's date of release for a good month, and had counted down the days. She also knew, through Chris's last update, Gian might need to lay low for a few days before she would see him, it really just depended on circumstances.

That, Cara had also understood.

What she didn't understand—or like, for that matter—was seeing a shot of Gian fresh off release, walking into what looked like a restaurant with his wife on his arm.

Then, the shot changed.

Gian stepping out of a car, moving to the other side, and then helping his wife out. She kissed his cheek, her wide-brimmed red hat that matched the color of her heels and dress, hid half of her face, but not enough.

Cara had not been able to forget what Elena looked like since the moment she had seen those wedding pictures. It was burned into her fucking retinas.

"Gian Guzzi, heir apparent and new boss to the Guzzi Crime Dynasty is free today," the anchor said. "We were unable to question the purported Don on his release, or the investigations the police say continue to be active, as he moved directly from the jail to a restaurant, where he seemed to meet with his father-in-law, while his wife was close by. Guzzi's father-in-law, Gabriel Canali, is another well-known gangster from an Ottawa organization, a leader of a Camorra clan, who was also recently released from jail."

The anchor continued talking, but Cara shut the television off, and tried to focus on eating her food. She no longer had an appetite.

Cara didn't want to be that woman—jealous because she saw Gian with his wife, and not her. She didn't want to become irrationally angry anytime a news program mentioned something about Elena.

She had *no right* to feel those things.

And yet she did.

Cara quelled her irritation and useless jealousy by rolling her hands over her unborn boy's movements. Each little kick and jab, calmed her a bit more.

There wasn't much else she could do.

It was the loud knock on her apartment door that broke Cara from her daze. She wasn't expecting visitors.

Cara quickly got up off the couch and made her way to the door, when the knocking became slightly more persistent. "Just a second, I'm coming."

She pulled open the door to find an unknown, older woman standing behind it. For a long moment, she only stared at the woman, taking in her ashy blonde hair, green eyes, and the way she smiled ever-so-slightly at the sight of Cara. The woman's gaze dropped to Cara's slightly rounded midsection, and then just as fast, flew back up to her face.

"My, you are quite a beautiful thing, aren't you?" the woman asked. "He always did have an eye for the ones that could stand out in a crowd. I believe it's because he never learned how to blend in, either. He always had to be front and center, a prince waiting to be a king."

Cara held the door, unsure if she wanted to close it or not. "Do I know you?"

She looked familiar.

"Under different circumstances, I am sure we would have known each other very well," the woman said softly. "It's Cara, right? Cara Rossi?"

"I am dangerously close to shutting this door," Cara warned.

The woman laughed, her crow's feet becoming more apparent around her eyes. It was that laugh, and the way her features changed enough, that Cara thought she might know exactly who this woman was. It also could have been the French accent coloring up the woman's words that did it for Cara, too.

But that woman wouldn't come here, would she?

She wouldn't seek Cara out, right?

After all, Cara was the whore, the mistress, the piece of ass on the side. She wasn't worthy of the family name, she couldn't sit beside her man in church, and her very presence was a dirty word for some.

Surely *that* woman, would not come to Cara.

Surely not.

"Celeste Guzzi, Gian's mother," the woman said, smiling softly again. "It's nice to finally meet the woman I'd heard all those rumors about nearly a year ago. Gian wouldn't budge an inch, when I asked. Your aunt is an old friend, from way, way back."

"Oh," Cara said dumbly.

"She thought I might like to meet you." Celeste's gaze dropped to Cara's stomach again. "For obvious reasons, sweetheart. And she was right."

"Not that you've given me a reason to think this, but to what, tell me to crawl in a hole somewhere?"

Celeste frowned. "Not at all, dear."

"Sorry, knee-jerk reaction."

"I can understand why."

Cara stepped back, widening the apartment door a bit more. "Would you like to come in, and maybe have a tea or something?"

Celeste nodded once. "*Oui*, I think I would."

"Does Gian know you're here?"

"Oh, no." Celeste laughed as she walked into the apartment. "I get to wait until tomorrow for breakfast to see him. We're going to have *so much* to talk about now."

Cara shot Celeste a look from across the way. "I'm not sure if you mean that to be a good or bad thing."

"Well, it's both. I understand the predicament my son found himself in, and not just with you. Between his grandfather, all the rules and expectations they shoveled onto him over the years, and then his wife ..."

"I'm not sure I want to know anything about her," Cara said, trying not to sound trite.

Celeste shrugged, as if to say, *do what you will*. "Perhaps you should learn about Elena, or at least, learn why she is where she is with my son. I wish more people had looked beyond the surface when they married years ago, or for that matter, paid attention to it all. No one thought to, and it's no wonder he's found himself—" She looked over to Cara, then said, "It's no wonder he's found himself in this situation. A man or woman can only be so unhappy in every aspect of their life, before they eventually start looking for something—or someone—to fill that void."

Cara turned the electric kettle on. "I never thought about it in that way."

"You don't know *her*. Elena, I mean," Celeste said, her assumption spot on. "But that is not my place to say, either."

"Is it your place to be here?"

The older woman didn't even hesitate. "No."

"Yet here you are."

"Here I am, Cara." Celeste smiled wider. "Now, tell me about my first grandbaby."

Cara stared at the tubs of ice cream in the store's freezer, trying to decide which flavor—or rather, favors—she wanted to buy. Shrugging, she pulled several mini tubs out and dropped them into her cart. If she couldn't decide on just one flavor, then she would try them all.

Winning, Cara thought.

Pregnancy was no fucking joke.

Neither were the late-night cravings.

"Is that one any good, do you know?"

The question came from Cara's left. She had been so involved in her task of getting the last, but most important, thing on her grocery list, she hadn't been paying attention to her surroundings.

Cara found the woman who the voice belonged to, and damn near tripped over her own two feet. *Elena Guzzi.*

Elena stood only an inch taller than Cara, but that was probably because of the sky-high heels the woman had on her feet. She certainly didn't look dressed to be grocery shopping in a black knee-high, pencil skirt dress with a beige trench coat overtop. Her makeup was flawless— impeccable, with nothing over or under done. Even her blonde hair laid straight down her back, and not one stray hair was out of place.

She was beautiful.

Perfect, even.

Yet, cold in her eyes.

Cara recognized her instantly, but Elena looked at her as though she didn't have the first clue in the world who she was.

"I-I'm sorry?" Cara managed to ask, finally coming out of her shock.

Elena leaned over Cara's cart, balancing her basket with nothing but wine inside, on her hip. "That one right there—the peanut butter one. Is it any good?"

"That one is, but I don't know about the rest."

"Oh, good. I like peanut butter." Elena moved around Cara's cart, seemingly unaware that she was being watched like a bug under a microscope. "Although I don't think I have the same excuse as you do to be snacking on these, do I?"

"Pardon?"

Elena pointed at Cara's stomach peeking out beneath her opened jacket. "How far along, if you don't mind me asking?"

Oh, God.

Cara did not want to be having this conversation with her lover's wife, especially considering the woman didn't seem to know who in the hell she was. Didn't that make it even more wrong on some level?

She was going to hell.

"Twenty-nine weeks in a couple of days," Cara said quietly.

"Almost there, then. Boy or girl?"

"Boy."

Elena smiled, but Cara couldn't help but notice how it didn't *feel* true. It certainly looked warm enough, but the iciness in Elena's gaze was hard to hide. Cara wondered if that was just a part of who Elena was inside her soul—perpetually cold, always distant.

Cara didn't have any right to speculate on those things, anyway.

"Have you thought of any names?" Elena asked as she put a couple of tubs of the ice cream in her basket.

"Um, his father likes Marcus. A family thing, I guess. I haven't said yes or no to it."

Cara's awkward tone did not go unnoticed.

Elena shot her with an apologetic look. "Oh, my gosh. I'm so sorry. You probably think I'm a creep or something, randomly questioning a stranger in a grocery store about her pregnancy. Don't mind me, really. Babies just make me curious, and so does pregnancy."

Cara knew better than to ask, and she should have just taken the chance to get out of the conversation while she had it, but she didn't. "Why is that?"

"I lost a baby, nearly four years ago, shortly after I married my husband. We haven't been able to … well, you know."

Guilt and shame compounded hard in Cara's chest, squeezing the fucking life out of her heart.

"I'm sorry," Cara said lamely.

What else could she say?

I'm sorry your husband knocked me up?

Elena smiled widely at her, as though her admission meant nothing, and neither did Cara's apologies. "Well, enjoy your ice cream, and have a great day."

"You, too."

Cara watched Elena disappear down the aisle. It was the strangest, most random interaction of her life.

Worse, was the fact Cara didn't even know if it *was* random.

Cara balanced the four bags of groceries in her one hand and arm as she tried to get the main doors to her apartment building open. She felt his presence slide in beside her before he even spoke. He slipped the bags from her grasp easily, and his sweet kiss landed on her cheek without a word.

An arm slid around her waist, and Cara's body reacted as though heaven had just come to wrap around her soul. She leaned into Gian's embrace as he kissed her cheek once more.

"What did I tell you, *mon ange*?" Familiar, comforting dark eyes looked her over, before moving onto the contents of her grocery bags. "Come on, tell me."

"About what?"

"When you need something, Cara."

"Gian, I am not getting someone to grab my groceries. I can handle it—"

"Then take someone with you to help you carry all this shit, love."

Cara shrugged. "You showed up. All is well."

Gian sighed, and gave her a quick kiss on her forehead. Cara smiled, and managed to get the main doors open at the same time. Quickly, the two slid into the building, and Gian led the way. His arm stayed firmly tucked around Cara's waist, his palm hidden under her jacket, resting flat to her swelled stomach.

"I didn't expect you so soon," she said as they climbed the one stairwell to her floor.

"I should have come sooner," he replied. "Things got in the way."

"Like what?"

"Life," Gian said roughly, "and nothing that matters, to be honest."

Once the two were safely hidden away in Cara's apartment, she stood back and let Gian put all the groceries away. He never missed a beat, sliding things into cupboards as though he had lived there for as many years as she had. He really did pay attention, and he didn't forget things.

At least, not where she was concerned.

"I want to apologize for something," Gian said, his voice muffled by the freezer as he shoved in the mini ice cream tubs.

"What's that?"

"My mother showing up here the other night."

Cara's tension released in a laugh. "She's a wonderful, interesting woman."

"Wonderfully interesting is one way to put it." Gian closed the freezer door, and looked back at Cara. "Still, you shouldn't have been put in that position. I should have told her first, and then—"

"You're right, you should have."

Gian nodded. "She let me know that. *Repeatedly.*"

"I like her."

"She likes you," he replied with a smirk. "I knew she would, it was just everything else that I didn't know about, I suppose."

Everything else, like his wife.

Cara thought to tell Gian then and there that she had run into Elena, but only decided against it because what would be the point? His wife clearly hadn't recognized her, and she hadn't done anything wrong or rude. If anything, wasn't Cara the one in the wrong, just by being pregnant with Elena's husband's child?

The meeting was random. Nothing more, nothing less.

Cara did have other questions, though.

Things she wanted to know.

"Gian?"

"Yes, *amore?*"

"Why did you marry her? Why her, Gian?"

Chapter 9

"Why her, Gian?"

Gian tensed at the question, but only because he knew there would be no one, easy answer. It was several events, mixed-messages, and dumb feelings that had led him into the mistake of marriage with Elena. A sense of duty.

When he stayed silent, mulling over his reply, Cara took a seat at the table. "So, you're not going to tell me?"

Gian meet her gaze, unashamed. "Of course, I'll tell you. It's just not an easy question."

"You've asked me before, if I wanted to talk about her or the marriage. What is so different this time? Because *I* asked?"

"Because I wasn't expecting it. Because back then, I was prepared to explain and knew how to say things. When you spring it on me, I don't have time to consider ways to wall myself off from shit I don't like to feel."

Honesty was the best policy.

Gian had learned his lesson about lying.

Cara played with the tablecloth as Gian got one of the mini tubs of ice cream from the freezer, and then spoons from the drawer. He pulled a chair out from the table, and set it opposite to Cara, so the two were facing one another.

"Wine would probably be better for this conversation," Gian said with a smirk, "but since you can't drink, neither will I, and the ice cream will have to do."

"It's that bad for you that you need wine?"

"Whiskey, preferably. Even beer wouldn't be enough." Gian shook the ice cream container. "And today, it's ice cream only."

"So, why her?"

Gian handed Cara a spoon, and used his own to pull through the top of the ice cream. He stared at the rolled-up treat on the tip of the spoon, considering whether or not he wanted a bite before he spoke. His mouth worked first.

"I met Elena Canali shortly after her twenty-second birthday, at a restaurant, actually. We married when she was twenty-three. Just a random pass by, she was at one table alone, and I was at another with a date, of sorts. I recognized her, but only because we had previous run-ins with her father. Gabriel is a boss of another organization—one not entirely like ours, less controlled, but still Italian-based. Not that it matters."

"Then get to what does," Cara urged.

Gian sucked the ice cream off his spoon, then waved it at Cara. "I'm picking out important details. Think, stuff I overlooked, or should have paid more attention to. Things like a boss's daughter being alone, without any sort of watcher or protection."

Cara frowned. "All right."

"She was exceptionally beautiful, and it's one of the first things someone notices about her, even from afar. I was not an exception to that rule. She kept looking over at me, ignoring the fact I was with a woman at my table, and I caught her staring a few times. It made me curious."

Cara took a bite of the ice cream, too. "She is beautiful, but cold, too. Even in your wedding pictures, I could see it. It's strange."

"It's not strange if you know her," Gian murmured. "Back to my story, though. I let my date go early; my mother had set it up, and back then, I didn't mind playing into Celeste's meddling from time to time, but nothing was coming from that."

Gian shrugged. "Anyway, she left, and I asked for the bill. The waiter hadn't even brought it over before Elena approached me. By the time he did get there, we were already five minutes into a conversation about who was going to run for mayor that year in the city, as the Ford family seemed like loose cannons, which teams had the best shot at the Stanley Cup, and some movie she wanted to see that was coming out."

"Oh?"

"I offered to take her to see it," Gian said dryly. "Call that a first date, I guess."

Cara took a huge scoop of the ice cream. "And then what happened?"

"I mean, you could say we started dating, but it wasn't like that really, and it was clouded by all sorts of other shit going on."

"Like what?"

"Elena's father was in the midst of a street war with a gang, so I had to be careful about my involvement with her seeming ... to their side of things and making it appear like the Guzzi family would get involved. Petty street wars aren't worth much except a growing body count, and the Guzzi family doesn't get mixed up in those sorts of things unless it'll benefit us in some way."

"Details again?" Cara asked.

Gian laughed. "Sort of. I thought *I* was the one being careful, taking her out occasionally, or having her stay over at my place, but never hers.

She didn't meet my family or friends, and I didn't meet hers. It turned out, *she* was the one being careful. Elena didn't want her father to know about me, or that she was messing around with me—that's the best way to describe what it was, anyway."

"But you liked her?"

"Well enough," Gian answered, choosing his words carefully. "I liked what she gave me, the pieces of her on the surface, because she never went beyond that. I liked how she was attentive to *me*, only. Especially when we were together, other people didn't exist to her. She doted on the stupid male side of a man's brain that feeds off being *the* man, you know what I mean?"

Cara shrugged, but said nothing.

"Elena works best when she controls a situation, no matter what that situation might entail. And she does that with men, specifically, because she knows she is beautiful, and she knows that using her sexuality and her sweetness is disarming to men who aren't looking for her manipulations. They are unprepared for the attack, for the gut-punch or the knife in their back when they turn away. She makes you trust her, because why would she want to hurt you, this person she so clearly adores? And then she strikes."

"Huh," Cara said quietly, frowning.

"I know, I jumped ahead a bit in explaining that. It'll make sense in a second."

"Go for it."

Gian took a deep breath, and another bite of ice cream, letting the chocolate and peanut-butter flavors wash over his palate before he spoke again. "We had been doing our thing for a few months or so, when she came up pregnant."

Cara stiffened.

Gian didn't miss it.

"Or so she said," he added, knowing it wouldn't make a difference. The words were out there, and they hurt to know. "I had no reason not to believe her, or to think, if she was pregnant, the child might not be mine. Things moved very fast from that point—her father was suddenly involved, and all the things people heard or whispered about that man were right in front of my eyes and very true. He's dangerous and he's volatile. He's manipulative and evil. But aren't we all, in some way?"

Gian shook his head, adding, "Elena wanted to get away from him, and that much was clear. I understood why, too, because he used her and he abused her. He was angry that she had been seeing someone behind his back; he's so abnormally close to her, and controlling of her. At least back then. And when she refused to abort the pregnancy, he nearly beat her to death, and then had her sent to me."

He dropped the spoon to the table with a clatter. "I saw a different

Elena then, Cara. One that was scared and small, a victim of a man she just wanted to get away from. And to this day, no matter what that woman has done to me or what she might do in the future, I still see the Elena from that day. Bruised, and swollen, with a bloody, busted mouth, and dried blood matting her hair. I see her, and I never have to think *why?* I think, *why not?* Why not hurt, use, and manipulate to be free, to be happy? Why not use all the things your father taught you to do, in order to protect and advance him, to protect and advance yourself? It doesn't give her a pass, sure, but it certainly makes more sense, in a way."

Cara cleared her throat. "She was lucky she didn't lose the baby, then."

Gian chuckled darkly. "There was no baby to lose, Cara, but I'll get there. Corrado pressured me to do the right thing, with Elena, but also where our family was concerned. He didn't want to face a war with Gabriel on the streets, and he knew how dangerous the man could be. So, a marriage it was."

"And that obviously happened."

"Quite fast, within a couple of months of announcing the engagement." Gian took Cara's spoon from her, scooped some ice cream, and fed her the bite, waiting for her to finish before he continued. "Leading up to the wedding, we had to deal with the usual family things. Which put Elena front row and center for her father. His way of hurting her emotionally when he couldn't hurt her physically, was to shame and embarrass her in front of me, or others. *Does he know,* her father would say, *how you sucked the cock of the mayor's son to pay off my debt?* Things like that."

Cara let out a shaky exhale, and looked away. "That's terrible."

"It reinforced my belief that I was doing the right thing, though I didn't love her, and I knew what a marriage with someone meant in my world. It is for life, there is no out, except for death. But I thought, I was doing the right thing."

"And then?"

"And then a week after we married, I caught Elena drinking wine. From the moment we walked out of the church on our wedding day, something changed with her. She no longer focused on me like she had once done—all that attention, the doting and the adoration, was gone. She didn't need to pretend, you see. Not once she had gotten what she needed from me. I was pissed about the wine, because of the baby."

"But there was no baby, you said?"

Gian nodded once. "She tried to say she had miscarried. We weren't even having sex; we hadn't fucked since the night we married, so how could I say for sure that she was or wasn't losing the baby?"

"Was she?"

"No, there *was no baby.* I had her records at her doctor yanked, though it wasn't my right to, and found there was no pregnancy, at least not within the months she had been with me. Six months *before* we had met, there had been an abortion on file. One of several over the years. She was actually on the depo shot, and had been since the last abortion, so a pregnancy was highly unlikely to begin with."

"Oh, Gian."

"Don't do the pity thing," Gian said, shooting Cara a lopsided grin. "Not for me. I overlooked a lot of things because I didn't want to question a woman that was clearly in need of help. I was too busy feeding a hero complex and trying to do what everyone else wanted me to. By the time I realized how incredibly fucked I was, and how much Elena had manipulated me, it was too late."

"You were married."

Gian's smile faded. "For life."

"But—"

"There is no but, not for this. Not in the position I was, and while I wanted to send her back to her father with a fuck you and a smile, I couldn't do it. And she fought with me daily, she raged at me. I gave her the things she wanted, a beautiful penthouse, new cars, furs, nearly a million in diamonds. I gave her everything she wanted, just to keep her happy for a short while, but that was the problem."

"It only lasted for a short while," Cara said.

"I couldn't keep her happy, because she had gotten what she wanted from me, and as of that point, I was only a nuisance. So, I moved out, about a year after we married, though we hadn't been even sleeping together or using the same bedroom from almost the day we married. We did it quietly, we were careful about our public side, making sure it still looked like we were a happy couple. We didn't want to provoke her father, after all. Then, as time went by, we stopped pretending unless it was something big or important, like a wedding, a funeral, somewhere our faces might be shot on the news, or whatever."

Cara reached out and stroked Gian's cheek, surprising him at the tender touch. "I'm sorry."

"Don't be, *bella*. It's circumstance and details. That's all it's ever been, Cara. I don't have a paper to say I'm divorced, because I can't. Men like me can't be divorced without ruining everything we worked for. And a divorce might push an already violent man over the edge—something else my family can't afford right now."

"What about ... other relationships?"

Gian shrugged. "I haven't had other relationships. For a while, even after we separated, I was faithful. Then one night, I met someone, and I was out of her place before morning even came. I didn't have time to be in a relationship, or the effort it would take to keep up the charade. When you came along, I wasn't so jaded toward women, because I hadn't needed to be in a long time. I had no reason to distrust you, not when you showed your cards that first night, telling me what you did and didn't want. And my God, there was something about you that made me sit down and pay attention. It just blew up from there."

"And you were fucked again."

Gian smiled sinfully. "I didn't mind, Cara. Not with you. You made me love you, and I wanted to be with you, so I was going to try and do that. I just didn't know how. I *was* trying to tell you before you found out in Chicago. I knew I should tell you, but it isn't the kind of conversation that is usually brought up when you first meet someone. As time passed, it became more of me not knowing whether you were going to be with me, or go your own way, so I held off again. I asked what you wanted with me, in the future, and you only said me. You said *me*, love. I just didn't know how to tell you the situation without ruining us. I didn't want to ruin us. And then you were gone."

"I should have listened to this when you offered to tell me before," Cara said sadly, her hand still cupping his cheek, and her thumb stroking sweet lines on his jaw. "I'm sorry that I didn't."

"Circumstance and details have put me back in the position where I have to play house with a woman I despise, who I don't trust. I wish I could be rid of Elena, but I can't send her back to her father. Not that it would do me any good, because she would still be my—"

"Wife," Cara interrupted gently.

"Exactly. I'm sorry that I can't give you the things you deserve. I'm sorry that I love you, Cara, but I can't shout it to anyone who will listen, or make a huge show of getting a ring on your finger and walking you down the aisle. I'm sorry that I was selfish and put you in a position where your worth is tied to my choices. I can't make a home with you, not one that will ever feel proper or permanent, because I fucked up once, and here we are."

"*Gian.*"

"I'm sorry," he repeated. "I wish I could say something different, but it's the only thing I have right now. I'm sorry."

"Me, too," Cara whispered.

"Gian?"

Gian reached for Cara through his groggy haze of sleep, hearing her call of his name, and wanting to bring her closer. He found her side of the bed empty, and promptly opened his eyes wide. Cara stood in the bedroom doorway, rubbing at her eyes with the back of her hand. A quick check of the clock said it was way too early in the morning for her to be up. Cara didn't get out of bed before eight, not if she didn't have to.

"What are you doing out of bed?" he asked her.

Cara pointed at her rounded stomach, pouting in the darkness. "He makes me pee a lot."

Gian's tired laughter rung out in the bedroom, and he fell back into the bed. "Go to sleep, Cara."

"In a minute."

"What is it, *mon ange?*"

"Did you set up the crib?"

Gian cleared the sleep out of his voice, saying, "Yeah, it needed set up, didn't it? You fell asleep early, I had nothing to do."

"Could have woke me up. There's all sorts of things we could be doing that are fun in bed, you know."

"You need to sleep more than you need me waking you up to get a good fuck."

Although, he was down for that, too. Just not when he could see she was tired as hell.

Cara slipped into the bed, and tucked herself close to Gian's side. Rolling over, he brought her head to his naked chest, and let his hand rest on her lower stomach. A possessive, protective swell washed through his bloodstream at the feeling of his son shifting under his father's palm, one of the first movements Gian had felt of his child.

"Cara?"

"Hmm?"

"I would rather set up a nursery in the penthouse, if you would be willing to stay there, I mean," he said.

Cara let out a soft sigh. "I don't know about that one."

"I don't have to be there, if you don't want me to—"

"Aren't things complicated and difficult enough with all of this? Do we need to add in that sort of thing, too?"

"I'll do whatever you want, love. You know that."

"I do."

"But my son is, and will always be, non-negotiable between us. For him, and for you if you would let me, I will move the world. I won't compromise about my child. Not when it comes to caring for him, or providing him with whatever he needs, not to mention his mother."

"I should hope not."

"Then consider the penthouse now, and what it would mean to be somewhere that's safer, better watched, closer to certain places you frequent. It would also be easier for me to come, on that side of things."

"And go," she added quietly. "It would make it easier for you to come and *go*, Gian."

"I can't help that, Cara."

"I know," she murmured.

"Consider it, for him."

"And for you."

Gian smirked, pressing a kiss to her soft hair. "And for me, yes."

"Gian?"

"What, *amore*?"

"Shut up and fuck me now."

"Cara, you should sleep while you can. You need to slee—"

She was the one to shut him up, instead, by leaning up to catch his moving lips with a hard kiss, and in the next breath, she had climbed on top of him under the sheets. In no time at all, she had discarded his boxer-briefs, and the short nightie she had on did little to hide the fact she was naked underneath.

Cara shivered under his wandering hands, and she let him pull that damn nightie off her body entirely, baring all of her to him. The heavy swells of her breasts fit perfectly into his palms, and she sighed happily when he tweaked her nipples under his forefinger and thumb. Her back arched under his touch, moving her closer to him when he shifted in the bed to sit up. He traced the gentle curve of her stomach with his fingertips, watching pretty goosebumps bloom over her skin.

Her hands were between their bodies before Gian could even demand it, circling his length and fitting his cock at her cunt. He held Cara's face in his palms as she lowered down on his length, hard and fast. Heat shot through his cock, and straight up his spine, when she was seated on him fully. There was no waiting for her, no slowing or careful movements.

She rode him crazy, so wild. Her nails dug into the hard muscles of his arms as he dragged her closer for a kiss, keeping her there while their tongues warred until he was forced to pull away for a burning breath.

"Oh, my God. Oh, my God," Cara mumbled again and again.

A record on repeat.

All her pretty cries.

The way she looked riding him.

How her body shook and shivered.

It was all such a familiar tune.

Gian loved it.

She was so wet, her cunt squeezing the fucking life out of his body through his dick. He angled his lower half into her lowering body, making it so that her greedy little clit was rubbing against him every time she came down on him fast and hard again.

Gian wanted to give Cara what he knew she liked the most—his fingers tight around her throat, his body pounding into hers until she was a mess of tears and sweat into the bedsheets. But he held back, and only because he thought that might not be okay, given her state. Instead, he settled on letting his hand rest against the thrumming beat of her pulse on her neck, and his teeth leaving marks on her lips and tits. He let her set the pace, and how rough she wanted to fuck him, not the other way around.

His words spilling out were damn near constant, though, and unstoppable. Whispered harsh and fast in her ear, because he was worried he was going to lose all train of thought before he could get them out in their entirety.

"You're so beautiful, *mon ange*. My good girl, fucking me like you are. Take what you want, Cara, take my cock."

Cara's first orgasm came on like a tsunami of sensation that even Gian could feel, from the way her body tensed and then shook, to the loud, broken cry she released. Her eyes flew wide, the blue of her irises a darkened wave of color, while her pupils had blown wide in her bliss.

So fucking beautiful.

And apparently, it wasn't nearly enough. The second she had calmed, her demands came sure and quick in his ear.

More, and *now*, and *only you, only you, only you.*

How could he refuse?

How could he refuse *her*?

"Seems we have some work to do," Stephan said.

Gian nodded in agreement with the Capo. "Lots of digging and prying into whoever might be feeding the police information."

"There's a lot of men in this organization," Dom pointed out.

"I'm aware."

"It won't be too difficult," Chris added.

All eyes moved to the quiet enforcer in the corner, who had mostly been playing on his phone and sipping from a glass of water. While the rest of them drank whiskey or a beer, Chris drank water.

"And why do you think that is?" Gian asked his man.

Chris looked up at his boss, shrugging. "Once word begins to travel that the boss is looking for a rat, you'll find that the men who don't want any fucking part of that shit will be the first to point you in the direction you need to be looking. They all pay attention, they simply choose not to speak up unless they need to. Make it so that they need to, boss. That's all."

Dom's gaze swung back to Gian. "How do we even know for sure that the rat *is* in our family?"

"Gabriel is pretty convinced on that fact," Gian replied.

"And he is a voice of reason here?"

"No, but since we all know how he treats someone he likes, imagine how he treats those he doesn't like. If he says he doesn't think there's a rat in his family, it's because he's already made his rounds. It's our turn to do rounds on our end, now."

Gian let the men have their opinions, but he was firm on what he wanted. Soon after, the three men cleared out of his office at the mansion, leaving him alone once again. He had only called the meeting, because he had spent the week keeping a low profile, and trying to spend as much time with Cara as he could. When he knew he had no choice but to head home, he decided to call the meeting.

"You look stressed, Gian."

His attention flew to the new presence in his office. Elena leaned in the doorway, a silk robe cinched tightly at her waist and her arms crossed under her chest. Immediately, he was on edge at Elena's sudden entrance and it had a whole lot to do with the bare legs and black heels she wore. Why did she need a robe and heels like those on at the same time?

It was a dichotomy.

Unless she was looking for something.

He wasn't about to provide it.

"Do you need something?" Gian asked.

"I saw the guys leave. I thought I should check on you."

Right.

"I'm fine, about to head to bed." With that, he stood from his desk, closing his laptop down and putting away his papers. All the while, Elena never moved from her spot in the doorway, forcing Gian to come incredibly close to his wife as he passed her by. Her hand coming up to press against his chest over his dress shirt stopped him for a moment. "What, Elena?"

"I don't interest you at all, do I?"

His gaze lingered over the delicate column of her throat, to the peeks of her breasts at the top of the robe, and then down over her trim waist and the expanse of her legs. "You did once, but it was a game you used to hurt me with. Nothing about that interests me at all, Elena."

"Why her, then?"

Gian stiffened. "I beg your pardon?"

"What about Cara Rossi is so special? She's pretty, sure. Red hair, tall, slim. But she isn't ... spectacular, is she? Or did I miss something?"

He realized in that moment how delicate of a line he was walking with his wife. It was not one he wanted to walk at all, but it seemed Elena was not going to give him a choice in the matter.

"Cara—"

"Did you think I wouldn't know about her visit when you were in jail? Or how curious it is that you are bringing her to visit … not to mention, when she's pregnant? Or that you hole yourself up in her place for days, hiding away from the world?"

"Elena, that's enough," Gian warned. "This isn't your business, and you have no reason to care, either way."

"Someone told me she was pregnant," Elena continued, not heeding his warning in the slightest. "I had to see, so I did. I approached her in the grocery store. I don't think she even knew who I was, or if she did, it probably wasn't until after. A boy, she told me. Marcus for a name, maybe. You're going to give your bastard—even if he is a firstborn boy—your family's name? And not even for a middle name, but a *first* name, his given name. I don't understand, I guess, what about her that does it for you. Like I said, nothing about her is spectacular or amazing. She's just a woman."

"Because she isn't you," Gian said, "she is the complete opposite of you, Elena. And that is *everything*. Stay away from Cara, understood?"

His rage simmered through his bloodstream, but he managed to hide it for the moment. How long that would last, he couldn't say.

How dare she approach Cara?

How dare she seek her out?

Had Cara even realized?

"I will make your father look like a saint, if you hurt that woman or my child," Gian murmured in Elena's ear. "We both know the only reason you're still a problem for me is *because* of your father. You have things in this life that she doesn't, where I'm concerned. You have my last name, my homes, my money, and my grandmother's rings on your finger. And you don't deserve a single fucking one of them. You know it, too. So, try not to let your need to play games with the lives of others cloud the smart part of your brain that knows you're safe and comfortable in your good little life here, Elena. I don't love you and you will never have my children, because those are things *she* has. And if you try to take them away from her because you are jealous or bitter, I will scatter you from one end of this city to the other."

Gian smiled, but Elena stayed stone-cold.

"Just so we're clear," he added.

Elena stayed where she was in the doorway. Gian went to bed. Cara, however, got an enforcer to watch her the very next morning.

Chapter 10

"Eight weeks left—let the countdown begin," Jenny teased.

Cara huffed as she bent down to pick up the rest of the art supplies on the small kiddie table. "Don't remind me."

"You're thirty-two weeks pregnant, Cara. How can you not know it every second of your day?"

"That's my point. I don't need more reminders."

Jenny laughed. "Uh-huh. Are you nervous, is that it?"

"Excited, but mostly …" Cara waved at her very large stomach that made it hard to sleep, eat, and almost every other function of life, including breathing some days. "I'm just over all of this."

"Don't worry. It will all be worth it in the end. Once you have the little one in your arms, all of the hells of pregnancy and birth will be forgotten."

Oh, Jesus.

Birth.

That was another thing Cara was not looking forward to. Not by a *long* shot. That, she was scared of. Terrified, even. A *baby*—a small human—was going to come out of her *body*. Women might have been doing it for millennia, but sweet Jesus, Cara had *not*.

"Wow, you just went white," Jenny noted.

Cara tried to be nonchalant as she put all the supplies away into their proper places. "I guess birth makes me a little worried."

"When a baby gets in, Cara, it has to eventually come out."

"Yes, that is the only guarantee about pregnancy. I'm well aware of that."

"Women's bodies are made for this, too."

"Again, I know."

"Then perhaps you should stop squeezing that glue bottle before you bust the top of it off," Jenny pointed out.

Cara instantly dropped the bottle of glue into the container. "Okay, so maybe the idea of birth freaks me out a bit."

"A lot, you mean."

"Make it easy on me, Jenny."

The older woman laughed, saying, "You know I won't do that. My whole job is to make people talk about their deepest, darkest issues. Since no one else is around right now, I might as well work on you."

"I'm not in need of a therapist, but thank you." Cara shot the woman a smile. "Really, though, I know it'll be fine. I'm just freaked out because I'm twenty-seven, *very* pregnant, and it's almost at the end."

"Which means?"

"My whole life is about to change?"

Jenny nodded. "But you know that, too. You know little man is going to change things for you, from your daily life, to school, to work, and that's just the surface. Emotionally, physically, and mentally, change will come there, too. The fact that you know these things means the transition will come easier for you, from a woman, to a *mom*. Too many live in the clouds when they're pregnant, and then baby comes, and boom, back down to reality. It's a hard pill to swallow."

"You make motherhood sound … like war."

"For some, it can be," Jenny murmured.

"I'm lucky that I have people to help," Cara said, shrugging. "Like the ladies here, or my aunt and uncle. The father and some of his family, too."

Cara said that last sentence quieter, and offered little to no information about Gian, his family, or who she meant.

"You say that like you're leaving someone out," Jenny noted.

Cara frowned, and turned to face the woman. "It would be nice to have my sister, too. You know?"

"To wish for things you cannot have, is human."

"Maybe so, but I don't like to dwell."

"And I think it's more than acceptable for you to wish your *twin* sister was here for this, even if it hurts a lot to think about. You shared your whole lives with one another. Boys, graduation, smiles and tears, laughter … *life*."

Cara cleared the emotion lodging in her throat. "Yeah and this is one of the very few things we won't get to share, so that's a little hard. But it doesn't matter, right? What's done is done, so let's get up, brush ourselves off, and move on."

"It *does* matter, Cara. My advice is that you don't hold those feelings in, or push them aside in pursuit of happier days, especially not now," Jenny said, coming close enough that she could soothingly rub a hand over Cara's back. "Because even if you think not dealing with those thoughts and feelings is better, you're actually doing yourself, and the baby, a great disservice."

"How so?"

"Babies have a way of reminding us of everything we are without once they come into the world, although unintentionally. The wash of hormones, all the changes, and everything else comes together like the Big Bang to make one hell of a combination on new mothers. Deal with how you feel now, so that when he is here, those things don't surprise you."

Cara nodded. "Okay."

"And I am always here to talk," Jenny added.

"Sometimes, I think you just like making people cry."

"Hey." Jenny covered a spot on her chest with her hand. "My heart. Did we not just have a deep conversation, of which you will take something away to use to help yourself?"

"So?"

"Remember what I said, Cara. Seriously."

"I will," Cara promised, "and thanks for making me talk. Too many people are fine and happy with me brushing them off when I say I'm fine, or something similar. You don't."

"Not my job to," Jenny said, ticking a finger over her shoulder as she headed for the door. "Oh, well, hello there. Can we help you?"

Cara turned to look at who Jenny had greeted, only to see a waiting Gian standing in the doorway. "Gian."

He pointed at Cara, a sexy smile growing on his handsome features. "I'm actually looking for her, as she has an appointment today, and I would like to join her."

"You don't have to do to that, Gian. They just want to make sure he's turned properly now."

"My son, so yes, I do."

Well, now someone else could put a face to her baby's father when Cara refused to.

Jenny shot a wink back at Cara. "Well, there she is. Why do you look so familiar to me?"

"My family is well-known in Toronto. We're often on the news, or something similar."

It took the older woman a moment to put together *who* she was looking at. A horrible sensation of dread dropped heavily in Cara's stomach as she waited for it to click.

"Does the name Guzzi help at all?" Gian asked Jenny.

"Oh … my." Jenny lost her happy disposition, but quickly plastered on a false smile. "Are you sure you're in the right place, then, Mr. Guzzi?"

"Jenny," Cara warned.

Gian rattled off something that sounded like a business name, but Cara couldn't be sure. Jenny tensed, and then stared at Gian. "Really?"

"Yes. I thought I might take a look around while I was here, if you wouldn't mind."

"Does she know?" Jenny asked.

Gian's gaze darted to Cara, and then quickly back to the woman standing in front of him. "There was no reason for her to. It was a common thing long before her appearance and work here."

"And the use of the business name?"

"No affiliation to a family name that may make some uncomfortable to be attached to, except in details that no one has time or need to dig into," Gian replied with a smirk. "It does the same job as anonymous donations, of course, but simpler come tax time."

"I'll have to take your word for that." Jenny looked back at Cara once again. "Thanks for helping to clean this place up. I will see you on Monday, right?"

"Monday," Cara agreed.

Once Jenny was gone, Cara looked to Gian.

"What was all that about?"

"Pardon?" he asked.

"That vague, weird conversation."

Gian shrugged his shoulders, his lips curving teasingly at the edges. "I have no idea what you're talking about, *mon ange*."

"Gian."

He glanced away, shoving his hands in his pockets. "So, the woman who started this whole place—"

"Carolina Demaske."

"She was a good friend to my grandmother, on my mother's side, especially throughout her life, long after she no longer needed the safe haven that Carolina provided. There was a time when my grandmother had no one else but for Carolina, and it was a message she passed down on us all."

Cara took in those words and what they meant. "You donate money to the shelter?"

"Monthly," Gian admitted, "and it is just one of many that I donate to, personally. I know my mother and father, and even my sister and brother, donate to other places or things they want to support. Carolina's House has always been one I focused on, personally."

"That's ... wonderful, Gian."

"I have too much, I don't need it all, Cara. I can afford to give some away. Unfortunately, there are those who are not comfortable with taking money from a man with my last name and affiliations, so I have become smarter about donating, using businesses as a shell of sorts, where my name is too deep into the paperwork for people to care."

"And I take it, this started long before I ever stumbled upon this place?"

He laughed, dark and husky.

It nearly killed her every time she heard that damn sound come out of his mouth. It was so fucking unfair that all the pregnancy hormones running through her body made it even more difficult to control herself around Gian. All it took was one of his chuckles, a look, or a smirk, and she was a stupid pile of hormones and desire.

And oh, God.

Being *touched?*

Apparently, Cara's body had nerves where they never existed before. Gian *loved* that.

Cara was just ... overwhelmed.

All. The. Time.

"Long before you," Gian said. "I may have upped the amounts I donate over the last few months, but I tend to do that whenever I have a particularly good year, money-wise."

"Oh."

"So, the appointment?"

Cara picked up her jacket and purse off the back of a chair. "You don't have to come for that, I told you. It's just a checkup to make sure he's where he's supposed to be."

Once she was close enough for him to reach out and grab her, Gian did just that. Cara found herself tugged into his side, his arm wrapped around her lower back, and then he pressed a soft kiss to her temple. Cara's smile grew as her eyes fluttered closed.

"I want to go," he murmured against her skin. "And then I would like to take you out to eat, get you home, relaxed and comfortable, and see what happens."

"That does sound nice."

Gian's fingers danced over the column of her throat before he pushed her wayward curls aside. Just the feeling of his fingers against her skin was enough to make heat and lust bloom.

This was heaven *and* hell.

Cara had been trying to let Gian in more, and not be so guarded. Especially not where his wife was concerned, or even just them in general. She finally understood what he meant about circumstances and details muddling up a situation that most people only saw from the outside, and never what was below the surface.

He made her so happy.

He loved her so much.

Why did she have to give up those beautiful things, and Gian, because others said they were wrong? She wouldn't. Certainly not now.

"I love you, Cara," Gian said.

Like he could read her fucking mind.

"I know you do. You can say it in three languages, remember?"

He never forgot to tell her he loved her, in the loud moments, the quiet ones, and all the times in between. He never once forgot.

"And I can mean it in every one of them, Cara."

No, they weren't bad or wrong.

"I can't believe it's June already," Stephanie said.

Cara glanced over her laptop, the dissertation she had been working on for the better part of two hours finally drifting from her mind. She welcomed the distraction. "I can't believe I have one week left to finish this damn paper."

"You'll kill it, no worries there."

"Thanks," Cara said, smiling.

"But are you going to make graduation, or …?" Stephanie trailed off with a nod at Cara's stomach. "How far along now?"

"Thirty-three weeks, and I probably won't make graduation."

"That sucks."

Cara shrugged. "Late July ceremony is not going to coincide for me, unfortunately. I mean, I probably *could* make it, if I wanted to. But I'm going to be *really, really* pregnant, if I haven't already had the baby by then. I figure since I already took time off from the shelter for around that time, I should probably use it to chill as much as I can."

"I get that. And hey, the university does do the mini-ceremonies in the beginning of the new semester for those who took the summer to earn their final grades, or whatever."

"Yeah, Professor Madele told me about it. She made it clear that if I didn't participate in the coming one, I had better be there."

Cara leaned back in her chair, resting her hand to the top of her swelled stomach. She thought the baby boy was already like this father, constantly wanting to move, never satisfied with staying still, and far too restless for his own good. Even in the womb. She could only imagine what he would be like *after* birth.

Still just like his father, probably.

"Miss Rossi?"

Two men dressed similarly in plain black suits approached the table, one already holding out a badge to identify himself. Not that Cara would have needed to see the badges to know the men were cops, or detectives. Growing up the way she had, cops were easy to detect. They all walked the same, dressed the same, spoke the same, and smelled the same.

Like a *cop*.

"Detective Seeley, and this is my partner—"

"Yeah, that's nice, hello to both of you," Cara interrupted. "What can I do for you?"

"Actually, Miss—"

"Cara, please."

"Cara," Detective Seeley said, drawling her name out for longer than was necessary. "Actually, Cara, we were hoping you might be able to do something for us. Or rather, help us with some information regarding Gian Guzzi."

Cara passed her friend a look, although to Stephanie's benefit, the girl was trying to look *anywhere* but at the detectives. "Hey, Steph, could you give us a few minutes?"

Stephanie nodded quickly, and gathered her things. "Sure can. I was about to head out anyway. Call me when you wanna meet up to sprint again, Cara."

"Okay."

The detectives kept quiet until Stephanie was gone. Thankfully, the library was mostly empty, as it was only mid-day, and the girls had picked a quieter part of the library to work. One between the bookshelves, where only two tables were set up in the large rows.

"All right, ask," Cara said, glancing up at the detective once she knew they were alone.

"Can you confirm you have personal ties to Gian Guzzi?" the detective asked.

"Define personal for me."

The man's gaze dropped to Cara's stomach. "We have reason to believe he may be the father of your child."

"What reason is that?"

"Well, we can't exactly give that information away, Miss."

"Again, it's *Cara*. I'm not married, I'm twenty-seven years old, and I'm pregnant. We have far passed the *respectable lady* stage in my life, thanks."

"Is Gian Guzzi the father of your child?" Seeley asked.

Cara sighed heavily. "And if he is? I don't see what that would have anything to do with detectives approaching me mid-day, in the library of my university, when I'm attempting to finish my dissertation so that I can get my diploma before my son is born."

"Our apologies for intruding on your time," the shorter of the two men said quickly. "But we have reason to believe your personal affiliation to Gian may help us with our current investigations."

"And what investigations are those?"

Cara did not plan to make this easy on the police, but she also had to be careful with how much she pushed. Given her dual citizenship, trouble with officials could put her back across the border without so much as a paper to sign.

"Surely you're aware that Mr. Guzzi is affiliated to some … criminal business in Toronto? We're aware you visited him while he was serving time in jail, just a few months ago. We would like to discuss your relationship with him, and what else you may know."

Cara took her time to save her document, shut down her laptop, and put her things away. She knew that no matter what, she didn't have a choice but to play along with the detectives, and keep her nose out of trouble. That didn't mean she planned to give them anything.

"Would you mind a trip to the station, just so that we can get our questions and your answers on an official record?" Seeley asked.

Cara waved a hand, as if to say, *whatever.* "Could I make a phone call before we go?"

"If you think you need to."

"I think I do."

The detectives probably assumed Cara planned to call a lawyer. She called Gian. He and a lawyer met her at the station.

Cara answered *nothing* after that.

"I can't see anything," Cara grumbled.

Gian's hands rubbed her shoulders, his dark chuckles echoing in her ear. He kissed the spot behind her ear and then said, "That's the point, *mon ange.* It's a surprise."

She reached up to try and readjust the blindfold over her eyes, but Gian quickly rerouted her arms back to her sides.

"Nope, hands stay down."

"But—"

"Little ledge here, and then some steps, love, so be careful."

Cara rolled her eyes behind the blindfold, but managed to get up whatever stairs were there with Gian's help. "Can you at least give me a hint?"

"Where's the fun in that?"

"Where's the fun in being told you're going to have a nice night with ice cream and a back rub, only to be made to dress up and be taken out. In *kitten heels*, Gian. I couldn't even wear my comfy shoes!"

"You will be happy that I made you wear the kitten heels. Someone might take pictures, and those shoes you wear do not look nice with a dress."

"Says you."

"And you, when you're not thirty-four weeks pregnant, Cara."

She huffed under her breath, hating that he was probably right. Then, she had another thought. "Why would anyone take pictures?"

"You'll see," her lover replied vaguely. "Gilles will drive you back to the penthouse once this is all done and over with, as it's not the kind of event men are usually invited to and I have something to pick up across the city."

"What happened to Chris?" Cara asked about her previous enforcer, who still refused to call her by her name.

"Chris has other things to look after at the moment. Sometimes, it's better to put people where they get the best business done. Chris happens to be very good at getting information from people, and I need that right now."

"Because of the cops?"

"Amongst other things," Gian muttered. "We're not talking about that tonight. This is all for you. And I thought you liked Gilles?"

"I do, he just ..."

"What?"

"Talks a lot," Cara said.

Gian laughed, his hands tightening on her as he directed her around a corner, or so she assumed. "He is a talker."

"Chris barely talks at all, except to repeat orders or something."

"Okay, enough of this, smile, *bella*."

Cara didn't know what he was talking about, but the blindfold was suddenly pulled from her face, allowing her vision to clear. It took Cara a couple of seconds of blinking, and a few shouts of "Surprise!" from the people standing around one of Gian's restaurants for her to realize what was happening.

Pretty, pale-blue and green decorations littered the restaurant. Each table held different items—a spot for gifts, one for a massive cake decorated in similar colors, and the like. A banner hanging from one chandelier to another read *Baby Shower!*

Cara took in the people around her. Women she worked with at the shelter and the women *from* the shelter. Her few friends from university, and the professor she enjoyed spending time with and who had helped her through her difficult moments. And surprisingly, nearing the front of the guests, Cara found Gian's mother and another woman, who, guessing by her features and how she kept close to Celeste, was probably his sister.

Crystal, Cara thought her name was. Gian didn't talk about her a lot.

"You've been busy," Gian said. "And working far too hard, *mon ange*. Ma asked about a shower for you, because she wanted to—at least—send something over. And then a couple of weeks ago, Jenny contacted me about helping with something like this to surprise you. You're not too angry, right?"

Cara just *blinked*.

"Why would I be angry, Gian?"

How could she be angry?

"You don't like surprises," he said.

She had assumed, given the circumstances of the pregnancy and Gian's marriage, and how busy her last few weeks before birth would be, that something like a shower was out of the question. She didn't even think she knew enough people to have a proper shower, not that it was acceptable for her to plan her own, anyway.

She didn't have to worry about anything, apparently.

Gian took care of things.

Always.

"It's wonderful. Thank you."

Gian kissed the back of her head, never hesitating with all of the eyes watching them. "Enjoy your party, Cara. I love you, pretty girl."

"I can certainly understand why Gian adores you so much," Crystal said quietly, giving Cara a small smile.

"It's a shame things are so ... complicated," Celeste added.

Cara cleared the awkwardness from her tone before speaking. "Thank you for coming, and for helping them set up, and everything else. Really, it was too much."

"Nothing is too much. Not for my grandbaby." Celeste waved her hand as if to dismiss that statement. "What a silly thought."

"Cara, are you ready?"

She looked over her shoulder to find Gilles—the enforcer Gian had said was non-negotiable for the unforeseeable future—waiting at the front doors of the restaurant.

"Just a second," she told the man.

"I'll grab the last bit of stuff and put it in the truck."

"Thank you." Cara turned back to Celeste and Crystal, the last two guests she had yet to say goodbye to. Everyone else had already gone and the staff had mostly cleaned the place. Cara had managed to sneak a few keepsakes to put in her baby's memory box of the day. "Time to get home and sleep, I do have to put in hours tomorrow at the shelter. It was very nice to meet you, Crystal. Thank you for coming, again. Really."

The woman shrugged. "Maybe we'll do something again soon, Cara. It just all depends."

Cara didn't ask what their future meetings would depend on, because she already knew. Privacy. Public opinion. Gian's wife. She didn't need the verbal reminders. Her mind never let her forget, now.

"Okay, let her go," Celeste ordered. "And I want one more of those pretty blue drinks before we go, too."

One more hug later and Cara headed out of the restaurant behind Gilles, whose arms were filled with his fifth round of baby shower gift bags, filled with too many items to count.

"Do babies really need all of this?" Gilles asked.

Cara helped to open the back of the truck, since her enforcer's arms were otherwise occupied. "I don't think they need *all* of it, but it certainly is cute."

And Cara swore everybody oohed and awed over every little outfit, pair of shoes, and tiny rattle she pulled from the gift bags.

"But look at it. Look at *all* of it."

She did.

The truck bed was filled.

It was a lot.

"I'm grateful," Cara said, laughing.

"But it's too much for a baby, right? Since when do newborns care how many outfits they have, or if they have a swing thing that bounces? Does the baby really need twenty pairs of socks, or bibs that look like bandanas?"

"He'll use it all, eventually."

Gilles shook his head. "It's crazy. Women go nuts over this stuff, and I just don't understand why."

"I take it you don't have kids, then."

The man looked *horrified.*

"Jesus, no," he muttered, glancing up to the sky at the same time he made the sign of the cross over his chest.

"I'm not sure God will help to keep the babies away, Gilles. They're not demons or evil spirits."

He stared at her with wide eyes. "That depends on who you ask."

Well, she would give him that.

"To the penthouse?" Cara asked.

Gilles nodded, urging her around to his side of the truck. "The penthouse; boss's orders."

The backseat was also filled, as was the front passenger side, so apparently, she would be sitting directly behind him in the back.

Cara turned to thank Gilles as he opened the back door to help her climb in the lifted truck, but she didn't get the words out. The last things she saw were dimmed car lights, before the vehicle turned sharply off the road, and headed directly for them. She felt the strong hands of the enforcer shove her into the truck at the very last second, but it was all black after that.

She could still hear the sound of metal crushing against metal when she woke up in the hospital screaming.

Gian.

She screamed for him.

And for her baby.

Chapter 11

"Gian … *Gian!*"

Cara's hoarse, panicked cry had Gian sitting straight in the uncomfortable hospital chair. His eyes flew wide, not that he had been sleeping. He couldn't sleep, really. In his daze of watching monitors and waiting, he had settled into a headspace that kept his anxiety and rage at bay, but forced him into a still state of semi-consciousness.

"Gian!"

"Shh," Gian murmured, "it's all right, *mon ange*. Everything's fine. You're fine. The baby is fine. I'm fine."

He was leaning closer to Cara's hospital bed, instantly, already squeezing her hand that he hadn't let go of since he came into the room. His other hand swept through her mess of curls, sweeping the hair from her face so that her searching blue eyes could find his, and she would relax.

Again.

This was the third time since he had arrived that she'd woken up confused, in a state, and unable to calm down. The first two times, his presence had done very little for her. Nurses had rushed in, then, needing Cara calm again for the baby's sake, had administered something into her IV that put her back to sleep.

She was lucky.

So fucking lucky.

At first, Gian had thought a concussion was likely, given the gash on Cara's hairline, and the bump behind her right ear. The doctor had agreed, and every thirty minutes, Cara had been woken up, checked over as best as was possible, and then allowed to rest again. Not that she had understood much of what was going on.

Cara's frightened gaze finally met Gian's and for the first time, she relaxed without the help of added medication. She slumped into the bed, but not before her arm—tacked and taped with an IV and tubes—snaked around his neck, and dragged him closer.

"The baby is perfectly fine," Gian told her again before she could ask. He could already see her questions forming. "He's great, his heartbeat is strong and they brought in the portable ultrasound machine to look everything over."

Cara's hold on him loosened, but barely. "Okay."

"Do you want a drink, or something?"

"Water."

"Sure, *bella*. You have to let me go first."

She did but it took a while. He quickly got the glass of water ready, with a bendy straw, and then helped her to drink until she was satisfied. Her voice wasn't as dry when she spoke again.

"My head hurts and my side, too."

Gian nodded. "You hit your head pretty hard inside the truck, and—"

"He pushed me."

"Hmm?"

"Gilles," Cara said, her brow furrowing and her gaze dimming with memories. "He pushed me into the truck, out of the way, when the lights came out of nowhere."

Ah.

Well, yet another reason for Gian to thank the enforcer and make sure he was given a proper send off to the heavens. For now, though, Gilles' body was still chilling on a slab in the morgue.

"You probably hurt your bottom rib at the same time," Gian explained. "Not broken, but it took a hard hit, like your head."

Cara's fingers danced along her hairline, and she winced at the feeling of the stitched slice that was a good two inches long. "Ow."

"Don't touch," he said, moving her hand away and tucking it into his own. "It's going to be sore for a while, but it'll heal nicely, given the way they stitched it."

Her wince deepened into a scowl, and her body tensed.

"*Ow.*"

Gian looked over at the monitor, recognizing how Cara's body tensed with that specific pain. He watched the little paper coming out of the machine spike but quickly drop. It had been nearly forty-five minutes since the last time it did that, and this time, the duration had been significantly shorter.

According to the nurses, that was a good sign to see.

"What in the hell was that?" Cara asked when the spike dropped and tapered off completely.

"A contraction," Gian said gently. "You were having them pretty steadily for a while, and they gave you some meds to slow it down, if possible. It worked, anyway. Soon, the contractions will taper off to nothing at all, and it'll be fine. That's what these are monitoring."

He moved the sheets covering Cara aside, so then she was able to see the bands and circular monitors wrapped around her middle.

"A *what?*"

"A contraction," he repeated, "though they're pretty short and not spiking high when they do hit now."

"I shouldn't be having those yet, Gian. It's too soon."

He shushed her again, kissing her softly on the mouth to quiet her fears. "The accident set them off, but he's *fine*. They're stopping. They checked and there was no dilation. He's got a bit more time to be safe in you, no worries there."

How Gian managed to stay calm, and speak carefully as to not panic Cara more than she already was, he didn't know. Inside, he felt like a raging fucking hurricane. A very small part of him knew that right then, Cara needed his calm, controlled demeanor.

He could do that.

For a little while.

Cara blinked, her panic subsiding slowly. "Where is Gilles?"

Gian sighed, his gaze darting away. "He didn't survive the impact."

"What about the other car—the driver? Are they okay?"

His rage flooded back into his veins, hot and heavy, demanding attention and wanting soothed in some violent way.

Gian would get to it.

Eventually.

"Hit and run," he said as calmly as he could manage.

In other words: *entirely fucking intentional.*

Gian wouldn't tell Cara that, though. At least, not while she was recovering in a hospital bed. These were the kinds of conversations that shouldn't be had in a hospital, simply because the walls had ears that were always listening.

And the cops would be back soon enough …

Gian, on the other hand, would be looking for the fucker behind the wheel that killed his enforcer, and damn near took the love of his life and his unborn child away from him. *Soon.* He already had a suspicion of who might be involved, though he had no particular reason to suspect her, except he wouldn't put it past his wife.

That, and he didn't trust Elena as far as he could throw her. He certainly didn't have a reason *why* Elena would have set something like this up, but sometimes, she didn't need a reason. She just needed to be able to do something and she would. Especially if it meant hurting someone who had hurt her.

"All those things," Cara said quietly.

"What things?"

"The baby things. The gifts from the shower. They were beautiful and tiny. They're all ruined now."

"You don't have to worry about those things, Cara. They can be replaced. They're just *things*, they're not you or the baby. Some of it is probably okay, whatever was in the back under the truck bed cover. But it doesn't matter right now, don't focus on it or worry."

"I know, I just …"

"Your mind's way of processing," he supplied.

Cara nodded faintly. "I'm tired, Gian."

He could see that in her, too. In her dropping lids, slack lips, and weakened grip on his hand. Another nurse would be in to check on her soon, but he figured she could get a bit more sleep before that happened.

"Rest, *amore*."

"You won't leave, right?"

"Not tonight," he promised.

"Did you see the baby on the ultrasound when they checked him?"

Gian smiled, cupping Cara's face in his hands, and stroking her cheeks with his thumbs. "I did. He looked like he might have waved, but I think he was just swiping at the thing pushing on him. He didn't like that very much."

"He does that every time. And he's okay, you're sure?"

"He's beautiful and perfect, Cara."

Just like her.

So beautiful.

So, so perfect.

And fuck *anybody* who tried to ruin that or take them from him.

Gian stepped out of his Mercedes, and surveyed the cars parked around the Guzzi mansion's circular driveway. Too many cars for a Saturday. And none he particularly recognized right off the bat.

A flash of irritation settled in his gut, as he had come to the mansion for a fucking reason, and he wanted to deal with it right then. Not at some later point, when his wife was alone.

Despite it being the weekend, and knowing he *should* stay put as he had been doing for several months without fail, Gian didn't bother to even grab his keys out of the ignition. He was all too aware that he still needed to keep up appearances with his wife, but he also wasn't interested in playing to the mafia's politics at the moment. Once he was done with his business here, he was heading right back to Cara, to get her settled in at home and comfortable again.

Or as comfortable as she could be, given the circumstances.

Inside the mansion, Gian found his wife, and *several* of her very loud friends in the common sitting area. Drunk, apparently. On a Saturday afternoon.

Elena rarely had parties and it wasn't often she brought over guests. Gian might have even taken a second look when his wife said she had friends, because she never spoke fondly of anyone except herself and her dead mother.

Her friends, however, were not what Gian would consider suitable pals for Elena. All women who had made their names and money from marrying men with deep pockets. Men who happened to be beyond a certain age. A few of the ladies had too much plastic and silicone pumped into their bodies.

Sure, the women were Toronto Elite. They regularly graced the society pages. They were also constant, unrelenting, non-stop drama. Those stupid fucking Housewives reality shows had *nothing* on these women.

Gian certainly didn't approve of whom Elena called her friends, but the very sad fact was, she fit right in. Perfectly. Then again, Elena could fit in everywhere. She only needed to want to, and make an effort.

And hell, if her time and efforts were distracted by these awful *femmes*, then he didn't give a shit. As long as it wasn't on him.

Gian stood in the entryway of the sitting room, shaking his head as the maid attempted to clean up what appeared to be a wine spill. Her effort was fruitless, because one of the women leaned toward Elena, and clearly drunk, simply spilled more right over the same spot.

"Mariana," Gian said loudly, calling their maid out by name. He also gained the attention of the rest of the drunken women acting foolish, including his wife. "Mariana, if the ladies can't manage to keep the wine in their glasses, please stop refilling them. Why don't you take a break for a little while? You look like you need it."

Mariana stood quickly, her aging face flustered. "Yes, sir."

"Just about time to break up the party, ladies," Gian said, turning back to the room. "Sorry about that."

But not really.

"Gian," Elena whined, "you can't just come in here and ruin my lunch with the girls."

Gian arched a single brow at his wife, silencing her from saying anything further. Mariana scooted by him in the entryway, her head tucked down. "Actually, Mariana, take the rest of the day off. You won't see funds deducted on your pay. It seems Elena has forgotten that your job is *not* to cater to her every whim and fancy, but rather, to keep her house clean because she refuses to do it herself."

Mariana hesitated, looking back at him with wary eyes. "If you're sure?"

"Positive. Say hello to your husband for me. I haven't seen him in a while."

"I will. Thank you, sir."

Gian faced the sloppy drunks in his sitting room once more. "Elena, have your friends leave, or join me in the kitchen. *Now.*"

"Gian!"

Elena's mortified shriek grinded on every single nerve that Gian had left. He managed to ignore it, but it was goddamn hard. Not bothering to wait on his wife's decision, Gian headed for the kitchen, listening to the voices he was leaving behind.

"My, he's certainly in a mood, isn't he?" one of the women asked.

"Oh, he's always in a damn mood," Elena muttered. "Don't mind him. He'll probably head upstairs for the rest of the day. We won't even know he's here."

"We never see him out with you, Elena."

"It's better that you don't, trust me."

Gian rolled his eyes upward, feeling the tension headache beginning to build in his temples. Fuck no, he would not be staying. Even if that meant coming back to find the entire mansion trashed from Elena's nonsense.

"What in the hell do you want?" Elena hissed at his back.

Gian had heard her enter the kitchen behind him, but he focused on his task of getting a glass of water. That way, he could resist the urge to put his hands around her throat and choke the fucking life out of her.

"No calls came in from you last night," Gian noted. "You weren't concerned when I didn't make it home?"

He looked back at her, noting her glazed eyes and messier than normal appearance. Drinking before supper could do that to a person.

Elena shrugged. "You come and go, Gian. This isn't the first weekend, recently, where you've stayed away until we have to be seen at church. What does it matter? You told me to fuck off, so I have. Isn't that what you want, for me to leave you alone?"

Yes, but he *needed* to believe she was actually doing that, too.

"And where were you, anyway?" Elena asked.

Gian stiffened a bit, but chose to answer partly honestly. "With Cara."

He decided not to mention the accident, or the hospital. His best defense against Elena's games—or any that she might be playing—were to let her set a trap, and then subsequently fall into it with her usual lies and manipulations.

Elena sighed. "You don't have to just … throw that in my face, you know."

"I didn't mean for it to sound that way."

"Well, it does. And that's kind of awful of you. I'm aware you have a mistress, and that she's pregnant with your child, you don't need to add onto it by giving me a play-by-play of your activities with her. It's embarrassing enough."

"You asked where I was, and I told you."

"Yes, for *no* reason."

"Actually, there was one. Cara was involved in a hit and run last night. It seemed, from onlookers, that it was very intentional. A man of mine was killed, too."

"So?" Elena asked.

She didn't ask about the baby, or Cara, or anything else. She didn't make one of her haughty proclamations about his whore, as she so affectionately called Cara whenever she got the chance and wanted to hurt Gian. Nothing. Simply a *so*, as though it had no affect or bearing on her life, because it didn't. And Elena cared for nothing that didn't involve her in some way.

That was the only reason why Gian chose to believe—at least, for now—that his wife was probably not behind organizing the hit and run. However, he put Elena on a very short leash where giving her any sort of trust was concerned.

"I'm going to head out again," Gian said, "I may or may not make it to church on Sunday, it depends."

"If you don't come here before church, then can I not go, too?"

"I don't give a shit. Make an appropriate excuse, when asked."

Elena nodded. "I can do that."

"And I'll try to keep my … activities, a bit more quiet," Gian said. "I certainly don't mean to toss them, or this, in your face, as you said."

"Well, you do. Often. More than you realize."

"I'll be more aware of that, or try."

It was the least he could do.

"Oh, and Elena?"

"What, Gian?"

"You have no reason to be jealous or to compete with any of those women out there, so I'm not sure why you continue to play these games with them like you do."

Elena shot him a look over her shoulder. "Don't I?"

"What do they possibly have, that you don't?"

"*Freedom*, Gian."

"Well, we both know why that is, don't we?" he asked.

Elena only smiled fleetingly and coolly in response.

He would much rather see another woman smiling at him.

"Here, love," Gian said, offering Cara his hand to help her from the car. She took it, her fingers warming his as she carefully maneuvered her way out of the backseat. "There you are."

Cara eyed the walkway from the side of the road to her apartment building's entrance, and frowned. "That's a long walk."

For a heavily pregnant woman with a bruised rib and lingering headaches from trauma? Yes, it certainly was a long walk. He could fix it for her, and he didn't mind doing just that.

Gian chuckled, and before Cara could refuse him, he swept her up in a cradle-like hold. Her arms flew around his neck, her eyes wide. She was still as light as a feather to him, but he was careful not to jostle her too much in case it caused her unnecessary pain.

"There, that's easy enough."

"Gian, put me down."

Chris strolled behind them, carrying what few bags had been in the back of the car. The enforcer said nothing, only grinned as Gian ignored Cara's demands.

"You're fine where you are, *mon ange*," Gian said. "Enjoy the view."

"I'm too heavy—"

"No, you're not."

"The scale says I am twenty-five pounds heavier."

"The man that loves you says you're *perfetto, bella, mia tesoro*."

She pursed her lips, half-heartedly glaring at him. "Why do you always do that?"

"Hmm, do what?"

"Say the right things all the time."

Gian smirked down at her. "It's a gift."

"It's certainly something."

Chris stepped up to unlock the building door and hold it open, but stayed behind them as Gian carried Cara to the apartment.

"Just set the bags inside the door," Gian told Chris as Cara unlocked the apartment.

"Got it, boss."

It didn't take them long to get inside, for Cara to turn the lights on, and for Chris to head back out. Gian urged Cara toward the couch, despite her protests to want to clean, or cook. He wasn't having that shit—she was resting.

"You do realize that no amount of talking is going to change what I want you to do, right?" Gian asked.

Cara sighed heavily, resting into the couch. "I need to sweep, and pick things up."

"I will handle it. You will relax."

"This isn't your—"

"I will handle it, Cara."

She scowled. "You're so stubborn."

"You're one to talk." Gian smirked at the sight of her frustrations. "Now, what do you want me to get you to wear from your dresser? Something comfy?"

"I'm fine."

"Cara."

"Oh, my God, Gian. Don't hover."

He was down on his knees in a flash, resting his hands on her thighs. That wasn't nearly good enough for him, though, so he pushed the over-sized shirt she wore up high enough to get his palms against the swell of her stomach. Quickly, he leaned in and pressed a kiss to her skin, just above her naval.

"I'm not trying to hover," he whispered against her skin, "but I can't help it. Let me do things, Cara, even if you're capable and I'm driving you crazy. Let me help, because I love you, and I need you to be okay. I need to make sure you're okay."

Her fingers drifted through his hair with soothing strokes. "I am fine."

"Now, Cara."

"And the baby is fine."

"Again, *now*." Gian kissed her stomach again, though the baby was quite still. He figured that the boy didn't have much room to move around in anymore. "You don't allow me to do a lot for you as it is. And I understand why, though I want to do more."

"You do enough," she replied.

Gian shook his head. "No, I really don't. I shouldn't be living separate from you, or worried I might miss the call when he finally decides to make his way into the world. You shouldn't have two nurseries in two different places. I shouldn't have to keep a fucking wedding ring tucked away in my car or wear it on my hand, depending on what I'm doing or where I am that day. None of that is what *I should be doing*. None of it, Cara. And it kills me—it's killing me. So if that's how I feel, then I can only imagine what it's like for you."

"Gian—"

"Please just let me help, *amore*. Let me do something."

Cara ran her fingers through his hair again. "Something comfy, then. And a glass of water would be nice."

"All right."

"And you," she added quieter. "You and a blanket would be perfect."

"Get one of those ugly Rom-Com things you like on, too."

Cara smiled beautifully. "You always call them ugly, but you laugh when you watch them. I think secretly, you like them."

He shrugged. "Don't say that too loudly."

"Mmhmm. Blanket, water, comfy clothes, and you. Hurry, Gian."

Standing, he kissed her mouth, soft and sweet. He had to keep it short and pull away fast, because the longer he kissed Cara, the more he wanted to stay right there and keep doing exactly that. Between them, kissing *always* led into something more—fucking was not resting, Gian was forced to tell himself.

Even if he could think of a dozen ways to have Cara *be* resting *while* he fucked her. This was more difficult than he thought it would be.

Gian gathered all the things Cara wanted, including the large, fluffy comforter from her bed. He let her change out of her clothes and into the clean, comfy things he had brought her as he went for the water. By the time he got back to the couch with a glass in hand, Cara had draped herself in the blanket with only her head peeking out from a small hooded bit.

"You look like a human burrito," Gian said.

"Don't judge. Also, the movie is starting, so be quiet."

Chuckling, Gian settled into the couch. Cara crawled, in her blanket burrito, closer, and then snuggled into his chest. He was far more interested in her than the movie, but that was okay, too.

"Why Marcus, again?" Cara asked randomly. "That's the name you like for the baby, isn't it?"

"It is. A family name."

"But all the men I know about in your family don't have that name."

"All the first-born men have it somewhere," he replied. "Usually middle names, like me, and my grandfather. My great-grandfather, and my uncle who died, their first names were Marcus, too."

"Is that why you got the family name, then? Because he died, and you were a first-born boy."

"He died when I was a toddler, actually."

"Why did you get the name being born to a second son?" she asked.

"My uncle didn't have children, and he wasn't married. The name had to pass on to someone, and my parents agreed to give it to me, on the stipulation they chose my given name. Gian Marcus it was."

Cara glanced up at him, her brow puckered in that way of hers. It told him she was overthinking something, which wasn't unusual for her.

"What?" he murmured.

"It seems like it's an important thing to your family—the name, I mean."

"It is. It's very important to us. It's as important as our last name. This is a legacy, Cara. All the men carry it on in one way or another, and it begins with a name."

"But …"

"Just ask, love. Whatever it is, ask."

"He's not going to be … legitimate, Gian."

He stiffened, hating how she said that word a little quieter than the rest. The last thing she should be, or that he wanted her to be, was ashamed. Not of innocent life or love.

"He's still mine," Gian said firmly, "and he's still a first-born Guzzi boy, which means it's my legacy to pass on, like it was given to me once. It's my choice to make for my son, not someone else's. It may seem silly to others, something insignificant, but I *know* what this name means. I know what comes of it and what's expected of the man who is given it. He's my boy. He's *my boy*, with a woman I chose and love, not one that was forced upon me. Whether he's legitimate or not is fucking nonsense; it means nothing to me. He was made because he was meant to be and because I love you. I want to give him *my* names because he deserves them."

Cara glanced away. "All of them, even the surname?"

"Why wouldn't I?"

"Your wife, for one."

"It's not a card I want to pull, Cara, but she is well aware that to keep her place and her respect in it, she can say nothing about what I do, so long as she is treated well and is held up as the wife I married. Nothing more, nothing less."

"But isn't a baby with your mistress the utmost *dis*respect, Gian?"

"For some. Not for others. It depends on the man, and at the moment, I am the most powerful man at the table. I am the only one with the voice that matters. I speak, they listen. Her included. This—the baby, his name, all of it—is no different."

"I don't know what to think about that," Cara admitted.

"You don't have to think anything."

"Marcus Gian, then? I like the sound."

"Marcus Gian *Guzzi*," he said, kissing the top of her head.

"Marcus Gian Guzzi."

The enforcer standing in front of the old barber's shop nodded to

Gian in greeting as his boss approached. Sure enough, through the window, Gian could see inside the business, and the man waiting that he had been called in for.

Gabriel.

It was a meeting that, for all purposes, had been meant for Gian and his Capos. Somehow, Gabriel must have gotten word and decided to crash it.

"Has he been here long?" Gian asked.

"Since we called, boss," the enforcer replied.

Gian scowled.

That was long enough.

"*Merci*. Keep an eye on the road."

The enforcer agreed. Gian stepped inside the barber shop, noting the tension had already settled thickly in the air. His men, those he had called for the meet, had shoved themselves to one side of the business, while Gabriel and his men had stayed on the other side.

Resting back in the barber's chair, Gabriel looked to be in his glory. His forehead and thick neck were covered with hot, wet towels, while his cheeks and jaw had been slathered with a foaming cream. The careful hands of the barber—one who had cut his hair and shaved Gian from the time he was fifteen—made clean lines with a blade over Gabriel's face.

"Gian," Gabriel greeted without so much as looking at him. "You don't mind me joining your meeting today, do you?"

"You know I do," Gian replied, "and more so, that you're in my seat."

"Well, here I am."

Yes, there he fucking was.

Quietly, Dom and Stephan entered the barber shop. Better late than never, Gian supposed. Truthfully, he had been closer to the spot when the call came in, so he wasn't about to throw a fit at his consigliere and underboss.

"What do you want?" Gian demanded.

"Right now, a shave."

"No, *being* here."

The barber's hands stilled and he shot Gian a look. Gian could tell the man wanted him to relax, and not cause any problems for his business. As it was, the barber shop was well-known for the *Mafioso* that came and went daily, most notably, Gian at least once a week.

Carmen had always been able to shave Gian far better than any razor ever had.

Gabriel looked over to Gian, though only his eyes moved. It was disconcerting to have this man stare at him, Gian thought. He knew the things Gabriel was capable of and he purposely tried *not* to poke the man's beast. That was just good business.

"I want an update on our little situation," Gabriel said, "and to talk."

"The *situation* is being handled."

"Good, then you've found the rat amongst your men. And disposed of it, I assume."

Gian felt the coldness and distrust that automatically came from saying that word waft from his men. A few murmured between one another, but most stayed quiet. "No, I haven't found him."

Gabriel *tsked* under his breath. "Wasting time, you foolish boy."

"That's your one insult, Gabriel. Any after that, and I'll begin taking a payment for it. A pound of your choice."

"Touchy," his father-in-law muttered.

"No more than you." Gian stayed standing, although he waved to Dom and Stephan to find seats closer to him. Then, he turned back to Gabriel. "We're still working on that issue. It's not as simple as it seems, and whoever it is, they're not obvious."

"Or you're distracted."

"I beg your pardon?"

"Your whore, Gian." Gabriel smirked as Gian went cold all over. "Cara Rossi, that's her name, isn't it? *Quite* pregnant. While I certainly wasn't faithful to *my* wife, I would have never taken you for the type, too."

Gian's molars ached from clenching so fiercely.

He would not talk about Cara with this man.

He would not give Gabriel that ammo.

Gabriel said nothing more, letting the barber finish his shave and wipe his face down with the hot towels before he stood. Then, he faced Gian, as hard-assed and as big of a bastard as ever.

"You *are* distracted," Gabriel said, "and it shows. Otherwise, you would have found your rat by now. I gave you time to do it, but since you're too busy making a fucking spectacle of that whore of yours all over the city, time has now run out. I'm not going to jail again, Gian. For every week that passes without you delivering the rat to me, I'll take one of yours. And just so we're clear ..."

Gabriel looked over Gian's shoulder, and waved a fat finger at the line of men who had come to speak with Gian only. "Just so it's clear to *them*, every minute you spend with your whore is a minute you could have been working to spare one of their lives. Make the choices *wisely*, Gian."

Apparently, Gabriel intended to start his plan immediately. He had only just left the barber shop along with his men and gotten inside a waiting vehicle, when a black van pulled up. The enforcer outside the barber shop was grabbed and gone before anyone had blinked. Gabriel watched from the backseat of his car with a smile.

Gian was going to kill that bastard someday. *Somehow.*

Chapter 12

At first, Cara didn't notice the police cruisers and unmarked vehicles parked along the front of her apartment building. She was too busy reading the letter from her university, inviting her to take part in the autumn graduation ceremony for late graduates of her class. While she wasn't a late graduate, she had passed on attending the main event.

When Cara did finally notice the police attendance, she was halfway up the walk. The early July air was hot and humid, as the majority of the entire summer had already been. She cradled her thirty-seven-week pregnancy swell overtop the flimsy summer dress that helped to keep her cool.

"Cara Rossi?"

She turned to see an officer in full uniform approaching. Her nerves picked up another notch.

"Yes, that's me," Cara said.

"I'll escort you to your apartment."

"Why? Did something happen?"

The officer smiled thinly. "Normal procedure, that's all."

"Normal procedure for *what?*"

"Follow me, miss."

"What is going on?" Cara demanded.

The officer answered nothing, simply urged her toward the front doors of the building. Cara wondered if maybe her place had been broken into, though that seemed unlikely. She lived in a good part of the city, and the cost of her rent proved that little fact. Her building—in all the years she lived there—never once had a crime taken place inside or on the outside property.

It was possible that the cops were there because of her accident weeks ago. Her rib was healed and no longer sore, as was the gash on her hairline. Thankfully, that had healed with a scar that wasn't noticeable, due to skilled stitching by a doctor.

"Is this about the accident?" Cara asked. "I answered all the questions I could at the hospital the next day, and then another round the next week when detectives came with pictures of vehicles for me to look at. I don't know what more to tell you."

The officer still didn't answer.

Now, Cara was just getting peeved.

She didn't have to wonder for long, as the door to her floor was pushed open. From her spot way down the hall, she could plainly see evidence boxes and bags resting along the wall outside of her apartment door. Inside a few of the clear, plastic bags with red tape sealing the tops, rested items that belonged to Gian.

A shirt of his.

A book.

An empty bullet clip for his favorite Berretta.

Wait, where in the hell had he put that damn thing?

"You're raiding my place?" Cara shrieked, heading down the hall fast. "What fucking reason do you have to justify a search warrant on my apartment?"

She dropped her bag and the papers from her university, uncaring about the items. Inside her apartment, it looked like a hurricane had ripped through it. An officer identified her and Cara confirmed it, before another paper was shoved into her hands. She barely glanced at it, seeing what it was and only getting more irritated.

A search warrant.

Signed by a judge.

"Nice to see you again, Miss Rossi," said a familiar detective. The man walked toward Cara with a small stuffed animal in his hands. A tiny elephant that had managed to survive the accident weeks before and Cara had put on the baby's dresser as a decoration. "Cute little thing, this is."

Her baby's nursery?

Cara's rage spiraled out of control, and she pushed past the detective, heading for Marcus's room. Sure enough, even it had not gone untouched by the search. Each and every one of the baby's dresser drawers had been pulled open. Carefully folded, tiny clothes spilled across the room in piles, while cute knickknacks and decoration items had been upended in a messy search.

The closet, a space Cara had kept a few boxes of Lea's remaining things, was open. The boxes of her twin's belongings had also been ransacked and searched through.

"We have reason to believe you or your apartment, is a regular stop for Gian Guzzi," the detective said behind Cara, "and so, here we are to check for any information related to recent investigations into his business."

Disbelief swept through Cara.

"And what did you hope to find in an unborn baby's nursery?" she asked.

"Oh, we didn't expect to find much in this apartment at all."

"Then *why?*"

She had been the victim just weeks ago. She had been the one nearly killed by a hit and run driver. And now it was *her* that needed to be treated like a criminal?

Why?

"Gian will understand exactly why," the detective said smugly.

Cara's hands balled into tight fists, her fingernails cutting into her palms. "Where is my purse and cell phone? I want to call Gian and my lawyer, now."

"As soon as we're done taking a look through the bag, Cara."

Fuck him.

"Cara, just consider—"

"Gian, it's fine. I've almost got the apartment back to normal. The baby's room is all organized and ready again. There's really no need."

"Well, *no* need is kind of wrong. There is a need, *mon ange.* Thirty-seven weeks pregnant with my son is a very good reason to move into the penthouse now, while you have a bit of time left to settle in."

Cara sighed, and shifted the bag of heavy text books on her shoulder. "Okay, I know I was pissed off about the search on my place, but it's still not a good reason for me to upend everything right now to move into the penthouse. We're a little late into this pregnancy to be doing such a big move, Gian."

"Except *I* would like for you to, Cara."

"Listen, we'll talk more when I get out of the university's library."

"Don't hang up on me because you don't want to discuss this."

"I'm not. I'm at the entrance doors right now. I want to get these books out of my place. I will call you back."

"*When* you're out, right? I want to talk about this, even if you don't."

"I have to head over to the shelter, too," Cara reminded him.

Gian grumbled under his breath. "Isn't your time off supposed to start soon for the shelter?"

"Next week, yes."

"Don't work too hard, Cara."

She smiled. "Why not? You happen to be very good at massages. It gives me an excuse to ask for one."

"You don't need an excuse, pretty girl."

"I'll remember that."

"Do so."

Thankfully, Gian dropped the prickly topic of Cara moving into the penthouse. With a quick "I love you" and another demand for her to call him back when she could, the call ended. Cara headed into the university's library, ready to get rid of her textbooks she had needed for the year.

The university had a program that allowed students to drop off textbooks to be used for students the subsequent year who were low income, and couldn't afford to buy the expensive books on their own. A lot of private libraries would pay a small amount for the textbooks, but the university's program was non-profit. It was all by donation and they didn't charge the students to get the used books. Cara didn't care about the money, she cared about being able to help someone.

It didn't take long for Cara to get her textbooks dropped off and head back out the way she had come. She fully intended to call Gian back as soon as she could, but he would have to wait. As it was, traffic in the city had been terrible all day, and Cara was running short on time to get to the shelter for her shift.

She would usually take the bus, but flagged a passing cab instead. Just as she slid into the back seat and tossed her mostly-empty tote bag to the floor, something caught her eye across the street.

Or rather, someone.

Two people, actually.

Elena Guzzi was just coming out of a specialty boutique, her arms loaded with several bags. A large-brimmed hat keeping half of her face hidden, but Cara would recognize the woman anywhere. At the end of the street, Domenic—Gian's younger brother—waited for Elena, already holding the passenger side door open for the woman to get inside the car.

That was all Cara saw before her cab pulled away from the side of the road, leaving the scene behind.

Still, an angry ache had settled in Cara's chest at the sight of Gian's wife. After their first run in, Cara had been left feeling so ashamed for her involvement with Gian and the pregnancy. But after, once she had learned more of the story, and the things Gian told Cara, she didn't think that run in with Elena had been accidental at all.

And neither had her pity party lies about losing a baby, or not being able to have more children.

Was Cara imperfect?

Were her actions immoral?

Was she a sinner in this?

Absolutely.

Yes, on every single account.

But something told Cara that Elena Guzzi was not all too innocent, either.

None of them were.

Cara held the hands of the young, high-risk domestic abuse victim across from her while Jenny continued to explain what was going to happen from there on out. Melinda, at only twenty-two, had just been dealt another difficult blow in what was an already horrible time in her life.

Two weeks after the beating her husband had served down on her, and the woman was at least beginning to look better. The black and blue bruising on her face had faded to a yellow that was easy to cover. Her broken nose was no longer swollen, and she was able to open her right eye again. The busted vessels in her left eye were also healing, and no longer drew attention, as they had when nearly the entire white of the eyeball had been a bloody, ghastly red.

Melinda tried to smile when Cara offered her hands a squeeze, but it faltered at the last second. Outside appearances were deceiving, and there had never been a better example of that than a woman who had learned to hide the signs of her spouse's abuse.

This woman had been hiding hers since she was eighteen.

"So, he got bail," Melinda whispered.

So soft spoken.

Still afraid.

Never weak, though.

Cara repeated that sentiment to Melinda when the woman was willing to listen. She was not weak. She was brave, courageous, wonderful, and deserved beautiful things. All the beautiful things she wanted would and could be hers.

"He did get bail," Jenny said, "and since this is his first charge on his record, we expected that. The restraining order is still in place and the police officer on the case was kind enough to alert us that he is free on bail, until the next court date."

Melinda wet her lips, her gaze darting between the floor and the wall. "He knows where I am."

"The restraining order is still in place, but should he come to the shelter, we have policies in place that will keep you and everyone else perfectly safe."

"Except he doesn't care about those kinds of things. He never has. He said he would kill me; he almost did. He's—"

"Melinda," Cara said softly, "take a breath. Take a moment to breathe."

The young woman did, but Cara could plainly see it didn't help all that much.

"This is the first time I've ever left him," Melinda mumbled. "This wasn't even the worst beating, it was just the first time someone helped. I don't … He won't … I'm scared."

Jenny nodded. "I know. We consider your situation to be high-risk, which means at the moment, the shelter is currently on a level red watch."

"What does that even mean?"

"It means that because there is a risk of an altercation between you and your husband while we get things settled with the court, your divorce lawyer, and everything else, everyone here will be more alert for a problem. Until we have a reason to move you—say, he shows up here, or approaches you when you're out with one of our escorts—then the shelter is where you will remain. So, while you are here, because of the risk level, the staff and volunteers, and even the other women currently housed here, will be on a high alert for safety."

"So, wait and see if he tries to beat me to death again?" Melinda asked.

Cara winced. "*We* understand the situation and why you're afraid of him showing up. But given this is his first actual arrest and the past years of abuse haven't been documented officially, the courts were already unlikely to deny him bail. Trust that we will do absolutely everything to keep you, and everyone else, safe while we go through this process. And if at any single time, he gives us even a small reason to suspect he's planning something, you will be moved with a police guard. Okay?"

Melinda agreed, but she didn't look entirely convinced.

Cara understood that, too.

It was hard to trust others to keep you safe, when all you knew was keeping yourself alive.

"Are you good to go back to your room?" Cara asked.

"Or, supper is getting ready to be served in the kitchen, if you're hungry," Jenny added.

Melinda shrugged. "Food would be good."

"Wonderful." Jenny waited until Melinda had gone from the office and the door was closed once more, before she turned to Cara to speak. "I didn't want to frighten her more, but the officer who alerted us to the granted bail thought we should know."

Cara stood, rubbing a hand over her stomach to soothe the jabs of the baby boy hitting her rib. "Know what?"

"The officer figured he would keep an eye on Allen Farger for the day, as he had time, and he said there was something about the guy that bothered him."

"So?"

"He lost him about an hour after he started tailing him," Jenny said.

"Like in traffic or something?"

"No, like Allen seemed to know someone was following him and deliberately lost the officer."

Well, shit.

"Why would he do that?" Cara asked.

Although, she was pretty sure she knew the answer.

"Because he didn't want to be seen or bothered doing whatever in the hell he was going to do." Jenny loosened her ponytail, and tipped her head side to side, stretching her neck. "*That* was why I put the shelter on level red watch, not because of the bail."

"Don't you think Melinda should know?"

Jenny frowned. "Tonight is the first night that young woman has even felt comfortable with eating dinner in the main dining room, around others. She is medicated just to be able to sleep. She is terrified enough, so no, I don't want to pile more on to her, and watch her regress. We've got a long way to go with this one, Cara."

"Yeah, I see your point."

"What time were you planning on leaving today? You should rest, you're nearly thirty-eight weeks pregnant, Cara."

Cara dismissed the suggestion. "I'm fine and I think after I make a call, I'll stick around."

"You really should relax. Once your baby gets here, you'll have no time to rest at all."

"Don't worry about me, Jenny."

"I worry about all my girls, regardless of who they are, Cara."

Yeah, she knew that, too.

"I'll be fine," Cara assured her boss once more.

Fifteen minutes later, Cara had holed herself in her small office, and finally gotten Gian on the phone. She probably should have called him back earlier after their conversation while she dropped off her books, but the hectic pace of the shelter that day hadn't given her the chance.

"*Mon ange,*" Gian said the moment he picked up Cara's call from her office phone. "How's my girl?"

"Honestly?"

"Of course."

"Tired. A little stressed. Craving that shredded ice with the cherry flavoring you brought me last week. Nothing I can't handle."

Gian's chuckles were dark and wonderful on the other end of the line. "I can have some for you when you get home. Just let me know when you're leaving."

Cara blew out a slow breath. "Yeah, that's the thing. I probably won't be out of here until later than I thought. I know you were going to come over, but why don't we just figure something out for tomorrow instead?"

"Cara, you're supposed to be taking it—"

"Easy, I know. But shit came up."

"Are you actually going to take your time off for maternity leave starting next week, or what?"

"Yes, Gian. I am going to take my leave."

"You make it hard to believe, that's all. You work harder than I do, *amore*. And that says something because I never stop."

"I promise I'm going to take my leave. But tonight, I'm going to stay later. We have a new woman on the floor—domestic abuse, and it's a risky situation right now. I feel like she just needs someone to talk to a bit more, and maybe she'll feel less anxious about the shelter and what we're trying to do to help her."

Gian grunted something under his breath that Cara didn't understand before adding louder, "Your soul is too good for this world, love. You better take your leave, and enjoy every minute of it. You deserve that, Cara. So fine, we'll do something tomorrow, but something tonight, too."

"I'm going to be too tired for anything tonight, Gian."

"I'll surprise you."

"With what?"

"I'm actually not too far away with my brother, having dinner. How about—"

Gian's sentence cut off, and a nothingness sounded in Cara's ear. She looked down at the office phone, only to see the call had been cut off, but there was no dial tone. She hit the receiver button, but each time, the same nothingness came through the speaker.

"What the fuck?" Cara asked out loud to herself.

Then, the lights went out.

Instantly, backup emergency lights lit up over Cara's head in one corner of her office. There was absolutely no reason for the phones to cut out, nor for the power to shut off. Cara might have overlooked the power thing, as sometimes that happened in the city when a car accident took out a transformer, but she hesitated on thinking that was the issue.

Why?

Because even without power, the phone lines would work. The phone lines would have needed to be cut, deliberately, for them not to work.

Instinct made Cara grab her cell phone from her purse as she headed out of her office. The shelter was a complex-style building, comprised of different areas from housing wings, to the kitchen, the offices wing, and the downstairs section, where things like the daycare, reception, a small library, and more was set up for the women to use.

Cara went for the stairs first, deciding on heading down that way to see what in the hell was going on. She had just stepped foot on the lower floor when the first gun shots rang out. Screams followed.

"Holy shit," someone murmured from the front.

Cara stayed behind the safety of the wall that separated her from being seen by the people at the front entrance of the shelter.

"Allen," she heard Jenny say, "please put the—"

"Shut the fuck up. Where's my wife?"

Cara heard the patter of fast footsteps heading her way, and the second gunshot split through the air. The body of one of the volunteers landed so close to Cara's spot that she heard the woman take her last breath.

Oh, my God.

"Let's not do that again," Allen—Melinda's husband—said, his tone cold and bored. "Lock the place down. I'm not leaving until I get my fucking wife."

Cara took a breath, and then another. Her slight touch of PTSD from Lea's murder made things like gunfire into a huge monster she didn't want to battle. She certainly couldn't afford to battle it right then.

She didn't realize it but she had squeezed her hands so tightly, her fingernails cut into her palms. It was only the slight movement of her baby that brought Cara but of her daze, back into the present, and reminded her what she had in her hand.

A cell phone.

One that worked.

And there was still a whole floor of people that needed to stay where they were and go into lockdown mode. It was likely that because of the cut phone and power lines, the staff in the upper floors were not aware of what was happening downstairs. A proper alert couldn't be sent over the speakers to lockdown and hide-in due to a dangerous situation.

Thankfully, given the time of day, the bottom floor was mostly empty. A lot of the staff and women would be in the kitchen on the second floor, readying for meal time. A lot of the woman might even still be in the housing wing, readying to head to the kitchen.

Cara hit the stairs running, though she tried to keep her steps as quiet as possible. Already, she had her phone turned on and was dialing nine-one-one.

"Nine-one-one emergency services, what's your emergency?"

Cara rattled off the address to the shelter. "Active shooter, at least one dead."

"You're sure it's *active*, ma'am?" the woman asked.

Another gunshot rang out from down below as Cara headed for the housing wing first. "*Very fucking sure, thanks.*"

"Okay, please remain calm and on the phone."

Cara pulled the lock-in bar from above the housing wing's entrance doors and set it up as firmly as she could against the bottom, hearing some of the women come out of their rooms. The dispatcher continued to ask Cara questions, and she rattled off as much information as she could while she placed the metal bar in under the doors, opened it wide so that it used the cement walls as support. Now, the door couldn't be opened from the other side.

"Ma'am, do you know—"

Cara ignored the dispatcher, and turned to the women coming out of their rooms, and the few staff there, too. "There's an active shooter on the main floor. Door one to the housing wing is closed, secure, and locked-in. I'm going to exit out door two and head toward the kitchen. Someone needs to put the lock in bar behind me. *Do not open those doors.* Do not open them until you hear police declaring a non-active situation. Get in your rooms, close the doors, lock them up, and get under your beds, in your closets, or your bathrooms if you have one in your unit. Turn the lights off. Be extra quiet. Police have been notified, so let's not get on a dozen cell phones and block up the emergency lines. Okay?"

She could plainly see the questions the waiting people wanted to ask, and their fear. She was grateful that they simply nodded, and she continued on, heading for the exit door.

"I take it the shelter has codes in place for this sort of thing," the dispatcher said. "That's good, very reassuring."

"Just because we have them, doesn't mean we want to use them."

"Good point. The police are on their way."

Cara's phone vibrated, an incoming call on the other line, but she focused on making sure the housing wing did as she asked, and locked in the exit door that led to the stairs. Instead of going down the stairs to the bottom floor, she went down the U-shaped hallway that would lead her into the offices and kitchen area.

Once again, her phone vibrated with a call on the other line.

Cara checked it, seeing Gian's number.

"You're still on the line, ma'am, aren't you?" the dispatcher asked.

"Yes, but—"

Another burst of gunfire rang out behind the doors that lead to the offices wing where Cara had first come from. The noise and shock alone sent her spinning back into the wall again.

Shit.

Shit, shit, shit.

She couldn't lock in the offices wing when she knew there were people inside that might be able to get out. Not to mention, the lock-in bars were *inside* the doors, not outside. Because the people within needed to be safe, and keep the bad guys *out*.

Cara hadn't meant to, but in her panic, she had clutched her phone the wrong way, and ended the call with the dispatcher. She could hear the shouts of Melinda's raging husband just a few feet beyond the office wing's doors when her phone started ringing.

Loudly.

Loud enough for someone to hear behind the doors.

Utter fear sent Cara running for the only safe zone left. *The kitchen.* Attached to the dining hall, she could get inside, have the doors locked down, wait for the cops, and hope for the fucking best.

She slammed into the back section of the kitchen like a bat out of hell, shouting and waving at the staff to help her get the lock-in bar in place. Her words mostly came out in a jumbled, panicky mess of jerky sentences and orders in the dark space with only the dim emergency lights up above.

Someone seemed to hear her, though.

Or they understood.

They just got the lock-in bar spread at the bottom of the door when the first kick hit it. Then, another round of gunfire sent Cara and the man who had helped her get the bar in place, flying backwards. She stumbled over her own feet, suddenly thankful the doors were metal and could take a bullet or two.

"The other door," Cara mumbled to the confused, frightened staff working in the kitchen, "get the lock-in bar in the other door!"

A nagging pain started to ache in Cara's side, but she pressed the heel of her palm against it to soothe it as best she could. Her phone rang once more, and Gian's number lit up the screen.

Even though every single part of her *screamed* to pick up the call and hear his voice, because it would calm her like nothing else, Cara didn't do it. She didn't want to scare him, or worry him. The situation was … well, bad.

Really fucking bad.

Cara decided to call the emergency line back, just to let them know an update on the situation, and why the call had been ended in the first place.

"Nine-one-one, what's your—"

"Active shooter at Carolina's House on the Fifth," Cara interrupted, keeping an eye on the locked-in door. "I was just on the phone with a dispatcher, and accidentally ended it. We have the housing and dining wings locked in, but the main entrance, bottom floor, and offices are not secure."

"Units are on route to the scene, and one has already arrived, ma'am."

"Thank you."

She still didn't relax.

Not for a minute.

And especially not when the dispatcher said, "We have a confusing report coming in from the first unit, could you clarify the situation? One shooter or two?"

Cara's brow furrowed. "Just one, why?"

"There are running vehicles outside of the shelter's main entrance and a witness told police that two men entered the shelter five minutes ago. With weapons visible."

"This began at least fifteen minutes ago," Cara whispered.

"Yes, I can see when your first call came in, ma'am."

Cara wasn't sure *why* she felt the need to ask, but the question spilled out anyway. "What are the models of the vehicles outside the shelter that the witness saw the men come in?"

"Um ... a Lexus and a Mercedes."

Gian.

Chapter 13

Gian couldn't get rid of the image of the brain matter splattered across the welcome sign behind the shelter's receptionist desk. He'd *thought* something was wrong when his phone call with Cara ended abruptly. He knew something was wrong for sure when—after driving like a bat out of hell—he found the front of the shelter dark, without the usual warm lights brightening the entrance.

Inside, two dead women sent him running for the offices wing. Dom stayed in the entrance to help the frightened, shocked women that had been spared.

"Cara!"

Gian checked office after office, but found nothing. A few of the staff had locked their doors, too, but he didn't think Cara would be in an office with someone else. She had called from her office phone, and that was why he went looking there first. He'd put together what she had said about the risk level for an altercation due to a new woman at the shelter, and figured … the altercation happened.

Halfway down the hallway, he heard a snarling voice coming from behind the exit doors. He wasn't sure where that led to, but he knew the shelter was sectioned off to make it feel more home-like, and less like a complex.

"Get those fucking doors open," a man barked. "Right now, or I'll blow your fucking head apart."

"Please, listen. The doors *can't* be opened. Please don't—"

"Open the fucking doors!"

"I can't open them!"

The woman's resounding cry that followed her statement had Gian picking up his pace. Already, he had his favorite Berretta at the ready. He shouldn't be walking around with a gun, anyway, not with the cops being so hot on his ass, and the time he had just served for illegal weapons possession.

Gian figured having a gun now was a damn good thing.

"Bitch, I'm gonna kill you."

Gian's foot hit the latch on the wing exit door at the same time he aimed his gun and turned toward the voices. The guy with the semi-auto rifle pointed at the cowering woman on the floor didn't see Gian either.

Not until it was too late.

The trigger pulled back smooth and easy under Gian's finger. The bullet plugged into the forehead of the guy, sent his eyes flying wide, and then he stumbled back several steps. His head cracked morbidly against the wall on his way to the floor.

Gian considered putting another bullet in the fucker, just for good measure, but the horrified shriek of the woman stopped him. He passed her a look and recognized her instantly. Cara's boss.

Jenny, he thought her name was.

"You okay?" Gian asked.

Jenny just stared at him, blinking.

"Did someone call the cops?"

She still didn't talk.

"Where's Cara?" Gian demanded.

Jenny swallowed hard, her gaze darting to the corpse bleeding out between his eyes on the floor, and Gian standing just a few feet away. "Probably inside the kitchen and dining area, if she's not locked in her office."

"She's not locked in her office."

"You killed him."

"He was going to kill you," Gian offered with a shrug. "Which was the better option? I think we both like this one more. I can have the carpets replaced before the weekend is up. It'll be like he never even happened, no worries."

The man might have hurt Cara.

Or Gian's child.

Rage filtered in through Gian's numbed senses, but he pushed it down. It was done with, and handled. A problem came up, and he fixed it. It was just what Gian did.

"RCMP, show your hands!"

Gian tossed his Berretta aside the second he heard the police shout their warnings from behind the doors where he had just come. He shot Jenny a smile as he put his hands behind his head, and moved down to his knees on the floor.

This way, he was not a threat.

This way, it would be faster.

He *really* needed to see Cara.

"Gian!"

Gian turned at the familiar sound of Cara's shout. Just in time, too. She barreled into him, her arms snaking tight enough to choke him, and then she pulled him closer still. Her kiss landed fast and hard against his mouth, taking his breath away.

Finally, he could *feel*.

He wanted to hug Cara, to bring her in closer, but all he managed to do was press his cuffed hands along the swell of her stomach. It was enough and the baby's kick had his heart beating a little faster.

"Hey, it's all right, *mon ange*," Gian soothed in Cara's ear. "All's well, now."

"What is this?" Cara demanded, pulling away to grab the cuffs. "They arrested you?"

The cop keeping watch on Gian near the back of the police cruiser gave a little shrug when Cara glared at him.

"Details," Gian said, "nothing more. I had a gun on me and no papers for it, not to mention a license for a concealed weapon. It's just details."

"Gian, those *details* put you in jail for five fucking months last time!"

"Yeah, not so loud, Cara. And it was a little more than one gun last time, but it doesn't make this look very fucking good on me at the moment."

She frowned. "But you were the one who … who …"

"Came in and saved the day?"

"I mean, yeah!"

Gian sighed. "Just relax. You don't need to be worrying so much that you worry my son right out. All right? Also, there's a couple of EMTs here, so have you been checked over yet?"

"I'm fine," Cara said, huffing.

She might have thought so.

Gian needed to be sure.

"Officer, could you have this woman checked—"

"Gian, stop it!"

He ignored Cara, and nodded toward her when the officer grinned. "I mean, if you wouldn't mind. I'm not going anywhere, really."

"I'll escort her over, Mr. Guzzi."

"You ass," Cara muttered under her breath to Gian.

"Just get checked, love. And the baby—his heartbeat and whatnot. I'll still be here, where the hell am I going to go?"

Cara's narrowed gaze didn't relent, but the officer was quick to urge her toward a waiting ambulance, fifty feet down the street. Gian took the second he had alone to breathe, and get whatever story he needed to tell straight in his brain. Not that it was going to help him on the legal side of things.

All too soon, the officer was back, without Cara.

"Well, Mr. Guzzi, it's time to head down to the station."

Gian looked in the direction Cara had gone. "Could I at least wait for an update on her?"

"She seems fine, and the EMT got an earful when he was a little rough-handed checking the baby."

"Oh, is that so?"

He couldn't even try to hide his rage, or the way his tone edged dangerously.

The cop eyed Gian, amused. "You killed one man tonight. Isn't that enough?"

"Not when it comes to her."

"Let's go, Guzzi."

Gian rested his head against the cinderblock wall of the jail cell, thankful he was alone for the moment. He'd been shoved into the cell with a half of a dozen other detainees, but throughout the evening and into the morning, the others had been moved elsewhere, or released once they'd slept their drunken stupors away.

He reached for his pocket to pull out his phone, and cursed under his breath, realizing he didn't have it on him. Everything—from his phone to his keys, and the bit of change alongside his wallet—had been taken from him.

This was not where Gian wanted to be.

Not again.

"You're looking mighty comfortable."

Gian didn't bother to even turn his head at the new—yet familiar—voice. The RCMP detective that had become a second shadow of sorts for him loomed just beyond the bars.

Seeley looked at a file in his other hand. "Quite the mess you've found yourself in again, Gian."

"*Oui.*"

"Why on earth would you think it was a good idea to go in guns blazing, when you damn well know you're not to have any weapons, legal or otherwise?"

Gian shrugged. "I wasn't thinking."

That much was the truth. He had gotten that call from Cara, decided to head over, and shit had gone south from there.

"The cops said you refused to give a statement," the detective noted.

"I want my lawyer there when I do."

"It's the weekend. You know these jails don't bring in lawyers and have all that nonsense done on the weekends."

"Then my statement can wait."

"Make it easy on them, give them the statement," Seeley said. "What's it going to hurt? We already know what happened, just repeat it for them."

"When my lawyer shows up," Gian replied.

Seeley grunted under his breath. "You've got these damn Mounties split down the middle, Guzzi. Half of them think they should release you for what you did, and the other half thinks you're nothing more than a—"

"Criminal, I know. That half is right."

"At least you're aware."

"Is Domenic being held in another cell because we're brothers?" Gian asked, getting tired of the same old conversation that would go nowhere. He'd also been wondering about his younger brother, and how Dom had faired through the weekend. "I mean, I get why you wouldn't want us together. It would be a shame if we concocted some kind of story to get me out of here, right?"

Seeley's face turned to stone. "Domenic wasn't arrested."

"Oh?"

Gian didn't hide his surprise.

"No need to, as his weapon was registered and legal. He also didn't shoot anybody, and he was helping in the main entrance with victims. He was brought in for a secondary, more thorough statement this morning, though."

Something in the lilt of the detective's tone caught Gian's attention.

"Was he now?" Gian sat a little straighter on the bench. "Do tell."

"Where did you get your gun from?"

Gian said nothing.

"How long have you had it?" Seeley questioned.

Gian stayed quiet.

There had to be a reason for these questions, after all.

Frustrated, the detective pushed away from the bars with a scowl. "You've got everybody fooled, Guzzi, but not me."

"I beg your pardon?"

"You owe your brother—big time."

Gian hid his inner confusion well. "We do look out for one another when we can."

"Seems *this* is no different. Domenic took the rap on your gun. Said the illegal weapon was his, in his vehicle, and that you had grabbed it when you two arrived. There's no way to prove otherwise, especially considering he too had a gun on him, though his was legal and registered. Your charges have been dropped, except for the discharging a weapon, but—"

Gian released a dark laugh. "It'll be thrown out in court, given the circumstances."

Seeley's face reddened. "Likely."

"When am I getting out?"

That was all Gian cared about.

He had a pregnant Cara to get back to.

Life was waiting.

He didn't have time for this shit.

Seeley perked a bit at the question, happier than before. "We're a bit short staffed this weekend, and nobody seems to be around to properly discharge you. Shame. Monday, likely."

Gian resisted the urge to flip the man his middle finger. Instead, he rested back on the bench, much more comfortable than before. "*Merci*, Seeley. See you next time, we both know there's going to be one. Oh, and do see if someone will bring me something decent to eat. I have restaurants that will deliver."

"Good to see you're smiling," Stephan said as Gian approached his waiting underboss.

Gian stuffed his hands in his slacks pockets, enjoying the sunshine. "Why wouldn't I be? It's Monday, it's a beautiful day, and I am not in a jail cell."

"Lucky, boss."

"Very. Where's my brother?"

Stephan shrugged. "Dom said he had some shit to catch up on. I didn't mind coming down to pick you up and take you home."

Gian kept his features blank, but disappointment filled him. He hadn't been able to have a conversation with his brother while in the jail, and knowing that Dom was taking a charge on possession of an illegal weapon for him, he owed him thanks. He'd hoped to do that first thing, and then get on with his day.

"Your vehicle is still in impound," Stephan said.

"I'll worry about it tomorrow."

"Maybe not even then."

Gian cocked a brow. "And why not?"

"You have bigger problems to worry about at the moment, boss."

He wasn't so sure of that.

"Bigger than Cara being two weeks away from delivering my first-born son? Bigger than convincing her she needs to move into the penthouse, so I can take care of her? Bigger than barely escaping more jail time? Tell me what's bigger than those things at this very moment, Stephan."

The underboss shot a look down the street, as though he was expecting someone to be watching them. No one was, or so it seemed. Gian wouldn't put it past their shadows, though.

"You made another show, boss."

Gian tipped his head to the side. "*Excusez-moi?*"

"We're all walking a fine line out here on the streets, trying to keep our noses clean, stay quiet and out of sight of the cops, not to mention away from that fucking prick Gabriel. And then there you go, making a show of yourself and all of us again. All because of your mistress, boss. I'm not saying this to be disrespectful," Stephan added quickly, likely seeing the rage growing on Gian's features. "I'm saying it because someone's got to be the one to warn you and nobody else is stepping up right now. As it is, we've been battling the cops *and* Gabriel's men, not to mention tip-toeing around one another, thinking there's somebody among us that's feeding info to the police."

"I hear you."

"Do you?" Stephan asked. "Are you listening now, Gian?"

Gian bristled. "Try that again."

"*Boss*, are you listening now?"

"I didn't intend to make a scene," Gian said quietly. "Not with this or with Cara. I reacted. Like any man would have done."

"Any man that wasn't in your position, maybe," Stephan agreed.

Gian hated how Stephan made damn good points.

"It'll smooth itself over, surely. Over time."

"Except it won't, not really. Let's not even consider the cops for the moment, just Gabriel. Already, he's threatened us, he's taken from us, and he's pointed the finger at you each and every time as a reason why. Maybe before, the men in the family would overlook it. But the next time, when another Guzzi man shows up dead because of that fucker, they're not going to be so compliant and forgiving. They're going to remember your face on the television, and your pregnant mistress as the reason why."

Gian no longer felt as carefree as he had just a few minutes ago. "I'll figure it out."

Something.

He would figure *something* out.

"But today," Gian said, "I have a woman to apologize to, so that's where I need to go."

Stephan nodded. "The penthouse it is, boss."

"She didn't ask to be taken to her place? Cara doesn't live at the penthouse, and never lets me forget it."

Yet.

"Well, that's where she's been. Chris says she hasn't left, either. He's been keeping an eye on her, apparently."

Well, then … maybe something *was* finally working to Gian's favor for once. He would take what he could get.

"Oh, my God. You smell like a jail cell."

Cara's words were grumbled against Gian's lips, but he still heard them perfectly fine. His chuckles did nothing to quell the way Cara's nose scrunched up as she pulled away from him in the penthouse hallway. He wanted to bring her closer again—fuck the jail cell smell—but she had a point. He needed a shower, a toothbrush, and a clean suit.

"Sorry, *mon ange*. I'll get on it."

Cara smiled in that sweet way of hers, but a wariness still remained in her gaze. "So, about the charges …"

"Everything is fine," he assured. "Things have been taken care of."

"How?"

"Carefully."

That was the best he could offer, given the circumstances.

"Enough about me. How are you feeling? Would you be more comfortable at your place?"

Cara shook her head. "I don't want to leave."

"We don't have to. Not today, anyway."

"*At all*," Cara said, looking up at him to make her point clear. "Maybe I took some time to think about things while I didn't have you all up in my head voicing an opinion, too. I like the nursery you set up across from the master bedroom."

"I told you I wanted one here, just in case."

"It's … fully stocked and ready. Everything is set up in there. The walls are even painted a pastel blue."

Gian's brow furrowed. "Of course, it is. You're thirty-eight weeks pregnant, *bella*. I'm not sure when you think it would be appropriate for it to be done, but *before* the baby arrives is a good time for me."

"But I kept saying no about living here, Gian."

"So?"

"You have everything he needs."

"Why should you travel a bunch of stuff back and forth if you don't need to?" Gian asked.

"Why don't you demand things of me? I'm having your child, we're in … whatever we are, this relationship together. Why don't you want more? Why don't you demand more?"

"Because I don't think you want me to, and I'm not sure it would make a difference if I did demand you do what I wanted," Gian answered honestly.

Cara just stared at him, barely reacting at all. "And that's all?"

"I love you, Cara. I will love you whether you live with me or not. I will love you if you're *with* me, or not. I will love you even when you don't love me. So, we don't get to be entirely normal, and circumstances kind of fucked us up along the way. Who cares? You make me happy; you give me every reason to be happy. Why would I mess that up by demanding that you change what you're fine with giving me?"

She didn't answer right away.

Instead, Cara said, "I'd like to stay here."

"*Live* here," Gian clarified.

"I want to be with you, Gian."

"I think we can make that happen."

He'd been waiting for this day; hoping for it, really. Living there was one thing. Gian wanted to give Cara something far more permanent where the penthouse was concerned. Something that no one could take from her. He only needed her signature on already finished documents, but that could wait for another day.

The prettiest, widest smile bloomed over Cara's lips, and Gian couldn't help himself but take another kiss. Cara relented to his wants, letting him take and take until she was breathless and laughing.

"But you do stink," she said.

"Showering now, *Tesoro*."

Her tinkling laughter followed him down the hallway, but he didn't mind her teasing. He didn't waste time showering, because he had something far better waiting for him outside the bathroom. He quickly showered up in the attached master bedroom's bath, didn't bother to shave like he should have, and walked out with nothing but a towel in his hand to run through his hair.

He found Cara staring at herself in the large mirror opposite of the bed.

She let out a heavy sigh. "I can't reach it."

"Reach what, love?"

"The stupid zipper on this dress. I got it up earlier, and now I can't get it down."

Gian held back his laughter. "Why bother with a dress at all? You have those comfy clothes you like."

"I wanted to wear something other than pants with stretchy panels, Gian."

"And now you want the dress off?"

"I miss my comfy pants," she admitted with a pout over her shoulder.

"I'll help," Gian told her.

Gian tied the damn towel around his waist, not missing for a second how Cara's gaze dropped down to his hard erection before it was covered. He couldn't help it, really. She was near, and as beautiful as ever—more so, carrying his child, if anything—which meant his cock was ready to play and do its thing.

"How can you even want to fuck?" Cara asked.

"*You*," he corrected as he came to stand behind her. "I want to fuck you because you're within touching distance and you're *mia bella cara*. If I didn't want to, then there would be a problem."

"Gian, right now I have the sex appeal of a slug. You can't be serious."

"Do you want to bet?"

"Bet on what?" Cara laughed, letting him pull the zipper on the dress down her back. "That I'm as huge as a house, and not exactly a hot fucking commodity in the sex department?"

"Cara, you are …"

Her gaze found his in the mirror. "What? *Very* pregnant. Very uncomfortable. Very—"

"Much mine," Gian interrupted firmly, hoping to quiet whatever nonsense was in her head. He began sliding the dress down her body, taking his time to enjoy baring her skin and curves while he did so. "Maybe there's a bit more of you to enjoy right now, and I think it makes you sexier. Maybe you heat up a little faster when I touch you, and your shivers come from somewhere deeper. I like this," he said, letting his palm skim over the roundness of her stomach before drifting lower to slip under her lace panties. "I like that this is where I've gotten you, and the way you look because of it, pretty and sweet with my child. Why wouldn't I like every bit of this, Cara? What man wouldn't be crazy about *this*?"

Cara's breath hitched as the dress fell to the floor, and Gian's fingers glided along the hood of her clit. Jesus, she was hot to the touch and it was *glorious.*

"A-and after?" Cara asked softly. "After, when I'm not like this or like before, either?"

Gian grinned, leaning in to get a taste of the tender skin behind Cara's ear. Her responding shiver only made his cock ache even more—got him harder. "So maybe you'll be *plus douce … doux, mon ange.* Softer, in spots. Sweeter, in others. Maybe you'll have some new lines or curves for me to explore and love, but don't you think you've earned those things? Don't you think this body of yours and what it's doing, deserves to be adored and loved, no matter if there's a little more, or it's a little different?"

"I—"

"Because I think it does," he interrupted, nipping the spot behind her ear to quiet her. "I think something that's this beautiful should know, and I intend to make sure that you do, Cara."

"So, no slug sex appeal?"

"Not even a little bit. That's nonsense. You're as beautiful and as sexy as you've always been to me, and I don't see that changing. Not with time or life. Not with more children or age. It just won't, *bella mia.* You're perfect. For me, you're perfect. And I waited so long for you, Cara, so damn long."

Cara's trembling picked up, and her breaths came out in stuttered streams as Gian's fingers continued their slow and steady pressure on her clit with each stroke. "I'm going to come."

"Yeah, that's the point." His free hand slid under her throat, turning her face just enough that she had to stare at herself in the mirror while the orgasm raced through her body. "And look at how fucking beautiful you are. Like this, with me. Why wouldn't I want to see this, Cara? *Why not?*"

And good God, she *was* beautiful when she came.

Flushed skin and a trembling lower lip. Hooded eyes and red curls framing her pretty face. Shaking from top to bottom with the most pleased sigh falling from her godforsaken mouth. He loved every inch of this woman. Every single curve and line that she owned fit perfectly into his own. He loved her.

"*Gian.*"

"Hmm?" His fingers slowed on her clit as she hummed her way through an orgasm that seemed to go on and on for ages. He explored lower, finding her wet and hot at her slit, just like he expected and wanted her to be. "Talk to me, Cara."

"You said it all pretty well without me needing to."

"I do try," he murmured. "And I know you miss when I choke you, when it hurts so good, or when I use you harder; I know you want me to fuck you crazy, and I *will*. But never like this, not when you're like this, sweetheart."

Not when she was fragile.

Not when she was growing something oh, so precious.

Not when he could worship her for being *everything*.

He just couldn't do it. He wanted to love her differently, then. Not that it was a better way, but he liked it just the same.

Cara's gaze darted to catch his in the mirror, and love stared back. "This is good, too."

Gian tipped Cara's head back far enough that he could catch her mouth in another burning, long kiss. Her tongue tangled with his, while his fingers weaved into her hair to hold her in place for as long as he wanted. He couldn't quite get enough—not of her softness, sweetness, her taste and smell, or all the rest that made up her wonderfulness.

It was never enough.

"Show me how good, then," he urged. "Show me how good you are, how good you look with me, Cara. Show me you *see*, too."

Cara was bent over before Gian could get another word out of his mouth. Her pretty ass was high in the air, while she used the sides of the mirror for support to keep her steady. Gian used those few moments he had to admire the woman begging for his hands to touch her, for his cock to fuck her, and how absolutely perfect she looked bent over, ready, and so damn willing. He dropped his towel and filled her full of his cock while her gaze stayed locked on him in the mirror.

He felt every fucking inch of her take him in, squeeze tight around him, and promise something wicked and heavenly was on the way. Still, he kept his gaze locked on hers. With each hard thrust that she met, and every long pull that came a little faster than the last, he watched her.

She had to see what he did, even if he spent the rest of his life making it happen.

Gian would do it.

Happily.

Gian rubbed his forehead to ease the tension settling there, and went back to looking over the emails in his inbox. What he needed to do was get some sleep, but as he was already behind on work, he couldn't afford to take the extra rest.

It never ended.

Life was always getting in the way.

"Gian?"

The cell phone on his desk rang at the same time Elena's voice filtered in from the doorway of the office. Gian answered the phone, and held up a finger to ask for a moment from Elena.

"*Ciao, bonjour*," Gian greeted, not even checking the caller ID.

"It's time."

It took Gian far too many seconds and a few more blinks of his eyes to realize who was speaking on the other end of the call, and what exactly they were trying to tell him.

Cara.

And her words could only mean *one* wonderful thing.

"You're sure?" he asked.

Cara blew out a hard breath that crackled the speakers. "Oh, yes. Definitely sure, Gian. These contractions are nothing like those fake ones I was having. It fucking *hurts*."

Gian winced, and kept the panic he was suddenly feeling out of his tone. For one, because he knew Cara didn't need the extra worry, and for two, because Elena was just a few feet away, listening to one side of the conversation.

"Have you been timing it?" he asked.

"They're ten minutes apart now for two hours, so lots more of this to go yet. Also, that kind of sucks, because if they hurt now, just think, Gian."

"Think what?"

"Think how much it's going to hurt when it's like thirty seconds apart."

"You're going to be fine," he assured.

Cara was strong as hell.

Silent strength.

Steadfast love.

She just *was*.

"Water?" he asked carefully, mindful of Elena's presence.

"Not yet," Cara replied, "but the doctors said it's not like the movies, anyway. Lots of women's water doesn't break until they're in active labor, so."

"I'll head over."

"Don't rush, we've got time."

Gian chuckled, and shook his head. "You're kidding, right? Of course, I'm going to rush."

"Don't get yourself killed on the highway or something, Gian. I swear to God." Cara's next breath came out stuttered and her voice strained. "All right, I'm going to hang up because another one is starting, and I don't want to talk through it."

"I'll listen to you rage, if that's—"

155

"*Goodbye*, Gian."

He laughed when she hung up the phone on him. He had zero doubt that Cara would be just fine through labor and birth. If anything, she was too stubborn to get overwhelmed by something as silly as pain. It would likely be *him* on the floor in a panic, passed out or something equally humiliating.

Birth was not for the faint of heart, or so Gian was told.

"You're leaving?" Elena asked.

Gian closed down his laptop, packed it up, and grabbed the suit jacket off the back of the office chair. "I am."

"Congratulations are in order, hmm?"

He shot his wife a look. "I beg your pardon?"

"The only reason you would rush out at night after a phone call like that one is because your *goomah* is having the baby. Congratulations are in order, so congrats."

Apparently, Gian had not been as vague as he thought on the phone call. That, or Elena was just very perceptive.

She cleared her throat, and crossed her arms over her chest. She was ready for bed, by the looks of the silk robe she wore, her clean-face, and the messy bun of hair on top of her head. It was rare that Gian saw Elena in a state that was any less than perfect.

"I did try to be discreet on the call," Gian said.

"I could tell, but I'm also not stupid."

"I likely won't be around for a couple of days. Don't expect me, not that you'll mind, I'm sure."

Elena glanced away, her jaw tight and eyes hard. But there was a barely hidden sadness in her features, too. Gian hadn't expected that at all.

"Again, congrats," she murmured. "I hope he's everything you want, and everything we don't have, Gian. It's easier for you that way, isn't it? When everything you share with her, is nothing like what waits for you here?"

"You don't really need an answer for that, Elena. You already know."

How different they could have been, he thought. How entirely different their life could have been together.

If only she had cared enough.

Gian no longer cared at all.

Marcus Gian Guzzi made his way into the world nearly twenty-four hours to the minute that Cara had called Gian. He came into the world quietly, pink, slick and bloodstained. He didn't cry at first, but not because something was wrong.

No, he didn't cry because he was born with his eyes wide open, already looking for the people that belonged to only him.

The smallest thing to have ever scared the very life out of Gian.

The most beautiful thing to have ever graced his life, next to his mother.

An amazing, tiny, brown-haired, dark-eyed creature that was nothing like Gian had expected, but *so much more*. Ten perfect fingers, and ten perfect toes. Soft, warm skin, and facial features, right down to the dimple in his cheek, that matched his father.

Features that matched the Guzzi genes.

Cara had been so quiet through the process, measured breaths and quivering words. She wanted Gian close, but she barely spoke to him at all. He went off her cues, to give her what she wanted, and didn't ask to be told what to do. It wasn't him doing this wonderful thing, after all. It was all on her.

It was only when, in a birthing pool of her choice, she had pushed Marcus out into the world that she did so with her first and only cry.

And it wasn't so much a cry as a roar.

It was kind of perfect, too.

Hours after, once Cara had finally drifted off to sleep, and Gian was awake in the private room, holding his blinking newborn son, he took that silent moment to be amazed.

So amazed and in wonder.

His child was *everything*.

Gian lifted the swaddled boy a little higher, bringing him closer so that Marcus's hazy gaze could catch his father's. Sure enough, the baby stilled under his swaddling blankets the moment he locked onto Gian's face, and everything was right and good and beautiful in that moment.

"Sweet boy. First of my legacy and house, and the seventh of your name. With blood made of gold, luck, and dirt, child. You don't know what awaits you; you have no idea how amazing you're going to be, but you don't need to know, not yet. You have a whole life for me to teach you all of that, so it can wait. *Guzzi Principe*, this world is yours. This whole great, big world is all yours, Marcus."

Like all Guzzi boys, Marcus was born a prince.

And like all Guzzi men, he'd eventually be a king.

Chapter 14

"A little more, please."

Cara tipped her head down, the action causing more of her curls to fall over her shoulder. "Like that?"

"A bit too much, actually," the photographer replied. "Now we're more like a curtain of hair, instead of a few stray curls."

"Here, let me help." Gian stepped into Cara's view, and in front of the white backdrop. He smiled down at her, his fingers sliding along the column of her throat to push back the hair that had fallen over her shoulder. Cara had all she could do not to shiver, and guessing by the way Gian's grin deepened, he saw it, too. "There, perfect."

"Step back and let me see, Gian."

At the photographer's demand, Gian gave Cara a wink, and did as he was told.

"Yes, that's much better," the woman said. Then, her camera started up again, capturing images of Cara in a stone-still pose, with a sleeping, one-week old, naked Marcus in her arms. "You do seem to have a good eye for this sort of thing, Gian. Do you dabble in photography at all?"

Cara shot Gian a look that she hoped kept him quiet from discussing his little hobby with *her* and cameras. In his spot in the corner, now sitting back in the corner chair and watching the session, he seemed content and pleased. In his suit and shined leather shoes, his dark gaze staying pinned on her, he had never quite looked more handsome. He barely reacted at all to Cara's unspoken warning.

"I certainly have an eye for someone," he murmured.

"I hope you put it to use."

"Oh, I do. I most certainly do."

"Gian," Cara said quietly.

His husky laughter filled the penthouse's living room. The photographer had chosen it amongst the many others, because of all the floor-to-ceiling windows and natural light. Cara wouldn't have minded going in to the woman's studio, but Gian said it wasn't necessary. She wanted photos, Gian had the woman come to her. It worked.

"I think we're just about—"

Gian's cell phone started ringing. "Done."

The photographer smiled. "Yep. Just let me pack up. Cara, you can keep the muslin wrap for Marcus, as I don't reuse items like those for other newborns. I have to say, he was one of the easier babies to photograph this week."

"That's because he spent an hour and a half on my boob before you got here," Cara half-joked. "Milk-drunk."

It wasn't a lie.

It *was* kind of funny.

The truth was, Marcus happened to be a wonderful baby. Sure, he clusterfed at night before bed, and he liked to have his spaces quiet and dimly lit, but Cara figured that was just his way of transitioning into the world at a slower pace. Marcus rarely cried, he barely fussed. And then there was Gian ... She swore the baby just *knew* his father was in the room, even when he couldn't see Gian.

Marcus was attached to Cara, yes.

Gian was entirely different.

"Here, let me take him, *mon ange*," Gian said, coming to stand at Cara's side again while the photographer packed up her things. "Go get in that new dress I brought back for you from Ottawa yesterday. He'll be okay with me."

Already, Marcus's hazy brown eyes fluttered open at the sound of his father's voice. He tried peering around, but was only satisfied in his knowledge that his father was near when Gian scooped him from Cara's embrace. Then, the baby blinked up at his father and promptly fell back asleep.

"Gian, that's not an at-home kind of dress."

He smiled, and kissed her cheek. "Maybe not, but it *is* fit for a queen in her castle. Go put it on. I'll get him into a diaper and clothes, too."

Cara thought about Gian's ringing phone that had interrupted the end of the session, even though he hadn't picked up the call, and wondered ... "Is someone coming over?"

"A couple of people, actually."

"Who?"

"Family." His stare dropped down to Marcus. "Mostly for him, though."

Oh.

"I'll go change," Cara said.

The nervousness in her tone must have been clear to Gian because he reached out and stroked her cheek with two fingers. "All you have to do is smile, beautiful girl. The world is so much better when you're smiling."

He always says the right things ...

159

Cara still couldn't shake the nerves as she slipped out of the flowy white dress that she had used for the photo session, and into the form-fitted coral Dolce & Gabbana number hanging in the closet. She figured the dress had been a silent apology of sorts from Gian, as something had come up in the week, and he'd rushed off to Ottawa to take care of it.

For the most part, he had spent the first couple of days after Marcus's birth with her, then one night at the penthouse, before heading back to the mansion. He had promised to come right back the very next night, but the Ottawa thing came up, and ruined those plans.

Quickly, Cara checked herself in the mirror as she slipped on a pair of black pumps and a diamond choker. Another expensive gift that she had woken up to the morning after Marcus's birth. Gian had only shrugged and smiled slyly when Cara asked where it came from.

Thankfully, her fit and slim form was bouncing back rather fast. She thanked breastfeeding, good genetics, and the fact she had been in decent shape before and throughout the pregnancy for that little gift from God. Of course, things *were* different.

Her body was still different. Slightly wider in the hips. Her breasts were bigger. And her stomach had softened slightly, even as it flattened back down.

She had worried about the changes, both selfishly and vainly. She wished now that she hadn't spent time on that nonsense at all.

Cara came out of the bedroom and into the main section of the penthouse to find the photographer had left, but the new guests had arrived. Her presence wasn't noticed as she hung back in the entryway, and watched the newcomers *ooh* and *awe* over her son in his father's arms.

Gian's mother and father, and his siblings, each took their turns giving little Marcus their time and attention.

"Oh, look at his little fingers," Crystal said softly.

"Guzzi eyes," Domenic noted.

"Not *just* the eyes," Celeste said of her grandson. "Look at the boy—he's Gian's spitting image, my God."

"He is, isn't he?" Gian asked, his pride shining through.

"*Oui*, he looks just like you did when you were brand new. *Doux bébé*," Celeste cooed, running her fingers through the wisps of Marcus's dark hair.

"And her," said the quiet, tall man standing just a few feet back from the others. "He looks like her, too. You can't miss *that*."

Cara shifted as the man's gaze fell on her in the entryway. It seemed she had not gone as unnoticed as she previously thought. She knew who he was—Gian's father, Frederic. She didn't know a lot about the man, as Gian didn't offer, but she had heard things in passing.

He did not approve.

Not of her.

Not of her child.

Not of Gian's choices.

Just the way Frederic's cold gaze passed over her, and darted back to the baby boy in Celeste's arms, Cara knew all of those things were true.

"He does take after Cara quite a bit, too," Gian said, losing the happier tone from earlier. He turned to Cara, extending an arm and opening his hand wide for her to step forward and take. She did, still unsure and unsettled in her heart. "Remember what I said about today, Dad."

"I came, didn't I?" Frederic asked.

"*Sì*, but remember, too. This is not *your* home. Your rules do not apply here. Mine do. Hers do."

Dom cleared his throat, and quickly diverted the attention back to the baby. While it helped a bit, Cara still couldn't shake the coldness she had found waiting for her in Frederic's gaze, or how he all but dismissed her presence, even when he was standing directly beside her.

It was difficult.

A shameful feeling burned in her throat.

She couldn't expect anything different.

Cara only relaxed when Gian's lips pressed to her temple, unbothered by the people watching them. His lips moved with his words, whispering over her skin with assurance and love.

"You are never the lesser, not in your own home, *mia cara bella*. Demand respect in your space because it is yours, and do not let someone take it from you. You are the queen, and *this* is your castle. This is your home, and those who are lucky enough to be allowed inside should understand what that means. Smile. *Always* smile here."

He was right.

He always was.

It seemed like Cara had blinked—just *once*—and Marcus was turning one month old. Everyone had told her again and again that she needed to enjoy the time she had with her baby while he was a newborn, because before she knew it, he wouldn't be so tiny and new. Sure, Marcus was still a newborn, but just the fact that the first month had passed them by so quickly, in a haze of long nights, dirty diapers and so much more, was surreal.

And sweet.

The ding of the elevator brought Cara from her thoughts. She lifted her stare from her sleeping son in her arms, just in time to see Tommas enter through the penthouse's elevator with a wide smile and already opened arms.

"Cara."

"Tommy," Cara replied in kind, unable to stop her growing smile.

"Come here."

Before she knew what happened, her brother had wrapped her up in a tight hug that damn near squeezed the life out of her. She wasn't about to complain, though. It had been too long since she last saw her brother, though they did try to talk at least once a week.

"My God, look at this *bambino*," Tommas said, stepping back to give Marcus a good one-over. "He's going to be a heartbreaker."

Cara swatted her brother on his arm, laughing. "Don't start with that yet. He's just a baby."

"Prepare for it, Cara. Prepare."

She rolled her eyes, and turned to walk them in further. "Do you want a coffee? How was your flight?"

"Coffee would be great. And it was shit, but it always is when I'm not flying privately."

"How's Abriella?" Cara asked.

"Wonderful and beautiful," Tommas said of his wife. "Next time, she'll come, too. It's just not the right time with the little one."

Tommas, too, was a new parent. His son, Tommaso, was only a couple of months older than Marcus. Cara had seen picture after picture of her one and only nephew, as Tommas was like every proud father with a camera in his hands, but she had yet to meet the baby.

"I get it, no worries," Cara assured. "You didn't have to rush up here, either, by the way. I would have understood, Tommas."

Her brother shrugged, setting his bag to the side as they entered the kitchen. "Who else is going to come here and see this baby of yours, huh? I'm the only family you've got left—*I* need to be here for him. And you, too."

"Sit down. I'll get your coffee."

Tommas shrugged off his suit jacket and took a seat at the large kitchen table. Cara didn't miss how her brother peered around the penthouse, or the bit of it that he could see. She hadn't been the least bit surprised when he mentioned wanting to come down for a weekend to visit, but she *had* been a little shocked that he actually made time to do so.

Her brother had a busy life in Chicago, especially now that he was married with a child of his own, not to mention the fact that he was the boss of the Outfit. She suspected that her brother's time was already pulled thin in every single direction, and yet he made time for her.

Time for Marcus.

Cara appreciated that more than Tommas could possibly know.

"So, this is a nice place," Tommas said quietly.

Cara side-eyed her brother as she set a cup of coffee down in front of him. "Say what you're thinking, don't dance around it."

"When did you move out of the apartment?"

"A couple of weeks before the baby was born."

"Wasn't that when the issue happened at the shelter?" Tommas asked.

Cara made a face. "Yeah, around that time."

Tommas scowled, but hid it quickly enough by taking a drink of his coffee.

"That wasn't Gian's fault," Cara said, shifting Marcus to sleep over her shoulder as she took a seat beside her brother. "That was completely unrelated to Gian, Tommy."

"So you said before. A domestic abuse victim's husband, right?"

"Right." Cara rubbed a hand over her son's lower back. "And Gian just happened to … get himself in the middle of it, which was mostly what ended up on the news."

"And you, too. *You* ended up on the news, Cara."

"Not by our choice."

Tommas sighed, and looked around the penthouse again. "I guess he moved you in after that, huh?"

"Actually, I kind of did that by myself. He didn't really say a thing either way, because it was what he had been asking for the whole pregnancy. It was a few days later that he finally did something about me moving in."

"And what was that?"

Cara's gaze darted away from her brother as she admitted, "Signed the deed for the place over to me. This place isn't his, now. It's mine. No one can take it from me, no one can force me out of it. It's all mine."

Tommas let out an appreciative sound, surprising Cara further. "Well, then."

"I do like the penthouse."

"It's very high up."

"I feel safer here, Tommy. It feels right to be here."

"Are you happier here, too?"

Cara looked back to her brother to find he was searching her face for any sign of a lie or maybe even discontent. "I'm happy with him."

"Even knowing what you do—even after everything?"

"I don't excuse Gian. I only choose to love him. The rest is details. Those don't matter."

"They never should." Tommas nodded, and then reached for Marcus. "Now, give me my nephew. It's time for him to wake up and meet me properly. Where is Gian, by the way?"

Cara handed the sleeping baby over. "He thought I might like to spend some time alone with you first before inserting his presence, too."

"That's fine and great," Tommas replied just as fast, "but it doesn't answer my question."

"At the mansion."

Tommas' gaze cut to Cara just as Marcus woke up. "Is that where she lives?"

"Her name is Elena. His wife. You can say her name to me, Tommy."

"Again, not my question."

"It is."

"I see," her brother said softly.

"It's not always easy or pretty. I never thought it would be, though."

"But love, right?"

Cara smiled. "Yeah, love, Tommy."

"I haven't decided if I like you yet or not," Cara heard her brother say from down the hall.

She carefully closed the door to Marcus's nursery, not wanting to wake the baby up after his before-bed feed. It was like the baby thought he suddenly needed another round of milk before he could go back to sleep. Cara's well was dry for the moment.

"I don't think it's required for you to like me, honestly," Gian replied with a chuckle.

Cara kept her steps light and quiet as she walked down the hall, heading toward the office where Gian had disappeared to with Tommas when she went to feed Marcus after supper. Just a foot from the opened doorway, she held back from going further where she could be seen, and listened to the conversation happening beyond the doors.

She knew better than to eavesdrop.

She couldn't help it.

All evening, from the time Gian had arrived back at the penthouse, the two men had engaged in very safe conversation with one another. They almost seemed to be circling around one another, too, as though they were being careful about their words and actions, lest one offend the other.

Cara was not sure if that was because of their respective positions in their organized crime families, or for her.

"I like that you love her," Tommas said, "and that counts for a lot."

"I love her entirely."

"And your son, too. That much is obvious."

"He's my greatest pride and joy, and she gave him to me."

"But I don't like the rest," Tommas admitted. "I don't like that she is pushed aside in the eyes of others, or given labels and names that she doesn't deserve. I don't like that it must hurt her to spend half of her week with you, and wonder the other half. I don't like that there are nights she is alone, caring for your child, because you have distractions elsewhere."

"Responsibilities—duties," Gian corrected fast and sharp. "Distractions implies something that is not and has not ever been *there*. Use the right word, Tommas. It's the least you can do if you're going to insult me to my face."

"I'm not trying to insult you, Gian. I only want to understand."

"You're like me, aren't you? You sit in my spot, too. You know these rules, this life, and those people. Divorce would mean ruining my family's legacy, at the very least. At the most, my life would be given up as a sacrifice. So here I am, doing what I need to do."

"Certainly not what you want to do."

"No," Gian murmured.

"I heard you were having some issues on the streets, and with the police."

"The police are expected, given what happened last year and before that. The streets, on the other hand … well, that's just my bastard father-in-law trying to force my hand with my family and men. He's been quiet the last month or so, surprisingly. And after everything he did, the issues he started, men he killed, and the threats … it's concerning. He's gone under the radar, too, making it harder to watch him. Even his men are out of sight for the moment. He wanted to make a point to me, or rather, make a point out of me. He didn't succeed, but that does not mean he's finished."

"Why is that surprising? Maybe he finally came to the realization that you're not going to give him what he wants."

"You would have to know the man," Gian said with a sigh. "Everyone always gives him what he wants, even if it takes a while. He simply has to find the right button to push with a man to get him to hand it over."

"And so, the quietness and the disappearing act is a bad thing."

"It is always bad when a man cannot see Gabriel coming, Tommas."

Silence hung heavily between the two before Tommas spoke again.

"And all of this for what? Why is he causing these issues?"

"He believes I have a rat in my family, and he thinks forcing my hand to cull through my men indiscriminately will fix the issue," Gian answered.

"Do you have a rat?"

"A big, fat one."

Tommas grunted disgustedly. "But you're not as concerned about the rat as you are—"

"Gabriel. Exactly."

"And why is that, now?"

"He's pushed every other button he thinks I have, Tommas," Gian said, "and it earned him nothing. I only have one thing left for him to come after, to make his point loud and clear."

"You're talking about Cara."

"Every part of me wishes I wasn't."

"But you've told me you keep her presence quiet, and that you're quiet about coming and going from here. You said you were *careful*, Gian."

"I can never be careful enough, I can only be mindful now."

"What does that even mean?"

"It means I have been watching and waiting for him to try and push that button with me, because he knows very well that it's there. I do all I can to keep her safe, because I put her in this position, even if she doesn't know it."

"Why not just kill him?" Tommas demanded.

"It's never that easy. Another person on my shit-list shows up murdered. I don't need the fucking attention it's likely to bring, unless he doesn't give me a choice. I've managed Gabriel this long, when others wouldn't have bothered at all, I can manage a little while longer. Surely. We've been entangled in this mess for years. I know his games."

"So just *kill* him."

"Tell me, why didn't you just kill the person standing in your way, Tommas?"

Tommas cleared his throat. "It wasn't that easy."

"My point, *merci*."

"And if he *does* go after Cara?"

"I'm doing everything I can to make sure that doesn't happen."

"But if he *does*," Tommas pressed, not even posing it as a question.

"Then I'll slaughter him. It'll turn all eyes on me—it'll cause a war between organizations. It's everything I can't afford to have happen right now, given the state of my freedom and *famiglia*."

"But?"

"I'll do it. I'll burn the whole fucking world down for her. Imagine what I would do to just one man."

Jenny's face lit up with pure joy as Cara turned the infant car seat so that a wide-awake, one month and a half old Marcus was visible. "Look at him!"

"I do," Cara said, laughing. "Every day, all the time."

"Oh, my God. He is too *precious*."

And just like that, someone else fell in love with Cara's son. She couldn't really blame people. There was something about Marcus's sweet face and gold-flecked brown eyes that just did it for everybody. When he smiled, they all *melted*.

"He looks like his father," Jenny noted. "Those eyes are just unreal."

"So everyone keeps saying."

Jenny carefully maneuvered Marcus from his car seat. The baby peered up at the new, strange person in his world, but still grinned behind his soother. "I'm so glad you brought him in to the shelter to say hello. Everyone misses you so much. We were starting to consider you were never going to come back."

Cara waved that off. "I'll be back. Four months is all I agreed to take off, and I can bring him in with me when I do start back. No worries there."

"Well, let's go say hello to everybody, sweet boy."

For the next hour, Cara strolled from office to office, and section to section, watching as yet more people fell head over heels for her boy. She had wanted to come to the shelter sooner, as her coworkers were just as much her family as her own brother, but things always seemed to get in the way. She had pushed it aside for far too long.

Cara was grateful she had made the time today.

"So, how's it been with the new baby?" another one of her co-workers asked.

"Busy. Tiring. Wonderful."

The woman smiled as she headed back into her office. "Babies will definitely do that."

Cara stepped aside as the mail cart was pushed through the office wing. The man who delivered the mail stopped long enough to give the baby and Cara a quick hello, and then went about delivering the last bit of his manila envelopes to each office.

"We will be so happy to have you back," Jenny said, "though I understand why you want to take as much time as you can with this beautiful little creature."

Cara took her son when Jenny offered the still wide-awake baby back. "I do want to get back here, though. I feel like I'll probably have way too much to catch up on, by the time I get back into the office."

"Don't worry, you haven't missed a lot, Cara. We've just spent the last month working through what happened with the shooting, settling back in, and getting everyone settled. Nothing too strenuous."

"Still …"

"Enjoy the time with your baby," Jenny said.

Cara sighed. "I am, trust me."

"And you are *always* welcome to come in just for conversation. No one is going to turn you away with little Marcus here."

She laughed. "Yes, not because you want me here, it's all about him, now."

"Well, look at him!"

"Oh, my."

The quiet exclamation from behind Cara gained both her and Jenny's attention. The previous co-worker that had been admiring Marcus stood in her office doorway with a manila envelope in her hands. Her gaze darted from whatever she was staring at, to Cara, and then back again. A pink reddened her cheeks.

"Something wrong, Nancy?" Jenny asked.

"Um. Uh. Well—"

"Spit it out."

An odd, heavy sensation settled in Cara's stomach. She wasn't sure why, but just the way Nancy looked at her again, and then back down to the item in her hands, it was unsettling.

To say the least …

"Whoa!"

Another shout from someone else echoed inside a different office.

"Did you get one of these?" Nancy asked, lifting the envelope for Jenny to see. She kept the items hidden behind it, though.

"I'm not sure."

Nancy's gaze darted to Cara once more. "You should probably check, Jenny."

"Just … Jesus," Jenny said, stepping forward and ripping the items from Nancy's hands. "Give it to me. What is wrong with you?"

Jenny didn't bother to hide the items that had been inside the envelopes the way Nancy had. Cara almost wished her boss would have done just that. She could plainly see photos of her *very* naked self in the most dirty, compromising positions. With each photo that Jenny flipped through, the images became progressively dirtier and worse for Cara.

"Oh, my God," Cara whispered, horrified.

She recognized those images.

They were ones Gian had taken of her.

Some from before her pregnancy, a few early in her pregnancy, and even a couple of candid shots late in the pregnancy, although those weren't filthy in nature, simply private.

Smudged lipstick. Cum up her back. A handprint on her ass. Her mouth full of cock. Her legs spread wide open. Her pussy wet and open. All of the images had her face clearly visible.

Cara's heart rammed hard in her ribcage, taking over all other sensations. Her blood rushed in her ears as she struggled to ignore the sudden flood of absolute *shame*.

"There were a lot of those same envelopes on the mail cart," Nancy said quietly. "Probably one for every office, Jenny."

Jenny stayed quiet for longer than Cara liked, but eventually nodded. "Okay."

"I'm so sorry," was all Cara managed to get out.

Anymore, and she was sure vomit would follow her words.

Jenny looked to Cara, a wariness and pity in her gaze. "This is a very deliberate act on you, Cara."

Was it?

Cara didn't know anything.

"Why?"

"The first time you come to the shelter since taking time off, and *these* get sent here." Jenny cleared her throat, uncomfortably. "Presumably to everyone in the offices."

"Oh, my God."

She was going to throw up.

"Who knew you were coming here today?" Jenny asked.

Gian. That was it, as far as Cara knew. And Chris, her enforcer, as she wasn't allowed to go anywhere without him. She didn't think either of those two people would have done this to her.

"I should go," Cara mumbled, grabbing for the infant car seat resting on the floor. "I'm so sorry."

"Cara, wait a—"

She didn't wait.

The shame wouldn't let her.

It ate her alive.

Chapter 15

Gian found Chris sitting at the kitchen table as he stormed through the penthouse. The enforcer had set little Marcus up in a bouncy chair, and was apparently reading the newspaper to the baby. Beside him, a row of overturned photographs and a discarded manila envelope sat on the tabletop, seemingly forgotten.

He hesitated at the sight of the overturned images, but only because he knew what he would see on the other side. He, too, had gotten a package delivered while dining with a business associate.

Apparently, so had his mother.

His father.

His brother *and* sister.

Several of his men.

People he worked with.

People who worked *for* him.

His aunt in Quebec.

His cousins.

Gian suspected there were more, but the people affiliated with his life were probably too shocked, embarrassed, or unsure to contact him and ask about the dirty pictures of Cara. He had found that with a few, they didn't need an explanation. Like the ones delivered to his parents—there had been no explanation. Some delivered to his men, or people he worked with, had included a simple note explaining who the woman in the images was, and how it related to Gian.

Others, like the ones delivered to *him*, or to Elena, had been written on directly. Or so Elena told him. Gian believed her, if only because his package had also held the naked images of Cara with red ink marked across the photos labeling her *whore* and *slut*. To name a few.

"Were those sent to you today?" Gian asked Chris.

The enforcer kept his attention on the baby. "Found the package under the wiper of my car after I ran in to get a coffee while Cara was inside the shelter."

Gian cleared the rising rage clogging up his throat. "I see."

"The doorman downstairs was nice enough to let me know that the front desk also received the same package of photos."

Gian's molars ached as he gritted his teeth in an effort to calm himself down. "Destroy them."

"I thought you would prefer to, if given the option. I didn't bother to look beyond the first one when I pulled them out. It was enough for me to know I shouldn't be looking at them. And then Cara came running out of the shelter like a bat out of hell … so, yeah."

"Does she know that you saw the pictures, too?"

Chris shook his head. "Didn't say a word, boss."

"Keep it that way."

"I planned to. This is bad, isn't it?"

Little Marcus seemed perfectly content to bounce in his chair, thanks to Chris helping by tugging on the bottom. The baby certainly didn't know his mother's whole world had just been turned upside down, and she would never feel safe or unviolated again. Not even in her own skin. How could she, when every time someone looked at her, she would have to wonder if they had done this to her, or if they had *seen*?

"It's bad," Gian said, "but not in the way some might think. Someone intended to embarrass me, to shame me, and what they did was far worse."

"They hurt Cara."

"Yes."

Chris sighed, and stopped bouncing the baby's seat as he turned to his boss. "Who would have access to those photos?"

"They're accessed only on my phone and you know how careful I am with that."

"But who would, boss?"

Gian had to seriously consider his answer, because he wasn't sure. Yes, his phone had a pin lock on it, but if someone picked up the device when his back was turned before the screen blacked out, they could easily see inside and explore his very personal and private life. Beyond that, phones were not infallible. Anyone with a decent computer program could plug one in and strip it of files, locked or not, with the owner none the wiser.

"Whoever it was would have needed to have my phone for a bit, I think. Some of those images are back from after the bomb was set on my car, when Cara and I were a new thing. It would have taken time to grab files that far back in the gallery."

"Then you're just knocking names off the list," Chris said with a shrug. "So, who was it?"

"Am I knocking names off?" Gian asked right back. "Because that leaves a few people who I spent enough time with to maybe set my phone down and look away, but that doesn't mean I did or would."

"Another question, then."

Gian figured he was the one who needed to be asking questions, but he didn't see the harm in letting Chris ask, too. "What?"

"Who would do it—do something that awful to someone like this?"

Gian scoffed, dark and hateful. "My wife. Her father. This stinks of them. It reeks of their kind of nonsense."

"You don't sound sure."

"I have never left my phone within reach of Elena, and she also received a package today with these photos, or so she said when she called to scream at me. I haven't seen Gabriel since before Marcus was born, and again, he had no access to my phone. It certainly stinks of them."

"Except *how*," Chris muttered.

"*Oui.*"

"Cara disappeared into the bedroom. I didn't want to interrupt her, and the *principe* is fine with me, boss."

Gian nodded. "Thank you."

Unsure of what kind of state he would find Cara in, Gian headed for the master bedroom. He opened the door to see a hurricane of devastation staring back at him. Clothes strewn about the floor in piles, wrinkled or torn. Jewelry scattered, perfumes toppled over, and makeup palates crushed in a strange rainbow of colors on hardwood. White sheets had been ripped from the mattress, and glass from the shattered mirror glittered on the floor and the shoes that had clearly been used to smash it.

Rage found him standing there.

Shame screamed through the silence.

Cara, so calm and put together, so strong even in her weaknesses, had clearly broke under a whole new kind of weight. It was not lost on him how she attacked the things that accentuated her life, beauty, or image. Her clothes, perfumes, and makeup. Her jewelry, and the mirror that showcased her reflection when she stared into it.

It killed him.

Because she was so beautiful. Because she was so wonderful. Because in her heart, she was everything sweet, good, and deserving of love, adoration, and respect.

Someone had taken that from her without care or concern. They had taken private moments of her life, things that only *he* was allowed to see or have from her, and showed them to the world.

And how dare they?

Cara's worth should never be tied to the acts of a bedroom, and yet, he feared they now would be for far too many. She probably knew it, too.

"Cara?" Gian called into the bedroom, taking a single step inside. "*Mon ange?*"

A quiet, choked sob echoed from behind the opened door of the attached master bath. Gian instantly headed in that direction, making sure to shut the bedroom door behind him.

He found Cara tucked into the corner of the bathroom, soaking wet from a still-running shower, and naked, though she clutched at a towel. She wouldn't look at him, not when he called her name again, or even when he got down on his knees and reached for her. She *flinched* away from him when he touched her, but he still pulled her into his embrace.

"I'm sorry," he said over and over.

"Why would someone do that to me, Gian? *Why?*"

"I don't know."

But he thought he did. He thought he might know. He still didn't want to tell her. How could he explain that someone had violated her privacy and life, simply to hurt him? Wasn't it bad enough that Cara had to know those photos were his to begin with? That he had not been careful enough with something like those images she trusted him with?

Cara shook from the force of her cries. No matter how hard he tried, Gian couldn't wipe the tears away fast enough before more ran down her cheeks.

"I'm so sorry," he told her again.

He couldn't make this better.

This couldn't be fixed.

Gian hated himself for that.

"Cara, look at me," Gian demanded.

She did, but the sadness that had been constant in her eyes for a week, stared back at him. He was so angry and disappointed in himself, because she asked him the same thing every day: *why* and *who*. He was no closer to being able to answer that for her, and each time he couldn't give her what she asked, he failed more.

"It'll be fine, a quiet weekend away," he told her.

Cara nodded, her attention drifting back to the sleeping baby in the car seat next to her. "Maybe it'll help to get away."

That's what he kept telling her.

He hoped it was true.

"Chris will keep an eye on you," Gian promised, "but if you need anything, if you want me, just call. Okay?"

"Sure, Gian."

He didn't for a second think she would call. She blamed him, in a way, and Gian didn't fault her for it. It had been his phone, his pictures. It was her job lost, her newly beginning career already stained and tainted, and her reputation destroyed with one selfish, vile act. It was her image and self-worth ruined, not his. And fuck him, because he couldn't even tell her who or why.

"Is it different?" Cara asked. "The Ottawa penthouse, I mean. Is it different from the last time I was there?"

Gian smiled. "A bit. I had some upgrades done. It needed them. I think you'll like it. Take some time to enjoy it, anyway. I haven't been able to yet. Not entirely."

"You could come."

"You don't really want me to, though, do you?"

Cara glanced away. "I just need to get out of this city and breathe, Gian."

"I know, *mon ange*." He wouldn't fault her for that, either. Leaning into the back of the SUV, Gian kissed Cara on her forehead, and relaxed a bit when her soft fingertips stroked his cheek. It felt like a silent promise that things would be better … eventually. Quickly, he laid his hand on top of his son's head, and Marcus's eyes fluttered open at his father's touch. "For *anything*, Cara, you call me."

"I will. I love you, Gian."

That, he didn't doubt.

Not at all.

"*Ti amo*, Cara."

Closing the SUV door, Gian smacked the roof with his palm, and caught Chris's eye in the front seat. He didn't have to verbalize his order for the man to do his job, Chris always did it without needing to be told.

Gian stayed standing on the sidewalk long after the SUV had disappeared out of sight. It was only as he headed toward the underground garage to get his own vehicle that his cell phone started ringing. Dom, he thought, or maybe Stephan. There was always too much shit for him to do, and he never got time to rest anymore.

He picked up the call without even checking the ID.

"*Ciao, bonjour.*"

"It's been a while, Gian."

Every inch of Gian turned to ice at the sound of his father-in-law's voice.

"Gabriel," Gian greeted as he closed in on his car. "I'd like to say it's nice to hear from you, but we both know that would be a fucking lie."

"Yes, well, I hear you've been looking for me."

Gian slid into his car, and started it up. "You heard correctly. I like to keep an eye on men who threaten me and my men, after all. You can't blame me for that."

"Of course, not. Have you found your rat yet?"

"That's not your concern."

"So, no," his father-in-law said rather cheerily. "As I suspected. Still too busy putting your attention and time where it neither deserves to be, or needs to be. Such a shame, Gian. I thought giving you some space and time to think might have changed your mind—especially now that the whore has had the baby. Babies change things, I thought. They make a man … see things a bit differently. It's not as fun with a whore when you're not just fucking her, but changing nappies and listening to a child cry for hours on end. I *thought* the baby would send you back to where you should be."

Gian's brow furrowed. "Where I should be? What in the fuck does that mean?"

"With my daughter. Where else?"

Oh, fuck that.

Gian had no idea where Gabriel was getting this nonsense, but he wasn't even going to indulge it. "My personal life is not up for discussion today."

"It is always up for discussion when it's a man like you, in your position."

"Was this ever even about a rat in my family, Gabriel?" Gian wondered out loud.

The older man chuckled. "It was. These are things you need to learn, and fast, Gian. Tell me, did *Cara* like the gift I sent out last week?"

All over again, ice and fire spread through Gian's veins, threatening to send him into a rage before he even knew what happened.

"How did you get those photos?" Gian asked.

"I have ways."

"You just signed your death warrant, Gabriel."

He figured the man deserved a warning, at least.

"Wrong," his father-in-law murmured. "You've signed hers, and the child's. As I warned you. I would have overlooked a lot of your personal business, until you began hurting what belonged to me."

"*What?*"

"I let you have Elena. You should have taken better care with her; I won't have her crying to me over something as stupid as you. Perhaps your man will make it out alive, though. The one driving them, I mean. I hope you said goodbye."

The phone call hung up.

Gian couldn't get his fucking car into drive fast enough. He hit the road already breaking the goddamn speed limit, but knowing he was probably too late.

Hospitals were both horrible and amazing places. Horrible, because just the smell alone brought memories of more deaths and nights spent in worry than Gian cared to remember. Amazing, because the smell also brought along memories of lives saved and time given.

The only thing keeping him sane as he sat in a hospital room, waiting? His son.

Marcus slept off the bottle of formula he'd downed as soon as the nurse had brought it in for Gian to feed the boy earlier. Although to be fair, Marcus had not wanted the formula at all or the oddly-shaped nipple that was nothing like his mother's breast, shoved into his mouth. In a hospital crib, swaddled in a warmed blanket, the baby had no idea how close to death he had come.

No idea at all.

Gian, despite tired legs and an aching back, kept watch over the boy. He tensed at every flicker of Marcus's lids, and each jerk of the baby's limbs beneath his tight swaddle. Marcus was perfectly fine—not a scratch or bump on his beautiful, innocent head. His car seat had made sure of that when the SUV had been run off the road, and then subsequently rolled down an embankment.

Still, Gian couldn't get the image of his son's car seat with a single bullet hole through the back rest, only a couple of inches higher than where his son's head would have been laying. He couldn't forget the pieces of broken window glass scattered across the baby's body, or the bloodstained blanket, colored red with Cara's blood.

Cara.

Pain shot through Gian like a lightning bolt.

His gaze darted to the closed door of the hospital room, and he had all he could do not to go out and demand someone give him more answers. He would get none if he did, anyway. Not until Cara's surgery was either over, or unable to be completed.

Three shots.

One through her hand.

One to her thigh.

The final one—the most deadly and likely to cause complications—to her chest. They had been aiming for her heart, though a shot to the head would have been quicker and cleaner. Gian figured it wasn't about quick or clean, it was about making a point.

A point he heard loud and fucking clear.

"Boss?"

The sound of Stephan's voice brought Gian from his internal war. The underboss stood in the now opened doorway, his gaze stuck on the phone in his hand.

"Dom wanted me to let you know that he got ahold of Tommas Rossi, and that your mother is on her way up now," Stephan said. "Tommas can't get out of Chicago right now, but he demanded updates every hour, on the hour. I guess your mother is in quite a state and is asking to see the baby."

Gian nodded, but the numbness was beginning to seep in, taking away his desire to talk, or even think. This was better, though, as he wouldn't feel so guilty when he left his child and Cara to recover in the hospital without him while he finished a job that was long overdue.

The guilt would come later, surely.

He would deal with it then.

"Mr. Guzzi," greeted the maid as Gian walked past the kitchen's entrance inside the mansion. "I was not told to expect you tonight, sir."

Gian cursed under his breath, but turned back to Mariana with a forced smile. "I wasn't expecting to be here tonight, either. Are you the only staff left?"

She nodded.

"Good," Gian said, "you're free to leave early. Now, preferably."

"But I haven't finished my—"

"It's fine. Please head out."

Gian waited for Mariana to gather her things, and then saw her out the front door. Satisfied he was now alone in the Guzzi mansion—albeit, his wife was *somewhere*—he went back to his task. Finding Elena.

It didn't take him long.

Elena rested in a Jacuzzi tub with bubbles that smelled of vanilla and overflowed to the floor. A half-downed bottle of wine sat on the edge of the tub, no glass in sight. Apparently, she was drinking it straight from the bottle. The steam in the master bathroom was thick enough to make Gian squint down at his wife from up above. He ignored her nakedness, as it did little for his desires, and it wasn't as though he hadn't seen it before.

"Elena," Gian barked.

She jerked awake in the tub, her flailing sending water and bubbles peppering the walls, floor, and Gian. He didn't bother to move, simply continued standing above her, glaring down.

Elena met his glare with one of her own when she realized he *was* there. "Gian! What in the fuck are you doing?"

"I could ask you the same thing."

"I beg your pardon?" Elena scrambled to sit up properly in the tub, using an arm to cover her chest as she reached for a nearby towel. She couldn't quite reach it, though, and Gian didn't offer to help. "What do you want?"

"Again, I'll hand that question right back to you, wife."

Her brow furrowed. "What does it look like? I wanted to take a bath."

"And drink a bottle of wine in the process, apparently."

"It's a half of a bottle."

"Details. Get the fuck out of the tub."

She narrowed her gaze. "I—"

Gian was not in the mood to play games with this woman tonight. He yanked Elena out of the bubbly, hot water by her wrist, not caring at all that she slipped and stumbled before righting herself with an angry huff. If looks could kill, he would have been dead right there on the spot.

"We're not going to play your games tonight, Elena," he warned. "I have a feeling you've been playing enough games with me as it is. I'm going to speak, you're going to listen. I'm going to ask questions, you're going to talk. If you lie to me, I will know it. If you spin bullshit with me, I will know it. Do you understand?"

"Could I at least get dressed?"

Gian grabbed the large towel hanging off the hook and shoved it at his wife. "Cover yourself up, it's the best I can do at the moment."

"You're an ass—"

"Yes, I'm aware," he interrupted before she could insult him. "You know, your father told me again and again that I needed to watch you. He tried to get through my thick skull that women like you can't be trusted. And after all the shit you already did to me, I should have listened to the man. Except I didn't, because I listened to too much of what you were saying. You're just as much of a snake as your father is."

Elena blinked, her brown gaze icing over. "What is this even about? Shouldn't you be fucking that whore of yours across the city? I—"

Gian moved forward, crowding Elena to the bathroom wall as his hand came up to clench around her throat. He squeezed hard, feeling her swallow under his grasp as she attempted to take in some kind of air. "*I* talk, *you* listen."

"O-okay, Gian."

"I don't know why, but it seems you've been feeding your father some kind of crazy bullshit where you and I are concerned. You have him believing you actually *care* about me on some level. You have him thinking I'm *hurting* you. That you're alone here, without me, and poor little Elena is just so fucking *heartbroken*."

Sarcasm oozed from Gian.

He couldn't even control it.

It was all lies.

"And what I didn't understand, Elena," Gian continued, "is why you would want to do that at all. We keep your father away and out of our life for a goddamn reason. He was always too fascinated with you, too close to you. Controlling. Vindictive. Dangerous. That's what *you* said. I saw these things myself, and I knew it was true. You wanted away from him, and you used me to do it, so I protected you for all these years, even after you lied and hurt me. I still *protected you*. Didn't I protect you from him?"

She nodded, though the iciness in her gaze hadn't left. She didn't look at him with fear, either, despite the fact he only needed to squeeze her throat a little tighter and she would have no air left to breathe at all. Gian figured that was because this was not the first time his wife had found herself in a position like this one.

"Then *why*?" Gian roared. "Why would you invite that man back in? Why lie to him, manipulate him with personal things about you and me that aren't even close to the truth? Why use a woman I love and my child—an innocent baby—as a sacrifice for your games? Why do any of that?"

Elena let out a slow, steady stream of air, as much as she could, and then smiled.

Goddamn.

It was cold.

Dead.

It burned.

Like her.

"Because look at you," she whispered, her voice hoarse and strained. "Look at you, Gian. Look at how angry you are, how ready to kill you are. Years ago, when you found me battered and beaten because of him, you were angry, but not like *this*. So calm and steady, but with rage so real it radiates. I thought it would have been enough back then to push you into killing him—seeing me like that, and what he did to me—but it wasn't. And because of that, I had to follow through, didn't I? To get away, I had no other choice but to follow through with the next part of the plan."

A heavy realization settled on Gian's shoulders like a dead weight as he took in his wife's words.

"To marry me, you mean."

Elena shrugged dainty shoulders. "I can't help that it's taken this long for you to finally find something you give a shit enough about to kill for it, but don't you ever fault me for using it, Gian. You know exactly who I am—I can't help that my father forgot for a time, too."

Yes, he knew.

She was a snake.

Just like her father.

Elena winked. "Hiss, hiss, Gian."

All that rage that had been beating at Gian's surface finally spilled over. The control he thought he had was gone, just like that. There wasn't a single part of Gian that was able to be rational in those few seconds. He took the greatest pleasure in seeing Elena's eyes water as he choked her against the bathroom wall—how her words struggled, and her body tensed with the urge to fight. It was one of the most beautiful sights he had ever seen, where she was concerned.

"You deserve to rot in hell, Elena. He almost killed them! Because of *you*."

"We'll be free," she croaked out under his hands. "Don't you get it?"

"You're—"

"*We'll be free, Gian.*"

He wasn't quite sure what it was that sent him jerking back from Elena. Partly, her words. Partly, her blue-lipped smile and happy eyes.

"You're fucking crazy," he said, pointing a finger at her. "You're insane."

"Why, because I figured a way out of this for both of us? All you have to do is get rid of the problem, Gian. He gave you a reason to do it, didn't he? A reason to justify all the problems that might come of it. You're angry, remember, he nearly killed Cara and the baby—your precious *things*. So, *kill him*."

"You think that'll fix this?" Gian asked, waving between them. "You think that's *enough*?"

"Shouldn't it be?"

"This is for life, Elena! And not because of your father's rules, but because of the ones *I* am forced to live by. You stupid, silly woman." He laughed darkly, taking another step back from his wife and shaking his head. "You're so blinded by your need to manipulate and control and gain by hurting others that you don't even realize how *fucked* you are. Killing him isn't going to get you the divorce. It will never get you the divorce!"

She stiffened, clutching the towel against her body with suddenly shaking hands. "But … but—"

"And the biggest problem is that I can't even kill you for what you've done this time," Gian snarled at her. "We've made such a fucking spectacle of this sham of a marriage—how unhappy you are, how distracted I am *elsewhere*. Killing you would do nothing but turn everyone against me when I need them the most. But Jesus, it might just be worth it, Elena."

Finally, a spark of fear lit up her gaze. "You can't kill me. I'm your wife, Gian."

Exactly.

And it had nothing to do with her, but everything to do with him. He was a made man—he chose this life, he lived by it, he spoke the rules, and he enforced them even when he hated them. No one could ever possibly understand the struggle it was to be *him*, and he wouldn't ever be able to explain it unless someone walked in his shoes.

No one ever would.

"The only reason I would ever give you a divorce, despite how it would ruin me," Gian said, "is so that when everyone finally stops looking at me, and you think you've finally gotten what you wanted, I could take it all away from you. I could kill you and no one would ever look to me, Elena. *That* is why I would divorce you, why I would sacrifice my name and legacy, because that is what you deserve. How badly do you want to be free? You've already taken everything from me. When is it finally going to be your turn?"

Elena only continued to stare at him, seemingly horrified and in disbelief, all at the same time. This was their life—he couldn't help the fact that she ignored things that were right in front of her face simply because she figured she could manipulate her way out of them.

That might have worked in her father's Camorra world.

It did not work in Cosa Nostra.

"You're going to get dressed," Gian said quietly, "put your makeup on, cover those marks on your neck with a scarf, and do your hair. Then, you're going to call your father, and tell him whatever you need to so that he comes over here tonight. You're going to sound pleasant and sweet and whatever else he needs to hear so that he doesn't think for a second that anything is wrong. And once he is here, you're going to do the same thing, and you'll look away when you need to, you'll say nothing to anyone about what happens here. Is that understood?"

Elena's hands trembled more. "Yes."

"*Yes*, what?"

"Yes, I understand, Gian."

He tipped his hand toward the bathroom door. "Hurry the hell up. I won't be far behind, so don't think I won't hear if you try to fuck me over, Elena."

Gian did exactly as he said he would, following behind his wife while she readied and then called her father. He said nothing as she convinced Gabriel to come to her, and Elena kept her act up the whole time.

He might have been proud, had he felt something at all.

He didn't.

Not an hour later, Gian had two snakes in his mansion instead of just the one.

"Daddy," Elena said, a false cheeriness coloring up her tone. "I've missed you."

"*Reginella*," Gabriel replied, the wet sound of a kiss meeting a cheek echoing down the hall to Gian's hidden spot. There was more affection in that one word than Gian had ever heard his father-in-law use before, especially toward Elena. It made him wonder—consider—just how much was an act those two put on for the world. How much of their vileness toward one another was simply what they wanted people to believe, not what was actually the truth. "You look tired, Elena."

"Long day," she replied. "Come in, sit down."

"I take it, your husband is not around."

"When is he ever around, Daddy?"

"Mmm," Gabriel hummed, "shame, really."

"He's just happier elsewhere at the moment."

"Not for long, *dolcezza*. I assure you."

"Oh?" Elena asked.

Gabriel's laughter rang down the hall, following along with two sets of footsteps. "That's not for you to worry your pretty little head over. I always take care of my *bambina*, don't I? Of course, I do. Now, where is that spiced rum I like so much?"

"In the main room. Are you supposed to be drinking with the medicine for your heart?"

"Never mind, *donna*. Don't lecture me on my health."

"I just—"

"Don't."

"Fine," Elena said with a quiet sigh.

Gian stepped out of the shadows of the closet enclave in the entryway after Elena and her father passed him by. He followed behind them a few steps, listening to their conversation as he screwed in the silencer to his gun.

What a mess this would be.

What a war it would start.

He wished he cared.

Gian stayed in the entryway of the main room while Elena directed her father toward the wet bar. It was only when Gabriel lifted a glass of spiced rum to his lips and turned slightly that he saw Gian waiting there, gun cocked and ready.

His finger was already on the trigger.

Gabriel took his drink, and swallowed it down without so much as a flinch before he said, "I trusted you, Elena."

The man didn't even look at his daughter when he spoke to her.

"You should have known better than to trust a snake you raised," Gian told his father-in-law. "She learned from the very best, didn't she, Gabriel?"

"*Elena.*"

Elena didn't respond, but she did do as Gian had previously told her. She moved toward him, readying to leave the room so that she wouldn't see what happened, or what came next.

"You could at least apologize to me, Elena!" Gabriel shouted at his daughter's back. "After everything I did for you!"

"Why should I apologize, Daddy? You never apologized for making me this way."

Gian waited until he heard the footsteps of his wife retreat to the second level of the wing, and then he pulled the trigger. He fired off three more shots, one with each step he took before he was standing over the dead body of Gabriel.

Just to make sure.

"*Cazzo*, Gian!"

Gian turned fast on his heel at the sound of his brother's voice. Dom stood in the entryway, his gaze darting between his brother and the body on the floor. "What in the hell are you doing here?"

He hadn't called for Dom. He hadn't even seen his brother before he left the hospital.

"I … I thought—" Dom's words cut off as his gaze cut to the side, looking at something down the hall before going right back to Gian. "Stephan said you had to handle something at the mansion, because of what happened to Cara and the baby. He didn't explain more."

"And what, you decided to follow behind me?"

"I thought you might need help."

Gian softened his stance a bit. Things had not been good with his brother for a long while. Longer than he was willing to admit. From the day in the jail all those months ago when Gian had needed to put Dom in his place, there had been a heathy distance between the two. It wasn't necessarily a bad thing. His brother became a better made man for it, a decent consigliere to his boss. Yet, the bond of what had been—between them as brothers—was seriously strained.

"If you want to help," Gian said, tipping his head toward the body on the floor, "then an extra pair of hands tonight would be great."

"Gabriel attacked Cara?"

"He did it. The bitch upstairs helped him along into it, but not much can be done for her."

That was all Gian was going to say about it.

Dom could fill in the blanks.

"I'll help," Dom said quickly. "Just tell me where to start."

"Find the bleach."

"There was something else, too."

"What's that?" Gian asked, tucking away his gun.

"Chris didn't make it through surgery. They put him on life support when his brain function failed."

Well, *fuck*.

Chapter 16

It was the pain Cara felt that woke her. It wasn't deep, or even sharp. Instead, it was a pulse skimming her nerves, being chased away by something cold in her veins.

The beep of a monitor had Cara turning her head to find the unusual sound. An IV pole with a morphine drip, and another for what looked like antibiotics, it seemed. She lifted her hand to find the tubes attached there.

Her other hand?

Wrapped in medical gauze and *ow*.

But almost as soon as she remembered the events that had gotten her in a hospital bed—being run off the road, the shooting that followed—the morphine chased the memory away again with its cold sweetness.

Still, Cara breathed deeply.

That hurt, too.

Worse than the hand.

It was only Gian coming in through the automatic doors of her room that distracted Cara. His attention was focused on Marcus, and a bottle of milk. He didn't notice Cara was awake as he tried to feed the baby.

"Come on, Marcus," Gian murmured, teasing the baby's lips with the nipple. "You have to eat, *principe*. I know it doesn't taste good, but it's good for you. It's not like Ma, I know. You *have* to eat, little man. What am I supposed to tell Ma, that you won't eat for Daddy? No, don't spit it—"

Gian sighed, his shoulders dropping as he used a burping cloth slung over his shoulder to wipe around Marcus's face. Then, the wailing started. Marcus's high cries resounded with his frustration and hunger.

"Okay," Gian soothed, "no crying. Ma's sleeping. Another walk around the hospital, more formula to spit on the floor while we go. Maybe you'll drink enough on the way to fill your stomach."

Gian turned around to leave the room, and Cara's panic flared. She forced herself to sit up in the bed, despite the pain in doing so.

"No, don't go, Gian."

How Gian heard her, she wasn't sure. Her voice was all but gone—too soft to make any impact. Somehow, he had.

Gian was already heading for Cara's bedside with one of his smooth, charming smiles firmly in place. Something was wrong. She could see it. His smile was forced.

Cara chose not to ask for the moment, instead, wanting her son. She held her arms out, ready to take the baby. "Let me see him."

Once Marcus was tucked into Cara's embrace, his gold-flecked brown eyes locked onto hers, she was finally *okay*. She could breathe, because all was right in her world. Her baby was okay.

Cara held Marcus a little bit tighter.

"I'm sorry," Gian said, keeping a hand on the baby's back to steady him. Cara hadn't realized it, but thin lines of tears streaked down her cheeks. With careful touches, Gian swiped the wetness away. "I tried, but he won't eat. I don't know if it's me or the shit they keep trying to shove down his throat."

"Probably both," Cara whispered through her tears.

"He doesn't want to sleep, either." Gian laughed hoarsely. "I just think he knew someone important was out of reach for a while."

"I thought he was a daddy's boy."

"Not when his mother isn't within crying distance, apparently. Kept his whole wing up last night."

Cara tucked the side of her face into Gian's palm, feeling his thumb rub soothingly across her cheekbone in rhythmic strokes. He kept her drowsiness at bay, and calmed her.

"I'm sorry for this, *mon ange*," Gian added quieter. "It never should have happened."

"I know."

And she *did* know.

She knew without him needing to tell her. Why would he want or wish for someone to hurt her and their child? He loved them; he protected them as best he could.

Cara knew all of those things because she saw him do it every single day. Sure, this was her greatest fear. It was all the reasons she didn't want to be in this life, attached to a man whose tomorrows were not guaranteed.

She also couldn't *be* without Gian. It wouldn't be living. It had just taken Cara a long damn time to settle those things with her head and heart.

Marcus turned into Cara's chest as he rooted for what he wanted to fill his stomach.

"Here," Gian said, handing the small bottle of formula over. "They said the narcotics will transfer through, so formula and bottles it is."

Cara frowned. "He's still new. I don't want to bottle-feed him. I'm better for him, Gian."

Her body ached to feed her child.

"Not my call," Gian said, leaning down to press a quick kiss to her forehead. "Besides, what's important is that he *eats*."

Cara nodded, but only because she knew Gian was right.

Marcus had to eat.

It was that simple.

Surprisingly, Marcus took the bottle with Cara feeding it to him. He drank it slower, and with a scrunch to his nose, but he certainly didn't give his mother the same kind of trouble he had given his father.

Gian took the baby to burp him—Cara didn't have the strength—and then placed a sleepy Marcus into his mother's arms. Cara took the time to look at her lover. A tired, strained smile stared back at her, but there was love, too.

Always love.

Gian dragged a chair closer to Cara's bedside, and took a seat. His arm curled around her lower half, while his other swept through her curls to keep them out of her face. His forehead pressed to hers, and his lips dotted sweet kisses along the seam of her mouth.

"This will never happen again," he promised.

"You can't know that."

"I can. At least, not by the person who did it, and not for the reasons it was done. It will *never* happen again, *mia cara bella*. Ever."

Just the way his tone dipped, and his dark gaze lit with fire, Cara chose not to ask more questions. They were things she didn't need to know, because she knew Gian.

She knew his love. She knew his providing, careful, strong hands. She knew his entire life and soul were the two things he was currently holding. It would always be enough for her.

"Let me help," Gian said, offering Cara his hand to help her from the limo.

She took it, muttering, "I'm fine, Gian."

"Maybe so, but you don't need—"

"Gian, you need to relax. It's been two weeks. The infection is gone. The doctor said I've healed well, internally and externally. I can get out of a car."

He stared at her. "So?"

"Gian!"

"Let me help you, *mon ange*."

Cara wasn't going to be given much of a choice, it seemed. She let Gian help her out of the limo. She *was* better, two weeks after being released from the hospital. It was only Gian that hovered over her like a goddamn hawk, now, constantly on edge and ready to kill someone for even breathing in her direction.

She wished she was joking.

Cara smoothed down her black dress as Gian leaned in the car to grab her clutch and wide-brimmed hat. Funerals were not Cara's favorite thing, not in the least, but this was one she refused to miss.

Even when Gian said she didn't need to go, or there were some people who may be uncomfortable with his mistress's presence. Even when he warned there would be media outside the church, although the private graveyard would be protected from unwanted attention.

Cara didn't care.

She *had* to go.

For Chris?

Of course, she did.

Cara fixed her hat, tipping the wide brim down enough to hide half of her face. She let Gian lead them into the church, her mind on her son at the penthouse with his grandmother. Her presence at the funeral would be enough; no need to go adding their child's intrusion, too.

Inside the church, Cara was acutely aware of the eyes that watched her. She didn't talk unless greeted, and only to offer her condolences to Chris's parents and younger brother, standing at his closed casket.

She had already met his mother and father once. It had taken a lot of begging on her part, but Gian took her down to Chris's ICU room where he was kept alive on machines until his parents chose to pull the plug on their adult son. She wanted to thank him—for everything.

It was in that hospital room where Cara finally learned why Chris had always used miss when he spoke to her, and not her name. His father used it for each nurse, to the female doctors, to Gian's mother, who kept watch on Marcus while they went inside, and to Cara.

Because respect is important.

Cara wanted to pay her respects and say goodbye because it was the very least she could do, after everything. Fuck anyone who thought she didn't belong there like they did, simply because she was who she was.

"Are you okay?" Gian asked as they took a seat in a middle pew.

Cara let him tuck her in closer to his side. "I am, Gian."

"But sad."

Yes, sad.

The funeral wasn't a big affair. Chris's father spoke, as did his younger brother. A friend got up to read something, as well. The priest finished it all off. Then, the mourners headed to the private graveyard to bury Chris in the cool October ground, while colorful leaves fell all around.

Gian and Cara were some of the last to leave the graveyard. Cara noticed a few men—some she recognized, like her uncle—stayed close to Gian after the graveyard cleared out.

The limo pulled up, and Gian opened the back door for Cara to climb inside.

"I have a dinner," he told her, "one I can't miss today."

Cara's brow furrowed. "You didn't say anything about that earlier."

"Came up last minute. I can't refuse, not if it'll mean peaceful streets for a while."

"Peaceful streets?"

"Chris wasn't the only man buried today," Gian said vaguely. "So, if this dinner will smooth over any possible problems with the new man in charge, I shouldn't miss it."

Cara quickly realized Gian was giving her a lot of information to take in, without actually saying a lot. She appreciated it.

"Okay, then I'll see you back—"

"*She* isn't going to show at the meet with the new Camorra boss, is she?" a voice called out from behind them. Gian tensed, scowling. Cara tried to look over his shoulder at the man making a scene over nothing. She recognized him as one of Gian's men, but she didn't know his name or how important he might be. "Wasn't bringing your *goomah* here enough, boss? We don't need to be rubbing her in their faces, too, considering."

Gian leaned in, gave Cara a quick kiss on her lips, and then closed the limo door. Or, he tried. Cara kept it open, unsure of what was about to happen.

"Don't drive off," she told the driver, not taking her eyes off Gian as he stalked toward his man.

The guy didn't even see Gian reaching inside his jacket. Or if he did, he didn't have time to react. Gian pulled his gun from within his jacket, and then *beat* the man with it. He beat him until blood spilled, and the man was unconscious on the ground. He didn't say one word while he did it. No one stepped in, either.

Then, as fast as that rage and violence had showed itself, Gian straightened to his full height, and it was gone. As though it had never been to begin with.

Cara, on the other hand, wasn't quite sure what to do.

"Would anyone—anyone at all—like to revisit this conversation?" Gian's bloodstained hands skillfully tucked the gun away. Not one man spoke up. "Good, then let's move on."

Yes, move.

That sounded like a great idea.

She closed the car door.

"Please take me home," Cara told the driver.

"When is enough going to be enough for you?"

Cara bristled at her brother's tone, and avoided looking at the laptop screen. Skype was a wonderful thing, for the most part, but not today. "Tommas, you don't—"

"I don't *what*, Cara? Know, understand, relate? Which one is it?"

"All of them!"

"I *know* you've lost your job. A job you worked incredibly hard for, and loved with every fiber of your being."

Cara tried not to show how much that comment stung. "I did lose a job I loved but I don't blame that on Gian. He wasn't the person who purposely distributed naked pictures of me, causing my boss to have to consider the ethical and moral ramifications of those images and my personal connections outside of the shelter. Gian didn't *want* that to happen, Tommas. Why would he hurt me like that or send people those photos? They were *his* private photos."

She had—at first—felt as though Gian could have done more to protect the images. She hadn't felt that he had done anything to help get those images out into the world to hurt her.

"Fine, move on from the photos," her brother said with a shake of his head, "because shit, Cara, they're just *one* thing in pile of things."

"Tommas, I didn't call you tonight to fight. I just thought you would like to see how I'm doing a couple of weeks after the accident."

"Accident?" He scoffed. "Say what it was. An *attack*. Something else that was—"

"If you say someone shooting me was Gian's fault, I am hanging up this fucking call."

"Did you do something to provoke someone into shooting you, or am I missing a whole bunch of shit?"

"He didn't pull the trigger, Tommas."

"He doesn't have to, where responsibility is concerned!"

Cara's fingers twitched to close the laptop screen. She didn't want to end the conversation this way with her brother. She knew Tommas was only expressing his concerns in the one way he currently could, and clearly, he was not doing it well.

Then, her brother said quietly, "I only want you to be happy, Cara.

Safe, happy, and *loved*. By a man who deserves to love you, and who can keep you safe while making you happy. I'm worried that you're so accustomed to coming second in his life now, that you don't even see that you do."

"Tommas, I love you."

Tommas nodded. "Yeah, I know."

"But you have no idea what you're talking about. On this, you're wrong. You're so wrong, it's sad. And sure, I know you don't have much to go on, but let me make one thing perfectly clear here. Gian puts Marcus and I first much more than anyone realizes, and those who do realize it, don't like it a whole lot. Because he shouldn't do what he does with us—he shouldn't be with us so much, or provide for us as much as he does. He shouldn't love us in public, or give us presence in his family. We're the secrets, Tommas, the dirty words in his life. His bastard son born to a *goomah* woman. He has every single reason to push us aside for his own respect and image, but he doesn't. And he *doesn't care*. We come first, even if it is to his detriment."

Tommas frowned, but said nothing.

"Frankly, I don't think even Gian realizes how often he puts us first to his own detriment. I don't think he cares either way, because this is what is right for him. He's a wonderful man, and I love him. So let's be clear here, okay."

"Okay."

"He's mine. I'm fine. I'm not leaving. Not him, this city, or this life. My son is healthy and happy, *with* his mother and father. I no longer give a shit who thinks what about me, Gian, our situation, or the rest. What I care about, is that I'm happy and my son is, too. That goes for you, too, so learn it fast. I love you but I don't have to like you if you're going to make it hard on me."

For a long while, her brother said nothing.

Cara expected that. She had always been the quiet one. Steadfastly strong, sure, but silent all the same. She didn't speak up unless necessary, and this had just been one of those things she left alone. Not anymore.

"I'm just worried about you," Tommas finally said.

"Don't be, Tommy. I am fine. I am going to keep being fine. It's what I do."

That was that.

Shortly after, Cara hung up the Skype call with her brother. Marcus was fed, fast asleep, and safe in his bed, she reminded herself. She had time to relax, and that was what she had intended to do. Instead, she had gotten into a verbal sparring match with her brother.

"He has a point, you know."

Cara jerked straight in the office chair, glancing at the doorway to find

Gian standing there. Solemn in his expression, with his suit jacket from earlier gone, his tie hanging loose over his chest, and his shirt sleeves rolled up, he looked … tired. Like his whole day had gone to hell in a handbasket, and he was just over it.

For the most part, Cara ignored the blood splatters dotting Gian's dress shirt.

"Who has a point?" she asked.

"Your brother."

Her brow furrowed. "You listened to my conversation?"

"Part of it," he admitted. "I came up on the last of it, I didn't mean to and I didn't want to interrupt. You spy on my conversations—don't pretend like you don't."

Fair point.

"And what was Tommas' point that you agree with, exactly?"

"Quite a bit of it, actually. I could do more, be more. I could do better things, be better. A better man. You deserve the kind of man he described, and so does Marcus, and yet, you're both very firmly stuck with me. Bit of a shame, *oui?* I'm sure there's someone out there who could have, and likely would have, made you a much happier woman. How fucking selfish of me to have kept you like I did, to have stolen you like I did, when you could have been someone else's everything, and you only get to be my something to the rest of the world. A fucking *shame.* I'm sorry for that, *mon ange.*"

Ouch.

That hurt.

"What did you just say?"

"Nothing," Gian said, waving it off and turning to head out of the office. "Nothing that wasn't true. I'm tired, Cara. I'll see you in bed."

Like fuck he would.

"Gian, don't walk away right now."

He kept going.

"Gian!"

Nothing.

Cara got up out of the chair, and headed after Gian, fuming and confused. She came up behind him as he shrugged off his dress shirt and tie in the hallway and tossed it into the laundry room without a care—bloodstains meant it would all need to be thrown out.

"Gian," Cara said firmly, grabbing his arm and pulling as hard as she could to turn him around to face her. "Repeat what you just said to me."

He stared at her with hard eyes and cold features.

His best defense.

Cara saw right through it.

"Your brother is right about the things he says. Maybe not in all the details, but in theory, he's *right.*"

"And didn't you hear what I said to him?"

"I heard you defending me when it's the very last thing you should be doing. I have done very little to be worthy of your loyalty, Cara. It would not be such a stretch to think you would like to have more from me, or this—whatever we are."

"We're us, Gian. And I like *us* perfectly fine."

"You like us. You like being my mistress and being seen as the dirty little secret in my life. You like being treated less than someone else, simply because you don't have my last name. You like having your child be pushed aside because—"

"You've never done any of that, and certainly not to Marcus."

"But others do. And if they haven't yet, they will in the future. Because that's inevitable, love. Don't you understand? He won't always be little, but I will always be married to someone else. As he gets older, as he becomes more present and not just a cute baby in the corner, he will become more of the awkward conversation people need to have, rather than what he is now. You don't deserve that, and neither does he, no matter what you've told yourself to believe otherwise."

"I haven't told myself anything."

"Clearly you have, or we wouldn't be having this conversation."

"*You* clearly know nothing about what goes on inside my head, Gian."

"Cara, I don't want to fight tonight. You asked what I felt was right regarding what your brother said, and I told you. There's no need for you to agree or disagree, or talk for hours on end about it. It's just an opinion."

"It's also the wrong one."

"Cara—"

"It's the wrong one!"

Gian scrubbed his hand down his face, sighing. "Just … let's have this conversation tomorrow. Okay?"

"No. Not okay."

"Well, I'm done for tonight."

With that, Gian turned on his heel and headed down the hallway again. Cara didn't even think before going after him once more. This time, she didn't bother to grab him in an attempt to stop him, but rather, scooted around his side and came up in front of him. She slammed a single palm into his chest with enough force to make her hand sting *and* make him come to a full stop with narrowed eyes.

"We're *not* done," Cara said calmly, "not until I say we are, Gian."

"Come on, *mon ange.*"

"I'm so fucking sorry that *you* have had to tell yourself some kind of shit to justify why you think I'm still here. I'm sorry you must have thought I was going to run at some point, because maybe that's just what you think I do. I'm sorry you don't think I'm a strong enough woman, or good enough, to do this with you, but I am. I have always been, Gian. And do you want to know the one thing I have never needed to know I was that woman?"

"Try me."

"For you to tell me. I don't need you to tell me anything. Not that you love me, or our son. Not that you'll be there, even when being here only digs your holes deeper elsewhere. I don't need you to tell me how you struggle, or that you worry about me, or that your biggest fear is that in thirty years, we're going to be just like your grandfather and his mistress. Locked away in a high-rise penthouse, hiding from the rest of the world on weekends, because we're so wrong and bad and isn't that just a fucking *shame*. Isn't it a fucking shame that you've got a mistress, so nobody talks about it, because I'll be your secret that's not really a secret?"

"I will *never* be that woman," Cara continued, "because you'll never be that man, Gian. I am not the one between us who needs to figure that out. What do you want to do? What do you need me to make you do so that you feel justified in what you think you've done to me? Do you want me to put you on your knees, Gian? Crawl across the floor to me, with your head low and your eyes down because you don't even deserve to look at me. Is that it? Do you want me to make you beg every time you come near me, or apologize again when I let you in close enough to touch me? Do you need to be *forgiven*, is that it?"

Gian's lips flattened into a grim line, but he stayed quiet.

Cara didn't really need him to talk.

"If that is what you're waiting for, Gian, you're going to wait a long damn time," Cara said, never once looking away from his gaze. There, she'd always found his heart and soul. He couldn't hide it staring back at her. "The things I needed to forgive you for, I already did. It's not my responsibility to forgive you for things you manifest all on your own, nor is it my job to tell you I already forgave you for the things you *did* do. I didn't do that for you, I did it for me. Because I love you. I have always loved you. I always will."

She poked him hard in the middle of his naked chest.

"And *that* is the end of the discussion, Gian, because I said so, not you."

"Well," Gian said gruffly, his hand coming up to enclose Cara's finger still poking his chest, "it's certainly the end of *this* discussion. I'm starting to think we need to have an entirely different one altogether, considering your mood."

"And what is that? Because there's nothing else for us to say about it."

He lowered her hand in his own. "There's lots to say, Cara. But you're right, and I'm sorry."

"I'm right?"

"About everything. All of it. Every single word you said is true. It's simply not a discussion I wanted to have because I felt a certain way about it all. Seems you didn't feel the way I thought you would, anyway. Much like with everything else about you and me, but that's fine, too. You're *right*, Cara. You don't owe me a thing, except what you want to give me."

She nodded. "Okay. And this *other* discussion?"

"Well ... that's entirely about us, too, *amore*."

"What is it?"

He stepped closer, taking her cheeks in his warm palms and making her look up at him. "Sometimes I do forget how incredible you are, Cara. Not because you're not showing it—you always show it. I just get used to not needing to do everything for you, because you've got it handled. Or not telling you the same things over and over, because you don't need to hear me say them. I forget sometimes how strong, resilient, and amazing you are. And that is a shame."

"Oh?"

"But I don't forget for one fucking second that you're mine, *mon ange*. I will never, ever forget that."

"You shouldn't," she said, barely above a breath. "I've always been yours, Gian."

"Maybe, but it is one of those things we sometimes need to be reminded about. Kind of like now."

Cara was going to ask what Gian meant, but found she didn't have to as his hands pulled her forward, and his mouth crashed down on hers. Her lips melded with his in a familiar battle—one she hadn't realized she had been missing. His tongue teased the seam of her mouth before she allowed him in to war with her own. There was nothing sweet or innocent about the kiss. Each stroke of his lips flamed a fire that had been dormant in Cara for a long while.

It wasn't Gian's fault on that end. The last time they had been intimate was shortly before Marcus's birth, and after that, it just hadn't been possible. She had passed her six-week waiting period to heal, and her doctor had given the okay to resume those activities, but Cara just ... hadn't thought about it.

Gian didn't give her a reason to. She was tired sometimes, and had other things to focus on. He never pushed, never asked or demanded anything unless *she* brought it up.

And good God, she was suddenly reminded why it was better when Gian demanded anything from her at all. It was better because he only had to speak, or touch her, and her whole body lit up like a fucking firework.

"Yep," Cara mumbled as her back hit the hallway wall. "Definitely missed this."

Gian's hot mouth traveled down over her throat, his hands skimming up under the silk nightie she wore to find her panties and pull them down roughly. *"Get these off right now, Cara."*

"Jesus, you're impatient."

"You will find out exactly why in less than thirty seconds, I guarantee it."

Oh, she already knew.

Cara could feel just how impatient he was, considering the hard length of his erection was digging into her thigh as he pinned her harder to the wall. "The bedroom is like two doors down, Gian."

"So?"

Up went her silk nightie.

She didn't see where it fell.

"Gian."

His response to her warning was the rattle of his belt buckle before his pants fell down to the floor, and his boxer-briefs followed. He stepped out of the items without even missing a beat or taking his hands off her body.

"The baby is sleeping almost right across the—"

His hot breath pulsed against the skin of her throat, wicked and promising. "You can, can't you?"

"Yes."

"You want this, don't you?" he grunted into her neck, his fingers sliding between her thighs to tease her sex. "You're so wet already."

Cara let out a breathless laugh. *"Yes."*

"Then shut up and let me fuck you, Cara."

That was that.

Gian's hands found the backs of her thighs, and his fingers dug in deliciously deep, holding her tight. He lifted her legs first, forcing Cara to find a very careful balance between his hard body and the wall at her back. His sinful mouth found hers for that first hard, deep thrust. It took her fucking breath away.

She'd forgotten how her body stretched for him. She'd forgotten the heat that tangled through her blood as she adjusted to his size and how full she always felt with him inside of her pussy. She certainly hadn't expected it to be damn near the same as it had been before, but it *was*, and Jesus, Cara was spun.

He was not easy with her, each flex of his hips coming harder than the last until the pace between them was simply *brutal*. She was sure his fingerprints were going to be permanently embedded into the back of her thighs, but she couldn't find it in herself to care.

"You can do better than that, *Tesoro*," he taunted when she didn't beg loud enough. And then he turned right around and uttered, "Fucking take it, Cara," through clenched teeth, while his hand found its favorite spot. Her throat.

Well, her favorite spot, too.

Cara thought, if it were possible, her body simply didn't have limits where Gian was concerned. She needed his rough hands, his dirty mouth, and the way he choked her to a sweet, blissful finish. She needed it every single time, however she could get it.

Like a damn drug.

Her fingernails raked lines over the backs of his shoulders when that beautiful release finally came flooding through her, hot and heavy. She felt him shudder—from the pain or his own orgasm, she wasn't sure.

But she heard his breath catch against her throat, and his fingers loosened on her throat as they trembled, and she knew then, anyway. His final two thrusts came harder, before his whole body tensed and she felt his release pulse inside her body.

Sweaty, breathless, and content, Cara hummed a pleased, happy sound as tremors worked their way up her spine and the orgasm faded. Gian took a slight bit longer to catch his breath, but that could have just been because he took his time dotting Cara's neck, cheek, and mouth with soft, sweet kisses all over again.

"Careful," he murmured as he pulled from her body and let her down to the floor. "Easy, Cara."

She laughed quietly. "Easy would have been the bed."

"That's no fun."

"It is, too."

Gian kissed her again, firmer that time. "I will give you whatever you want in bed in the morning, I promise."

Cara rubbed her thighs together, acutely aware of the sticky fluids there. "You made a mess."

"*We* did."

"Same difference."

"I should have grabbed a condom," he admitted.

Cara ran her fingers through his hair. "It's all right. I started the pill again, anyway. Though, it won't be effective for another two weeks."

Gian rolled his eyes upward, then glanced down the hall at the baby's closed bedroom door. "Right, the pill. The thing that didn't stop Marcus from making his way into being at all."

She patted his cheek with a wink. "There's other ways, Gian. Besides, Marcus is wonderful, and I don't regret him for a minute."

"I said nothing about regret and I didn't say I wanted to prevent anything, Cara. I *am* a Catholic, remember? Even if I'm not a very fucking good one in almost every other aspect."

Cara's gaze shot up to Gian's, only to find his amusement lighting up his handsome features. "Is that so?"

"We never talked kids, love."

"We just had one."

"Exactly." Gian scooped Cara up into a bridal embrace, walking them toward the bedroom as she snuggled in closer to his warmth and familiar scent. "I want a whole army of kids."

"Wow."

"Boys, preferably."

"You don't really get to pick, Gian."

"A baseball team, or a half of one."

"You're killing me," Cara said, shaking her head.

"Someday, Cara."

She smiled.

Maybe.

Chapter 17

It was decided.

The best sight in the morning was Cara on her knees, face buried into a pillow to muffle her sounds, while Gian got a mouthful of her cunt from behind, and stuffed her ass full of his fingers. He loved the way her body trembled with the need for release, and how sweat had slicked up her spine from being teased over and over.

Crazy red hair.

Flushed skin.

Sweet pussy.

Wild eyes met his over her shoulder, when he added a third finger to Cara's ass, and replaced his mouth on her cunt with just the pad of his fingertip massaging her clit. It was the way her hips swayed and her muscles contracted that drove him crazy. She was so fucking tight around him, and he couldn't fucking wait to get his cock feeling that, too. She always begged so well when something was filling her ass.

Yes, the very best.

"You want to come so badly, don't you?" Gian taunted Cara, kissing her lower back between each word.

Her reply came out breathless and high—so very pretty and strained. "You know I do, Gian. *Please.*"

"My greedy girl. So fucking needy. Come, then."

His mouth was back between her thighs in a heartbeat, sucking hard on her clit while his fingers pounded deeper into her ass to stretch her open. She loved that, he knew, though it had been a while. He was going to make sure it wasn't as long between this time and the next time.

Cara's cries turned the sweetest kind of desperate, and then muffled into the pillow as her body tensed all over. Gian chose not to complain about being unable to hear her coming, but only because he got to taste it, instead.

And sweet Jesus, she tasted heavenly when she came.

Like his own personal tart candy.

Gian had just gotten his cock lubed up, had a fistful of Cara's hair wrapped tight around his hand, when familiar soft cries broke through his lustful haze. A baby's cries, he realized. It took Gian far too long to realize it was *his* baby that was crying through the monitor on the nightstand.

Cara laughed when he stiffened above her and let go of her hair. Turning over, she leaned up and kissed him hard on his slack lips—grinning in a know-it-all sort of way. "Sorry, Gian. Raincheck on that for tonight. Either learn to fuck faster, or stop demanding I be so loud."

"But ... but ..." He looked down at his fully erect, lubed cock that was aching. "But ..."

He *really* needed to fucking come now.

Cara's palm patted him square in the middle of his forehead, as though she were stamping something there with her hand. "Parents call that being cock-blocked. Welcome to the club."

"Cara!" Gian shouted over his shoulder as she headed for the bedroom door. She only shrugged in response, slipping on a nightie and then a robe to fully cover up. "That's not fair at all, *mon ange!*"

"Shower, and take care of it yourself, I guess."

Holy sweet baby Jesus!

"I don't *need* to take care of it myself! Cara, I haven't taken care of myself in a decade, for fuck's sake."

Cara's head popped back in the doorway. "Seems you do, actually. No better time to get reacquainted."

She was *loving* this.

Gian knew he was bested—by a baby *and* his lover, it seemed. He could have waited, of course. Marcus liked to sleep in the mornings after his feedings, and Gian could always drag Cara back to bed and punish her for her smartass remarks, *plus* relieve himself in the process. It sounded like a good idea, except his fucking balls hurt like hell all of the sudden.

And that wasn't good at all.

Gian was a ten-minute kind of morning man. Ten minutes was all he needed to jump in the shower, get dressed, and head out for the day. It was a routine he had perfected over the years. That day, it failed him entirely. It took him thirty minutes just to get through a goddamn shower, and while he got the job done, he hated every fucking second of it.

Cara was right.

He was going to have to learn to keep her quiet, or settle with a faster fucking.

He liked neither of those options.

All dressed and ready for his day—albeit in a slightly shittier mood than he suspected he would have been, had he gotten to be balls deep in Cara before seven AM—Gian headed for the kitchen. His walk slowed as voices filtered down the back hall, and it took him all of three seconds to go from shit mood to *rage.*

"Thank you for letting us up to talk, Miss Rossi."

"Yes, Gian was never so kind, unless we had a warrant," Detective Seeley added with a chuckle.

"I didn't actually let *you* up," Cara replied coolly. "I was told I had guests and allowed entrance without asking for details. Not the same thing. My mistake. Don't think it'll happen again."

"Sure, well—"

"What do you want at seven-thirty in the morning?"

Gian held back from entering the kitchen, instead lingering out of sight in the hallway. There, he could still hear the conversation, but the detectives wouldn't know he was within hearing distance. Shit, he didn't know if they were aware of his presence in the penthouse at all.

"How long have you been living here, again?" Detective Seeley asked.

"I've *owned* the penthouse for a couple of months or so. Why?"

"Curious. Where is Gian this morning?"

Cara said nothing.

The detective chuckled. "You're not sure or he's with his wife?"

Gian stiffened, anger flooding him all over again. Using his wife to annoy, offend, or bother Cara in any way just seemed like a prick move on the man's part.

"Where Gian is can't be any more or less important than whatever the fuck you want," Cara replied sweetly.

"Little ears are listening, Miss Rossi."

"I'm sure my son will hear worse."

"With a mob boss for a father, I would tend to agree."

Another dig.

Cara only laughed. "Right. Moving on. What do you want, or again, you can leave. Mornings are busy with a baby, as I'm sure you know."

"We've gone over some of your interviews and statements with police after the latest attack, and wanted to go through other details with you that you may not have been aware of. Or rather, some suspicions we have that may be of interest to you, where Gian is concerned."

"I'm sure they won't concern me at all," Cara said flippantly, "but you can try."

"Never say never," Seeley replied all too cheerfully. "Shorty before your attack, you found yourself in a bit of an awkward situation, didn't you?"

"I'm not sure what you mean."

"Photos of you were distributed. See, the shelter reported the photos, as the owner assumed you too would be opening an investigation into such a matter."

Gian swore he could feel Cara's tension when she said, "I don't know exactly what kind of legal action I could have taken for those, but I assure you whatever the penalty, it would not have fit the crime or made me feel any better."

"Are you aware that Gian's father-in-law was the person to distribute those photographs?"

No, Cara was not.

Because Gian hadn't told her.

Fuck.

Cara handled the news with grace. "I had not known."

"I suppose you're also unaware that the man is also now dead," Seeley said quieter.

"I did know that but only because his funeral was plastered in the news. Seems to be a big thing in the city lately—organized crime, I mean. I'm not sure why the man's death should matter to me, though."

"You don't think the two are connected?"

"I—"

"You're not that stupid, are you?" the other detective interrupted. "Someone distributes racy, compromising photographs of you that effectively ruins you, and suddenly they show up dead."

"Again," Cara drawled, "I'm not sure why the man's death should matter to me. I wasn't aware he distributed the pictures. I didn't know him at all."

"Seems he knew you."

"Well, his daughter might," Cara replied carefully.

"She was the one who had been given the photographs in the first place," Seeley said as though the information were nothing. "All though, clearly she used the items for a purpose we did not intend, after pulling the files from Gian's phone."

It wasn't nothing to Gian.

It was *everything*.

He hadn't considered Elena having anything to do with the photos of Cara being distributed, because he'd *known* without question she hadn't had his phone. At least, not long enough to get inside the device. He even locked his fucking bedroom door when he was forced to sleep at the mansion.

Cara was quiet for a long while before she said, "You pulled my photos from Gian's phone."

"His first arrest included warrants for electronic devices, and we found some images. He was arrested again after the shooting at the shelter—"

"All charges dropped," Cara interjected with heat in her tone, "and for good reason."

"Nonetheless, he was taken into custody again and the phone was removed from his person. I can't help if a few image files were removed from the device at that time, too."

"That's fucking illegal! How *dare* you?"

Marcus whined at his mother's high shriek.

"It's standard procedure in a case like that for any electronics on a detainee to be searched," the detective said, "which is exactly what happened."

"But not for you to remove images, thank you very much. Not to mention, *my* images. And what business is it of yours—what effect would it have on Gian's previous arrest or the arrest after the shooting—to take my private photos and … why in the hell would you take *my* fucking photos off his phone like that?"

"We had proof he was in a relationship with you, clearly."

"But *why*? What did you need that information for and what good would it do you? It wasn't exactly a goddamn secret. Those images did nothing but hurt me, and other people. That was it—nothing more."

Gian knew exactly why.

He had never considered that it was the detectives who had removed his photos of Cara from his phone. Only because, like Cara, there was no real benefit to doing so for the police. He didn't use his phone to do any real business that would get him in trouble, and so he had never had an issue with handing the device over to cops during his arrests.

Clearly that had been a mistake.

While taking more photos off his phone after the shelter shooting had been … borderline illegal, it wouldn't matter if the detectives never intended to use those images as pieces of evidence they needed to legally obtain. It would only matter to *them* if the images could help them in some way.

Like for someone on the inside of Gian's life.

Someone they could hurt.

Someone they could use.

Perhaps, someone they were already using.

Elena had always liked her tit for tat. She gave something, she expected something back. It was always that way, no matter who she was dealing with.

Gian finally found his rat.

The fucking *cunt*.

"You need to leave," Cara said firmly, bringing Gian from his thoughts. "Now."

"We aren't finished talking quite yet, Miss Rossi. We thought this information might—"

"What, sway my opinion on Gian? You do realize I consented to those photos, I thoroughly enjoyed having my hair pulled, ass spanked, and his cum painted up and down my body in each and every one. I *liked* when he got the camera out to play. What I don't like, is that you assume telling me about his recklessness with the phone, or the way you came about the images, should affect my opinion on him. And as far as his father-in-law, may the man rot in pieces. I bet he got exactly what he deserved, and while I am sure you thought suggesting Gian did that would frighten me, it doesn't bother me a bit. Get out, now."

Gian waited in the hallway until the penthouse was quiet again, except for Cara's soothing hums to the baby in the kitchen. It was as though the meeting hadn't happened at all, but she still looked to him with sad, knowing eyes when he came out of his hiding spot.

He dropped a quick kiss to her forehead, lingering there for as long as he could, and then giving one to his son's head, too.

"I have to head out," he said.

Business like this couldn't wait.

Cara nodded, questioning in her gaze but never letting the words fly out of her mouth. "Okay. I love you, Gian."

He kissed her again. "Always, *mon ange*."

The Guzzi mansion was much quieter than Gian expected it to be for a weekday. He found there was no doorman waiting to take his coat and keys, as usual, and even the maid was nowhere to be seen. It rubbed him the wrong way, if only because he knew how much Elena liked to be attended. She liked being served as though she were a queen in her big castle. He hadn't minded indulging her nonsense, if it kept her happy and out of his hair.

Clearly, he had overlooked too much about his wife.

He had been stupid.

He should have killed her long ago.

Gian chose not to question the lack of people in the mansion, only because it benefitted him. He didn't need to demand someone get out, and no one would even know he had been there. A clean job was the best kind of job, after all.

It took Gian far too long to find Elena in the mansion, because she wasn't inside at all. He found her sitting outside, with her back turned to him, as she sat on a wicker chair and overlooked the back property. An entire empty bottle of wine rested on its side at her feet, a blanket spilling around her frame in the wicker chair that she was using to cover up with.

"Elena," Gian called quietly, already spinning the silencer into the barrel of his gun.

Easy.

Fast.

Simple.

He didn't even care about clean up, or the trouble that might come his way for this. It just needed to be done. Some things were just better *done*.

"Elena," he said again when his wife didn't respond.

Her shoulders moved slightly, and her head bobbed a bit, but that was all the response his wife gave to the call of her name. *But*, it did mean she could hear him.

"Your father warned me and I should have listened," Gian said. "He told me women like you know exactly what you're doing, even when everything says you don't know at all. You needed a short leash, he said. I thought, *why*. I give her everything she wants because she doesn't want me, so why should I worry about how far she goes? I should have *listened*, Elena."

Unsurprisingly, his wife didn't talk or move.

Gian took another couple steps across the large back deck, closer to her position. "The only thing you ever wanted was to be free, wasn't it? Something I couldn't give you, but by no fault of my own. It was your games—*your* schemes—that got us here, and you thought you could play your way out of them again. Get me locked up for good, maybe. File a divorce then, when it couldn't be contested and it wouldn't matter anyway. You would have it all and the rest wouldn't make a fucking difference."

Still, he got no response.

Elena's arm slipped off the arm of the wicker chair, falling out from beneath the blanket. Maybe it was the ashen tone of her skin, or the slackness in her opened hand, but Gian knew right then that something was very wrong.

He clicked the safety on his gun, and tucked it away, crossing the space between him and his wife in three short strides. He came around the front of the chair, already bending down to grab her by the shoulders.

Elena was conscious, but barely.

Glassy-eyed.

Slack-mouthed.

Discolored lips.

Gian's hands skipped to her face, and he tipped her head up to make her dazed gaze lock on his. Still, her eyes wavered, flickering between whatever she was seeing and whatever was just beyond her reach. She was cold to the touch, but not quite a dead-cold. Her breathing turned shallower with each inhale and no matter how high Gian tipped her head, he couldn't seem to clear her passageways.

"What did you do?" he demanded.

She smiled, chilling and fleeting. "This is even better, you get to be here. It doesn't hurt me at all, but it will for you."

What?

On her lap, two opened prescription bottles lay empty.

Gian's gaze darted back to the ashy face of his wife. "Elena, what did you do?"

"He'd have f-forgiven me for everything," Elena said, her voice barely breaking a whisper, "but not for what I did to you. He wouldn't have forgiven me for hurting you—I had to make you hurt him instead. Don't you see?"

"Who?" Gian demanded, holding her face tighter. "*Who*, Elena? Your father?"

What difference would that make, now?

Gabriel was *dead.*

She shook her head, though it was weak and faint, her eyes glassier than ever. "No."

"Who?"

"And if I can't be happy, Gian, then neither can you. *Neither can you.* I'll take it all away—all of them."

He swore he watched the life drain out of her eyes in that moment—how death crept in around her pupils, and darkened them for good. She almost felt colder in his hands in that moment, if it were possible. Perhaps it should have made him relieved, as his problem was gone, and she had done it to herself, but he only felt empty.

And lost.

Because *who.*

Who had she meant?

The empty prescription bottles clanged to the deck, and Gian broke out of his daze. He picked one up, just to look at it and see what exactly Elena had used to end her life. The strong painkiller was not what caught his attention first—it was the name written on the label, to whom the prescription had actually been prescribed.

Domenic Guzzi.

Two bottles.

Both empty.

Both Dom's.

Gian couldn't move; he couldn't take in air.

His brother wouldn't ...

Couldn't ...

Gian only came out of his stupor when he heard a faint buzzing coming from somewhere beneath the blanket covering Elena's body. He found her phone tucked into her side, and was surprised to find the device unlocked. A quick check confirmed his worst fucking fears.

A constant stream of incoming messages—each getting progressively more panicked and desperate than the last—from Domenic, which had started just an hour before. Several calls, one that was picked up, and the rest had not been. Gian scrolled up through the new messages to find what Elena had started messaging to Dom just an hour before.

He's never going to let me go.
He's got her, anyway.
I'm done.
This is it, Dom.
I love you.
Don't blame yourself.
It was him.
He did this to us.

And to top it off, she had even texted a picture of the empty pill bottles. Her intent had been clear, and even right up until the bitter end, she couldn't help herself.

Elena had to manipulate.

She had to hurt someone.

Elena's final words to Gian made a hell of a lot more sense when Domenic's final text came in. *He'll never be happy, either, not after today.*

Even in her death, Elena was selfish to those who had either cared, loved, or protected her in some way. Gian wasn't surprised at all.

This also wasn't the time for him to wonder about it. Something in his brother's last message told him that he had far more pressing matters to deal with. Unfortunately, it looked like Dom might have a few minutes ahead of him.

It'd been a while since Gian prayed.

It still felt like breathing.

Chapter 18

Cara had just set a sleeping Marcus into his wicker moses basket when she heard the familiar ding of the penthouse elevator ringing out in the hallway. She figured it was probably just Gian coming back, considering how long he had already been gone. Setting the wicker basket on the middle of her bed, where the baby was safe, she headed for the attached bathroom, slipping out of her robe as she went.

A hot, nearly-overfilled bubble bath was waiting.

After her morning, she deserved it.

"Cara?"

Shit.

Apparently, the bath was going to have to wait.

She had wrongly assumed the person coming into the penthouse was Gian. It sounded like Domenic. She quickly shrugged her robe back on and left the bedroom, tying the sash securely at her waist as she rounded the first corner leading out of the hallway.

"Cara, are you home?"

The buzzing of her cell phone echoed from the bedroom—she always put the ringer on silent when Marcus was sleeping. Surely, Dom could wait a second.

Cara nearly spun back around to go to the buzzing phone, but it stopped. Then, it started right back up again.

What the fuck?

"Yeah, just give me a second," Cara called back.

"Gian here?"

"No, he had something come up this morning." Cara was one step away from reentering her bedroom when Dom appeared at the end of the hallway. "I'll be right out. Did something happen?"

Dom shrugged. "Nothing you need to worry about."

Her heart stopped for a split second. "But something did?"

He didn't answer. In the bedroom, her phone continued buzzing away. Persistent and wanting her attention, clearly.

"Let me grab my phone," Cara said to Dom, "before it wakes up the baby."

Dom's strange, cold expression didn't change a bit, but he waved her off anyway. Cara didn't think it was entirely odd, considering Gian's brother was one of the few people she hadn't gotten close enough to that she considered him a friend of sorts. The man was always respectful and polite, but he didn't go out of his way to be friendly with her at all.

She hadn't minded. She understood some people—some of Gian's men or family—wouldn't be comfortable with her or her relationship.

Cara turned her back to Dom and headed into the bedroom, only to realize that was probably the biggest mistake of her life. She hadn't even taken a single step inside the room, before Dom was suddenly behind her. For such a big man, Cara barely heard him make a sound.

He had a fistful of her hair and was dragging her to the floor in an instant. The pain that radiated through her scalp and down her spine shot through her nervous system like a thousand needles. Dom didn't seem to mind her first struggle, easily overpowering Cara with his size, forcing her to her back, and then smashing her head into the floor.

Her tears were already starting to form in her pain and confusion. Those emotions were nothing compared to her *fear*. She had done nothing to Dom, nothing to justify his fists raining down on her body, or his mocking laughter as she begged for him to stop.

"Why are you doing this?"

"Don't talk," he snarled.

Why?

What?

While Cara had never felt close to Dom, or even friendly with him, the man above her now was not one she had ever seen before. It was like his entire face had changed, his expression—nearly dead looking—was one of a monster.

It was as though he wasn't seeing *her* at all. It was as though his eyes weren't looking at the mother of his nephew, or a woman who had never spoken badly about him or any of his family. He didn't care who she was, because she was just *something* to deal with.

Something to dispose of.

Her initial shock was quickly overcome by the scream she released. A scream that woke her sleeping baby.

Marcus's wail filled the bedroom. Cara's heart dropped into her stomach as Dom's next hit hesitated, and he glanced up at the bed, like he was just realizing then that the baby was in the room, too. And like with her, he didn't look at the small wicker basket with the familiarity of a man looking at something he *should* have cared for, on some level.

Cara's panic ran into overdrive just like that. She had been far too shocked and unsure before to really react, though she had tried stupidly to get out of the way of the slaps and punches. Now, with a single look at a man who she thought might kill her son for a reason she didn't understand, desperation really kicked in.

It kicked in fucking *hard.*

The taste of blood bloomed in her mouth, and pain radiated from her face to her chest, but Cara didn't care about any of it. All she heard was her crying son, and the racing beat of her heart. Her struggle under the weight of Dom increased and she struck out at him. All she had to fight with was her hands, her fingernails. But she used them the best she could, punching Dom as hard as she could and feeling her knuckles crack from the impact of busting his mouth. Her fingernails dug deep into his face, scoring lines from his eyes to his lips as she bucked and kicked out her legs in an attempt to gain some kind of traction.

"Don't fucking fight," she heard him snarl above her.

Cara didn't listen.

She wasn't sure how she possibly could.

"He couldn't just *let her be,*" Dom howled as his hands enclosed Cara's throat. He squeezed hard, taking away her air and making her lungs burn. "He'd never let her be happy, not like *he* wanted to be. Fuck him, and fuck you."

Blood rushed Cara's ears. Her vision blurred. Her lips tingled with numbness, like the rest of her extremities. She swore she felt her heart slow.

She wasn't sure how it was possible, but it was as though the world slowed down all around her in those moments. It made her far more painfully aware of the fact she was about to lose her life, and there was nothing she could do about it.

"Please don't hurt the baby," Cara managed to get out with what last bit of breath she had left. "Please—"

"Shut the fuck up! Shut up, shut up, *shut up!*"

Somewhere in the back of Cara's hazy consciousness, she was sure that she heard a ding echo through the penthouse. Not that it mattered, because Cara didn't even have the energy to keep her eyes open any longer, never mind pick up her fists to keep fighting.

Please don't hurt my Marcus.

Please don't hurt my baby.

I'm sorry for whatever I did, but don't hurt him.

She wasn't sure if she said those words out loud, but she thought them. Her mind screamed them until her throat felt raw and bloody, but that could have just been from the choking, too.

The happiest memory Cara could think of in that moment was waking up in the hospital the first night after Marcus was born, to find Gian singing a French lullaby to their son. She didn't know he could sing at all, and he hadn't noticed her awake. It was the sweetest sight—proof in an instant that no matter what, he was going to love his child.

And perhaps if one of them could make it out of this alive, she would want it to be Marcus.

He would always have his father.

Crack.

The loud sound accompanied a sudden intake of air into Cara's lungs. Her eyes widened at the absolute agony it caused for her to breathe in, but all she saw above her was the falling form of Dom coming at her. She couldn't even find the strength to move out of the damn way.

"Shit, Cara, just a second, baby. I got you."

That voice … it was so beautifully, wonderfully familiar.

She barely moved at all as Dom's dead weight was shoved off her. She clutched at her throat, taking in gulps of air. It didn't really help.

"Look at me," she heard the man demand. "Let me see your eyes. Don't take in such big breaths."

She couldn't focus on the blurry image above her, her pupils struggling to form the shapes it needed. Careful hands touched her face, and that hurt, too.

"Christ, *mon ange*, look at your face. Try to calm down and focus."

Cara did, but it didn't help. "My baby … get my baby, please."

"Shh. Marcus is fine, just angry."

"*Get my baby!*"

"Okay, okay."

In the time it took for Cara to smell the sweet scent of her child and have him in her weak arms, her vision had cleared enough for her to see again.

Gian.

He sat across from her, his gaze wary, and his hands outstretched to take her into his embrace when she was ready to move. She only shook her head, not wanting anything to touch her or her child in that moment. He checked her over from afar as she soothed Marcus in a daze.

"Don't look at it," Gian said when Cara glanced to the side at Dom's body.

The back of his head was blown apart.

Blood was pooling across her bedroom floor.

"I don't know what just happened," Cara whispered.

"He was going to take you away from me."

"But why?"

"Because he thought I took Elena," Gian said.

Cara didn't entirely understand.

She didn't think it was all that important.

Once again, the familiar ding of the elevator rang through the penthouse. Cara's frantic gaze darted to Gian, but he looked a hell of a lot calmer about an unknown *someone* coming into their place than she did.

"Calm down, it's probably just—"

"Boss!"

"Stephan," Gian finished with a sigh.

"*Boss?*"

"In the fucking bedroom, Stephan." Gian held his arms out to Cara once more. "I know you're scared and hurting, but I would really like to hold you right now, *mon ange.* Please."

Her skittish nod sent him moving fast across the floor. She felt better the second she didn't feel anything but him. His gentle fingers skimmed over her face, and through the tangles of her hair. He looked at the marks on her neck, muttered about a busted vessel in her eye, and mentioned a doctor that would come in and look her and the baby over once they had the mess cleaned up.

Cara didn't care, as long as Marcus was still happy in her arms and Gian was there.

"Holy shit," Stephan said from the doorway. "How did you make it here before me? I was closer by fifteen minutes, at least."

Gian shrugged, but didn't let go of Cara. "I drive fast."

"Chris always said you drove like a bat out of hell, boss."

"He understated it," Gian said deadpan. "This needs to go away, Stephan. This mess—the body. It needs to be gone, it can't be found."

Cara chose not to ask about that, either.

"I can do that," Stephan answered.

That was that.

Cara found Gian sitting on the middle of their bedroom floor, his suit jacket discarded, and his tie hanging loosely around his neck. He sat in the same spot Domenic had damn near killed her, and then subsequently lost his own life. Gian fiddled with his finger, and as Cara came closer, she realized he was spinning the wedding band around and around the digit. She rarely saw him wear the piece of jewelry—he said he didn't like it, and only put it on when necessary.

She supposed today would have been one of those necessary days.

Elena's funeral.

The last two weeks had been especially trying for Gian, she knew. Perhaps had it been any other man he'd killed, and not his brother, the heavy weight he carried around wouldn't be so present and obvious. She had gone along with him when he chose to tell his mother and father that Domenic would not be coming home ever again. Gian hadn't needed to do that, because as far as Cara knew, by Gian's request, Stephan had taken care of the body so that it wouldn't be found. As sad as it would have been for Gian's parents to realize something had happened and not have answers, Gian was not required to give one.

Yet, he had.

And the *sound.*

Oh, God.

The sound of Celeste Guzzi's heartache still resounded in Cara's mind. It was as though the woman's whole world had just fallen apart entirely. It had been a tug of war in the mother's eyes as she listened to Gian explain and apologize. Cara did not think she was as good of a woman as Celeste seemed to be in the moments that followed. A woman who faced the reasons *why*, and forgave all the same. A woman who loved a murdered child, and the child who had done the killing.

Gian's father, on the other hand, had not been so understanding. *Coward. Fool. Your fault. You did this. And for what, Gian, for a whore?*

Cara would never forget those words.

She suspected that neither would Gian.

"Gian?" Cara asked quietly.

He didn't look up at her, but his fidgeting stopped. "Hey, *mon ange.*"

"I didn't see where you went when you came in the penthouse."

"I needed a second."

"For what?"

Gian let out a heavy breath. "To think. Alone, for a while."

"I can let you—"

"No, don't go." He caught her wrist in a snug grip, and tugged her down. She sat opposite to him on the floor as his ring spinning started up again. "Last time to take it off."

Gian said that with a soft smile and a shrug.

"Then why haven't you?"

"A part of me thinks it's not real. As much as I hate this ring, I don't hate what it means, Cara. I just hated who it tied me to and how it chained me. It felt like it was choking me every time I had to put it on. I'm worried, that's all."

"About what, Gian?"

"That maybe the way this one has always felt will taint the way the next one feels."

Oh.

"We don't need to be worrying about that right now," Cara whispered, reaching out to stroke Gian's tense lines away on his face. "You know that, right?"

"I'm a boss. A boss needs—"

"To be happy. To take some time. To manage a family and his organization. To be a dad. To be my lover. To be a son. Have you ever taken the time *just to be*, Gian?"

"I don't have that kind of time, Cara, not in my position."

"And who the fuck is going to tell you what you should and shouldn't do for you at the moment, Gian? Who is going to tell you *anything*? You got one thing right—you're the boss, not anyone else."

It took Gian nearly an entire silent minute before he said, "But I do want to marry you. I have wanted to marry you since the moment I knew I loved you, *mon ange*."

"And someday, you can ask. Today doesn't have to be that day and neither does tomorrow."

He laughed. "That's quite a way to leave me hanging."

"You have to ask someday, Gian, that's all."

Gian's gaze dropped. "I found out some things today—coroner's report came in, and I went down after the funeral to go over it."

"All right."

"Elena was pregnant, maybe with Dom's kid, I'm not sure. I suspect it was. They had some tissue to test against my DNA, if I wanted—they suspect me of being the father. Not possible, but I didn't correct them. They don't need it on record that I wasn't the father of the child because it'll just give them something to look into, so I didn't ask for testing to be done. As it was, I deleted the messages, calls, and Dom's contact off her phone before I left the mansion that day. I took the pill bottles with his name on it. I knew I was going to kill him, and I was still trying to protect him. I did it again today. I realized I wasn't even mad at Dom for what he did with her, or for falling into her trap. I was him once, too. I'm pissed because of what came of it, because of what he did, but not for her. I miss my brother, but not the thing she turned him into."

"Anything else in the report?"

Gian shrugged. "Toxicology said there was a significant amount of prescription opiate use going back at least two years. It explained why they found bottles of painkillers with her name on it, and the ones I found and took with Dom's name on them. Doctor shopping, likely. She hid that well."

"Addicts sometimes do. High-functioning ones, anyway."

"She was at least four months along in the pregnancy, Cara, so she had to know."

Cara sighed. "I would think so."

"That day I found her, I thought she was selfish," he admitted, "because of what she did to Dom, something that was only meant to hurt me. She couldn't help herself, clearly, she had to manipulate and play her games even at the end."

"So?"

"So, then I learn she's pregnant, too, and it just verified those thoughts. I don't feel so awful for thinking them, now. I don't feel as bad for what she did, because I don't think it was ever about me. It was always about her, that's just who she was."

"It's done now, Gian," Cara said.

He nodded. "I was wrong when I told you freedom was always weightless. Do you remember that?"

"Of course. I remember everything you've ever told me."

"Sometimes freedom feels heavy, too. Like when you don't know what to do with it."

Cara pushed up from her backside to rest on her knees. She leaned forward and kissed Gian softly on his mouth, feeling his lips grow into a sensual smile the longer she held him there. "You've got all the time in the world to figure this out, Gian."

"With you."

"With me," she echoed.

"Because I don't care much about the rest," he said, holding her gaze, "as long as you're going to be there with me, Cara."

"I'm always going to be here."

Where could she possibly go?

Life and love had entangled her heart and soul with Gian Guzzi.

He was hers.

She wasn't going anywhere.

"He was wrong. All those years, what he kept repeating to me; he was wrong."

"Who?" Cara asked.

"My grandfather. Duty. Legacy. And only then, love. Always in that order. That's what he told me but he was wrong. At least for me. He used to say that if a man failed at his duty, his legacy would be nameless, and his love, hopeless. But that only works if a man loves his duty more than anything else in his life and I never did. I love you far more—I love my son far more. I would have no legacy without love, and then what would be the point of my duty at the end of it all? There would be no point, I suppose. I would have nothing worthy to pass on, nothing to watch grow. Or worse, I would have no one to pass it on to, no one to give all of my legacy. Yet, I do, and it was only because I refused to put duty first. I'm not sure if that counts as failing, or not."

"Oh, Gian."

"Yeah, I know." Gian slipped the wedding band off his finger one last time, and handed it up as though it was an offering for her to take. "A gift I didn't think I was going to be able to give you."

Cara pinched the tiny piece of jewelry between her fingers, staring at it for a long while before she said, "One woman to one man, Gian."

"For the rest of my fucking life, Cara. I promise."

Epilogue

"Marcus!" Gian whispered loudly down the hall.

Nothing answered him back.

"Marcus, you better not be waking up your brothers, you little monster."

Or his mother …

Marcus could be a handful for a nearly two-year-old child. Gian turned his back on his oldest son for two seconds, and the kid was gone. Like fucking lightning.

The further down the hall Gian got, the quieter he whispered for his son to come out of his hiding spot. "Marcus, Daddy has one of your cookies."

Muffled behind the twins' nursery door, Gian heard the sounds of Marcus making car noises. He quickly opened the door to find his boy playing on the floor between the two bassinets, his favorite toy car in hand. Marcus didn't even look up at his father, instead continuing to play as though he hadn't done anything wrong. Thankfully, it seemed the plush carpet was mostly muting the noise of the toy car.

"Marcus," Gian murmured, carefully sidestepping a particular spot on the floor that creaked loud enough to wake the devil. "You know not to come into your baby brothers' room when they're napping. Come to Daddy, please."

The boy rolled over to his back, and smiled up at Gian.

"Hi, Daddy," Marcus said, barely above a whisper.

Serene.

Innocent.

Sweet as could be.

Terrible.

Good God, the boy was *terrible*. He knew exactly how to wrap his mother or father right around his tiny little finger with nothing more than a smile and twinkling brown eyes. Gian fully expected that out of his three children—whether or not more kids came in the future was up to Cara— Marcus was going to be the one Gian had to watch out for.

"Let me check on your brothers, and then we're going," Gian told the still-smiling toddler.

Gian leaned over the wicker bassinets, his gaze drifting over the swaddled, sleeping twin two-month old boys. Even small, brand new, and beautiful, he could see his features reflected in the babies. The shape of their noses, their dark hair, and the curve of their lips. Marcus had been perfect, too, but Gian had forgotten how strange and wonderful it felt to simply stare at his children and *feel*.

When they slept, when they were quiet, and when they couldn't possibly know he was watching them … it was amazing. *They* were amazing.

And they had come from *him*.

Corrado preferred his thumb to a soother.

Christopher could only be soothed on the breast.

Gian vividly recalled the moment Cara had slid a positive pregnancy test into his hand with one of her sly smiles. He had never guessed that one baby would actually be *two*. Identical twins—boys, *again*.

Suddenly, their little family had become very big in a short amount of time.

He barely blinked, and he had three children. Three boys to raise. Three pieces of him to love. Others might have been scared at the changes in their life, but Gian was not one of those people. He had wanted a family of his own for longer than he cared to remember, but he had settled on the idea that he might not see those wishes through.

Yet, there he was, a father.

And there his babies were, all his.

"Daddy."

Little Marcus pushed up from the floor and tugged on his father's pant legs. Quickly, to keep him quiet and prevent him from waking up his baby brothers *and* mother, Gian scooped Marcus into his arms. The toddler peered into the wicker bassinets, curiosity lighting up his gaze.

For the most part, Marcus had no interest in his brothers. They were still too new, Gian thought. They didn't play like he did, they cried when Marcus wanted quiet time, and they took up a lot of his mother and father's attention.

He was a good big brother, though.

Or he tried to be.

That was all Gian asked of his oldest boy.

"Mook," Marcus said, clearly done with looking at his brothers. He patted his father on the cheek with a slightly wet hand. Likely drool. Gian ignored the ickiness of it. "Mook, Daddy."

"Yeah, we'll get you some milk, *bambino*."

It was better Gian did leave the nursery, anyway, as the twins hadn't been down for very long, and Cara had only fallen asleep in the next room shortly after. If he woke them up, but especially Christopher, then Cara would have to get up, too. She needed her rest; she deserved to sleep.

She had wanted a shower while she had the chance to take one, but shit, Gian didn't even think she was able to do that before she hit the bed. Out like a light.

Motherhood was tiring.

Tandem breastfeeding twins was exhausting.

Cara barely breathed a complaint.

Gian had always thought his lover was amazing, because how could he not think that when she had never proved him otherwise? Watching her navigate their twins simply reminded him of just how truly amazing she was. For him *and* their children.

Someday, he was going to be the luckiest man in the world—more so than he already was—and he would be able to tell their sons why they too were so lucky. Because they had a mother like Cara, who had loved them and given them every part of her that was good and beautiful from the moment she knew they existed.

Gian was just a sinner in nice clothes.

Cara was the angel.

Marcus hugged tighter to his father as Gian closed the nursery door as quietly as he possibly could. Downstairs in the kitchen, he found his mother wiping down the countertops. The room smelled like Lysol, and the dishwasher was running.

"Ma," Gian said, putting Marcus down to the clean floor. "You don't have to come over here to clean all the damn time."

"Nonsense," Celeste replied blithely. "This is how we *help*."

Their house wasn't dirty, anyway. They had a three-day-a-week maid. Cara was a bit anal on cleaning, too, and Gian picked up after himself and Marcus. Apparently, just the two of them made more messes than the twins.

That was a complete exaggeration …

Gian smelled the air as Marcus toddled toward the fridge, still voicing his desire for milk. Repeatedly. "And you're cooking something, too."

"A casserole. Cara doesn't need to be cooking all the time with the new babies."

"I *do* help, Ma."

Celeste eyed him over her shoulder, smiling slightly. "I know you do. You're a good man in that way, Gian. Of course you are, I raised you, silly boy. But other than your maid—who, by the way, needs a lesson on dusting higher than eye-level—who is here helping you and Cara?"

No one.

Gian had wanted to hire a nanny to help Cara, especially when he had to go into the city for most of the day, and didn't get back until late. Cara would hear *none* of it. A nanny was not going to raise their children, and if Gian brought one home, he wouldn't like what happened after. Or, that's what Cara told him. He chose not to test the theory out.

"We appreciate it."

Celeste's smile grew wider. "That's all I want to hear."

He wished it was that simple, though.

Unfortunately, his father was not of the same mindset that his mother was. Frederic and Gian had not quite made amends for the choices that had needed to be made years ago. His father had yet to meet the twins, and he hadn't even seen Marcus since the boy's last birthday. Gian suspected when Frederic did come to see them, it would not be when his only living son was in the house, too.

Gian wanted to feel guilt for his actions that pushed his father away, but he couldn't.

Had he made a different choice …

Had he been just a few minutes later …

"Mook, Daddy!"

Gian looked to Marcus. The toddler pointed firmly at the fridge, wanting what he wanted, and he didn't want to wait one more minute. His oldest son was like his father in that way.

Had Gian second guessed himself back then, he would not have what he had now.

Gian didn't regret any of it at all.

He quickly got his boy's drink set up in a sippy cup, and set Marcus into his high chair so he could watch one of his favorite cartoons. Satisfied that his boy and his mother were thoroughly distracted, Gian headed back upstairs.

He should let Cara sleep.

He *should* …

Gian had other plans. Now that his twins were born, he could finally get Cara down the aisle, as she had promised him all those months ago. The problem was, he had been overthinking this for too long. When to ask, how to ask, and all of that nonsense.

He realized one morning, while Marcus cuddled into his chest, and Cara fed the twins, that it was all rather obvious. Their best moments, and their best conversations, always happened in bed. He didn't know *why*, but it was true.

Gian didn't think this would be any different.

At some point, Gian stopped caring about what others thought—and their fucking opinions—regarding his unmarried state, his children born out of wedlock, and how it made him appear as a boss to other families.

Fuck those families.

Gian was too busy raising his own family to play into other people's politics. Besides, his ability to run a criminal organization was only dependent on his capability to keep control of the men, *not* which woman wore a ring and had his last name.

Although, he *was* working on that, too.

Just not to please anyone else but himself.

And Cara.

Slipping into their master bedroom, Gian found his wife was still sleeping happily. On the bedside table, the baby monitor lit up with the rhythmic sound of the twins' breaths.

Seeing Cara curled into the blankets on his side of the bed, holding tight to one of his pillows, made Gian pause. Instead of waking her up like he had planned, he sat down in one of the rockers in the corner, and simply watched his lover.

Marcus was fine with his grandmother.

The twins were okay.

He had time.

They so rarely had time lately.

As he watched Cara, her dreams flickering behind her closed lids, Gian found his peace. Too often, his days and duties and stresses got away with him, and he forgot about the important pieces in his life that brought him happiness. Beautiful things like Cara.

Gian hadn't realized it, but he'd pulled the small velvet box from his slacks pocket, and was flicking the lid open and closed. Why he was fidgeting, he wasn't sure. He wasn't nervous, but *anxious*.

The two-carat ruby, set atop a crown of diamonds on a white-gold band, rested inside the box, nestled amongst a velvet bed. He thought, when he had found the piece, that it fit Cara better than any other ring could. Certainly, better than normal diamonds, or something else of equal flashy appeal.

Red, like her hair and her lips.

Red, like the color of her passion and her love.

Red, like the hurricane they were together and apart.

Red was the color of all extremes, both good and bad. It was the color best described by the strongest human emotions—love and anger. Red was the color of blood, of a man's heart, and he thought if it were possible to see inside his soul, it would be a crimson shade, too.

Just like Cara and her love and soul.

A ruby was perfect.

He slipped it back into his pocket for the time being.

"Gian?"

At the sound of Cara's sleepy call of his name, Gian was up off the chair and crossing the room. He slipped into bed with Cara easily, his arms snaking around her body to pull her in close. There, he could hold her still, feel her warmth, and hide away from the world for a short time.

"Afternoon," he murmured into her hair. "Chris and Corrado are still asleep, so you can rest some more, if you need to."

Cara sighed. "I swear, I have an internal alarm now. I wake up *before* the twins do, in preparation for them."

Gian kissed the top of her head. "That might be very true."

"There's no 'might be' about it, Gian. The boobs know."

His laughter rocked them both in the bed. Cara's lips curved into a sweet smile against the column of his throat. "They do have a job to do, now."

"Apparently." Cara tipped her head back so she could look up at him, her wild red curls splaying over the pillow. "Gian?"

"Hmm?"

"Will you marry me?"

He stiffened in the bed, his gaze darting down to meet hers. "You couldn't even let me ask, could you?"

Cara shrugged, her sly smile teasing him. "I saw you looking at the ring. I figured … well, I should save you the trouble."

"You're supposed to let me ask, Cara. I've waited a long time for this."

"It *is* a beautiful ring."

"*Cara.*"

"Ask," she whispered before pressing a quick kiss to his lips.

Gian let his fingertips dance over Cara's side, tickling her. Her giggles rang out at the same time a quiet set of matching, perfectly-timed cries started from the baby monitor.

"Shit," he muttered.

Cara winked as she pushed up from the bed. "I may be queen of the house, but I still answer to the little ones. Fun is over. The princes call, Gian."

And they would keep calling, he knew.

Marcus, too.

Plus, every other person that interrupted their daily life time and time again.

Gian grabbed Cara's wrist at the last second, stopping her from climbing off the bed. He could deal with getting the ring on her at another time. He only needed to *ask*.

"Marry me, Cara," Gian said. "Please, marry me?"

Cara crawled back over the bed, kissed him hard once, and replied, "Do you expect any other answer but yes?"

"Not really, but I'm worried that if I don't ask *right now*, I will never get the chance to ask. So please, Cara, will you let me love you like this, too? I'm already happy, whole, and lucky because of you, but will you marry me, too?"

"Yes, Gian."

He pulled her back for another lingering kiss, and then swatted her ass as she clamored off the bed and headed for the nursery. It wasn't long before he was following after her, too, scooping one of the two twins from their beds to help Cara in whatever way he could. He headed for the changing table with a slightly happier Corrado, while Cara sat down into one of her rocking chairs to feed the less than pleased Christopher.

Less than a minute after the twins had woken up, a loud, chocolate-stained Marcus made his way into the room, too. He made a beeline for his mother.

Their life was busy and messy. Time was already a rare commodity. He got his yes, though. That was all that mattered.

Time could be made.

He figured that was a lesson worth learning early in their family; time could always be made.

Seventeen Years Later

Gian stared up at one of the many paintings that hung in his home. He had far more expensive pieces than this particular one; art was a good way to hide vast wealth in material things that could be easily liquidated, after all.

But this painting?

This one he could never sell.

To him, it was priceless.

Sitting on a gold chair that looked almost like a throne, in the middle of a forest that was just beginning to change to autumn, the woman stared straight ahead, as though she owned the whole world. She seemed unaware of the fact time had stopped around her—the artist catching colorful leaves as they fell, and a bird looking down from one of the trees behind her. Blue eyes, red hair. Dressed in a royal purple, knee-length gown with the heels to match.

And damn, didn't she look good acting a Queen.

Then again, Cara always looked amazing.

Surrounding their mother in the portrait were her boys—five of them. Gian had commissioned the piece when their last boys were only nine. Those same boys were fourteen now, and he still looked at the painting every single day.

Nearly nineteen-year-old Marcus shuffled past his father in the hallway with a cigarette tucked up behind his ear, a sly smile as he glanced down at whatever was on his phone, and swinging a set of Mercedes keys in his hand all the while. Gian let his oldest son pass him by, but only because this was nothing abnormal for Marcus.

Or any of their boys, really.

Gian was not the most important person in the room, not when his children were just coming home after being gone for days, or even a few hours to school. Marcus no longer lived with them—he hadn't since he turned eighteen—but he knew better than to stay away from the Guzzi home for too long. Three days, four at the max, was enough.

Then, Cara started to miss her son.

Marcus didn't like those phone calls from his father when Cara started complaining. To be fair, Gian didn't like her complaining.

Gian headed after his son, ready to eat.

No, Marcus didn't greet his father first. He moved across the dining room floor quickly, dropped his phone into his pocket, and then bent down to kiss his mother's waiting cheek. She sat at the head of the table—a spot that *should* have been reserved for Gian only.

It wasn't his spot to have.

It had never been.

It was Cara's spot in their home.

Head of the house.

She always had the floor.

The only Queen of his family.

Gian made sure not a single fucking soul ever forgot it, either. Including their *five* sons.

To be a Guzzi *principe*, those boys were never allowed to see their mother as anything *but* the queen that had birthed them. They worshipped Cara, the ground she walked on, and the very air that came out of her body. In their eyes, their mother did no wrong. Each one of their sons would defend their mother to the fucking death, and they wouldn't think twice about it. They didn't let anybody say a bad word about her, not without some kind of apology that usually included blood.

When they walked into the house, Cara was who they looked for. Cara was who they greeted first in every situation—their father second. Cara was served before them, him, and guests alike. She never had to ask a second time for anything, not when she had five sets of ears listening the first damn time. She wanted for *nothing* in their home.

His sons' greatest fears?

Failing their mom.

They didn't know it, but they could never fail Cara. She loved them too much to see their faults. Gian saw their flaws, occasionally, because he was their father and he had a different role to play, at times, with his boys. But no matter what, he was damn proud of his sons.

Gian liked to think he had a big hand in how his sons treated, loved, and respected their mother. Fact was, his boys just loved Cara. And all he needed to do was occasionally remind them *why* as they'd grown up. They did the rest themselves, honestly.

"Hey, Ma."

Cara preened up at her oldest son, happy as could be. "How was your week?"

"Busy."

"Not too busy, though," his wife said, shooting Gian a look.

Marcus shrugged. "It's good, Ma. I like being busy. Keeps me out of trouble."

Cara pursed her lips. "Mmhmm. I'm sure. Sit, your brothers are almost home from school."

She wasn't wrong.

Gian had only taken his seat at the other end of the table when four pairs of footsteps echoed down the main hall. Two sets were closer than the others. Loud, raucous laughter followed his four other boys. Nearly seventeen-year-old Christopher and Corrado moved through the dining room first, going straight for their mother. Seniors in high school, the two boys were often more different than they were alike. Which was strange, considering they were identical twins. One was more daring, the other reserved. One was louder, the other quiet.

Perhaps it was just how his first set of twin boys fed off one another. One helped the other to stay calm, the other pushed his brother to take risks.

Gian wasn't entirely sure.

He let his boys figure out this life thing all on their own.

"So, wait, she tried to—" Fourteen-year old Beni—short for Benito— quieted when he realized the entire dining room was looking in his direction. He shrugged off the dirty look his twin brother—Benedetto— gave him, especially considering Cara was now interested in whatever she had heard.

"You're an ass," Bene grumbled. "Told you to drop it."

"She?" Cara asked quietly. "Who is this *she*, Bene?"

"Ah, Ma. It's nothing."

Bene—said with an 'ay' sound at the end—and Beni—said with a hard "e" sound—were the complete opposite of their older twin brothers. Where Chris and Corrado made a great effort to be different from one another, Bene and Beni did not.

From a young age, the younger twins had stuck to one another like glue. They spoke alike, dressed similar, and rarely allowed people close enough to understand their strange bonds. Gian could bring forth a dozen memories of his youngest twins having conversations with one another in a babbling language as babies and toddlers that no one could understand. Or how one would *always* know the other was sick or hurt before anyone else did. It took Cara and Gian years—until the twins could speak properly and communicate—to understand why one would wake up in the middle of the night in a terror, only to figure out the next morning, the other twin was sick with some bug or other.

Cara had quietly mentioned once that she had shared a similar—albeit less intense—kind of bond with her dead twin. It scared the shit out of Gian, not *because* his boys shared something so strange and wonderful, but because *what if*. Cara had never thought her twin would be taken away, and he didn't want to consider that might happen to one of his boys, too.

Because what if it did?

He did not think Bene or Beni were like their mother. He did not believe one could survive without the other, not like they currently were. They were too close, too dependent, and their lives were too intertwined. Cara told Gian all the time not to think about it. Live and let live, she would tell him. Love and let love.

Some thought the boys were a little odd or strange, but Gian didn't. Then again, he had watched his boys grow from the day they were taken from their mother's body and put into his arms. Of course, he didn't find anything odd or strange about them.

There were some who could not tell the two apart, although their parents had never had that trouble.

Gian would *never* forget Cara's tired laugh when the ultrasound technician very quietly informed them that their pregnancy was once again a multiple. Not one baby, but two, and identical.

Cara had turned to him and muttered, "You got your baseball team, Gian."

They hadn't even known the genders.

Cara always seemed to know.

She also got her tubes tied after that pregnancy.

Cara smiled, took her kisses from her youngest boys, and waved them off to their respective seats. "I will be asking about this *she* later, Bene."

Gian chuckled, his attention going to the maid as food was brought in.

"It's just some girl that he—"

"Beni, shut up," Bene barked, tossing a piece of garlic bread and hitting his twin straight in the forehead.

Beni answered back by throwing a handful of croutons, peppering his twin.

Chris and Corrado laughed, already stuffing their faces, despite grace not having been said. Marcus, on the other hand, rolled his eyes like it was any other day. The only singleton Guzzi brother, with no twin to share, Gian sometimes thought Marcus felt left out in times like these. He certainly couldn't have grown up lonely with so many siblings, but did he sometimes wonder why *he* had been the only singleton?

Gian didn't wonder at all.

Marcus was still a *principe* working his way into being a king, sometimes stumbling a bit on his way to the top. He never could have shared that kind of spotlight with someone else. He was too focused, too driven, and way too goddamn competitive.

But that was good, too.

Gian thought to correct his sons before they got out of hand, but he found himself distracted by the amused, soft smile Cara shot across the table at him. He couldn't very well correct his boys when their mother enjoyed their antics.

Head of the house.

She always had the floor.

Queen of his family.

Sitting right where she belonged.

Always.

Bio

Bethany-Kris is a Canadian author, lover of much, and mother to four young sons, one cat, and three dogs. A small town in Eastern Canada where she was born and raised is where she has always called home. With her boys under her feet, a snuggling cat, barking dogs, and a spouse calling over his shoulder, she is nearly always writing something ... when she can find the time.

Find Bethany-Kris at:
Her website www.bethanykris.com,
or on Facebook at www.facebook.com/bethanykriswrites,
on her blog at www.bethanykris.blogspot.ca,
or on Twitter - @BethanyKris.

Sign up to Bethany-Kris's New Release Newsletter here:
http://eepurl.com/bf9lzD

Other Books

Seasons of Betrayal

Where the Sun Hides
Where the Snow Falls
Where the Wind Whispers

Gun Moll Trilogy

Gun Moll
Gangster Moll

The Chicago War

Deathless & Divided
Reckless & Ruined
Scarless & Sacred
Breathless & Bloodstained

The Russian Guns

The Arrangement
The Life
The Score
Demyan & Ana
Shattered
The Jersey Vignettes

Find more on Bethany-Kris's website at www.bethanykris.com.